UNDEAD WATERS - BOOK ONE

WAVES OF UNDEAD

Raine,
Watch out for
biters on the beach!
Cheers,
R Cuthbertson

First edition: June 2025

Cover Design by Nightsky Graphic Book Design | Stella Ehrhardt |@nightskygraphics

ISBN 978-1-0692631-0-0 (Paperback)
ISBN 978-1-0692631-2-4 (Ebook)

Published by:

DARK COAST
PUBLISHING

https://rcuthbertsonwrites.com/

Printed in Canada
at Hemlock Printers on FSC-certified paper

AUTHOR'S NOTE

Waves of Undead is, needless to say, a work a fiction. The geographic locations, however, are very real, and very dear to me. This story primarily takes place on the southwestern coast of British Columbia, Canada, in Ladner, Tsawwassen, and Tofino. These are all places that I have called home, so I wish it to be known that I hope none of the events on these pages transpire.

The likelihood of an infected outbreak remains very slim (questionable bacteria discovered in the melting permafrost aside). Alas, Tofino *is* geographically in a tsunami hazard zone. Though I wrote about a tsunami striking Tofino's shores, I pray the day will never come. I wish only prosperity to that slice of paradise, and only clean, glassy waves of a surfable size.

CONTENT WARNINGS

The story you are about to consume contains blood, body horror, gore, violence, and many other themes that may be triggering to some individuals.

For a further list of content warnings, see page 254 at the back of the book. Please note that spoilers may be contained therein.

TYPOS HAPPEN

If you happen to catch a typo that I missed while in some sort of editing-zombie state (I may or may not have uttered *braaaaains* several times during the making of this book), please feel free to email me at rcuthbertson.writes@gmail.com. I'll fix it for future print runs and digital versions. In return you'll receive a heartfelt thanks and a metaphorical gold star. Or a gold brain, if you prefer.

A NOTE TO MY AMERICAN READERS

You may notice that some of the spelling includes extra letters compared to what you're used to. That's intentional, though I appreciate your concern.

For some reason, Canadian English sometimes follows the rules of British spelling and sometimes leans toward American English. I know. We're confusing. I'm confused.

On with the show.

DEDICATION

To my mom, who will always be my number one fan. Thank you for encouraging me to see this through. Without your support, this story would still be drowning in the depths of my hard drive.

WAVES OF UNDEAD

UNDEAD WATERS | BOOK ONE

R. CUTHBERTSON

PROLOGUE

With his heart drumming against his ribcage, Mark tried to focus on anything but the blaring siren warning people away from the beach. He gritted his teeth, lay on his surfboard, and paddled out with the receding tide. A wave of this magnitude would break much farther out than the usual surf, and he knew if he wanted a chance to ride the big one, he'd have to paddle farther out of the bay.

The exertion gave Mark a coughing fit. He spat a mouthful of dark blood into the Pacific. Crimson diffused into the teal depths around him.

Stealing a glance over his shoulder at the shore, he was relieved that he couldn't see Lara. *You better be on high ground by now,* he thought. When she dropped him off at the entrance to the beach, he told Lara to meet him in the water. He should have tried to find her when the alarm sounded, should have protected his wife and made sure she escaped nature's wrath, but Mark was so tired of fighting, of running from death, that he cared little for his own inevitable demise. He trusted that she'd have the sense to seek high ground, even if it meant leaving him behind.

Another mouthful of blood spluttered from his lungs. He spat it on his board this time and watched his vital fluid trickle between nodules of white wax.

When the alarm went off, Mark had been surfing the southern end of Cox Bay, nicknamed Land of the Lefts by local surfers. Hundreds fled, clogging the two major arteries that were the exits of the beach. Screams from shore had replaced the birdsong that usually emitted from within the slanted foliage of cedar, pine, and hemlock. Now the beach was empty, save for abandoned towels and surfboards.

Mark pushed his tired muscles and headed west out of the bay toward open ocean. A watery hill grew on the horizon as the tsunami formed in the distance. Mark grabbed the GoPro from the nose of his board and started recording himself selfie-style.

"Cox Bay is totally going off today, dudes! I'm about to ride the big one, and I guarantee...it's going to be gnarly!"

He laughed at himself as he clipped the camera back onto its mount. Mark wasn't usually one for dramatic exits. He hadn't said goodbye to everyone he loved before he embarked on his "Bucket List" adventure with Lara. He was reluctant to record his last words, but fairly certain that no one would ever find the camera after the mess that this wave would create.

He turned around and paddled for shore as the behemoth wave approached behind him. When he felt the tail of his board rise, Mark gave two last strokes with his long arms and popped up onto his feet.

Looking over his right shoulder, he saw a hundred thousand tons of water crest into a barrel. He was inside the largest tube he'd ever ridden. The sound was deafening, yet he felt at peace as he glided along the face of the sixty-foot wave. He bent his knees several times to pulse the board farther down the tube.

He was halfway through the bay when the wave hit the shallow sandbar under the water's surface. The tube morphed into a washed-out wall of sand, seaweed, and unstoppable chaos.

Mark regretted his reckless decision when his mind flipped from calmness to fight or flight. He tried to stay in front of the spray, for fear of being torn apart by the strength of the surrounding wave if it overtook him.

It only took a millisecond of imbalance for the nose of his board to dip under the surface of the water and throw him in the air.

The pressure from the wave that engulfed him was unbearable. Mark covered his head with his arms. He was an ant in a washing machine, unable to tell which direction was sky or sand. His lungs screamed for mercy and his brain begged for oxygen.

3

Just when he was about to give up and inhale the briny water, he surfaced. He drew in a breath and opened his eyes in time to see his surfboard whip through the air toward him. Covering his head again, he ducked beneath the surface to avoid being hit by the board.

Mark winced when he was thrown against a tree at the shoreline. He bounced off the cedar and was projected toward a pine. The board, still attached to him by his leash, got stuck between two tall trees and held Mark there, tethered and helpless.

He attempted to reach for his left ankle to unhook the Velcro, but the constant surge of water was too strong. It flowed endlessly. Mark looked around desperately, searching for anything that could help free him.

A few feet away, a ball of waterlogged fabric floated at the water's surface. Mark recognized it as a tent he had seen on the beach earlier that day. It had become tangled between two pines.

Mark heard a crack as the Styrofoam and fibreglass of his surfboard gave in to the pressure of the water, and he felt himself drift toward the tent.

A groan escaped from within the soggy polyester.

"Hello? Is there someone in there?" Mark could hear movement within the tent. He reached for it and pulled at the floating flap of fabric. A lump formed in his throat when he saw her purple wetsuit and dark, waterlogged curls. "Lara!"

The sound of his voice caught her attention, and Lara turned to face her husband. Beneath her freckles, her usually warm complexion was pale; her lips were blue, and broken blood vessels encircled her hazel irises. Her left arm hung at an unnatural angle.

"Hold on, love. I'm here," Mark said to his wife.

The surging water subsided slightly, and Mark unstrapped himself from his board. His lungs were on fire from the effort, and another coughing fit plagued him. He wiped his blood-soaked strawberry-blond stubble with a neoprene-covered wrist.

Mark heard the polyester shift as Lara exited the tent. When he looked up, she let out a feral shriek and waded toward him.

"Lara? It's okay. We'll be alright. I'm sorry I didn't come for you, babe, I'm so sorry."

Mark opened his arms to her approach and reached out to embrace his wife. She grabbed him and squeezed so tight he could almost feel her nails through his wetsuit. She leaned in toward his shoulder, nestled into his chest, and let out another inhuman hiss.

Her lips felt like ice against the exposed skin of Mark's neck. He felt a searing pain and let out a scream when her teeth tore into his jugular.

5

ANA
30 JUNE 2018
08:45 PDT
YVR AIRPORT
RICHMOND, BC

"Last call for flight OA2112 to Tofino. All passengers, please make your way to Gate B."

Ana peeled herself from a blue pleather bench and made her way through a sea of travelers toward the gate for domestic departures. Hesitation made her feel like she was wading through water with every step she took toward the pilot. She handed over her boarding pass with hands that shook from nerves and caffeine.

Bright morning sunlight caused Ana to squint as she stepped onto the tarmac and marched between faded white lines toward a Piper Navajo Chieftain, an eight-passenger plane that would carry her to paradise. She sat in a vacant seat across from a petite woman with brunette ringlets.

Fuck, it's already hot, Ana thought as she felt her clothing stick to her. She had flown from YVR to YAZ on countless occasions and had hoped that an early departure would provide some respite from the sauna-like experience felt at 5,000 feet.

The captain welcomed his passengers and recited his pre-flight safety spiel. Ana half-listened as she yawned and pulled her golden hair into a loose ponytail. She noted her reflection in the round window. The bags under her green eyes boasted of another sleepless night. She felt slightly nauseated, as though butterflies were emerging from chrysalides in her stomach.

The propellors spun, and a passenger in the front row cheered.

Ana pulled her phone out of her pocket and sighed. *How long until you realize I'm not home, Paul?* Ana stared at the screen, as if willing her twin to respond to the voicemail she left him early that morning.

After she released another heavy sigh, she selected a song for takeoff: "The Passenger" by Iggy Pop. Restless despite her exhaustion, she readjusted her long legs and shifted in her seat.

The plane jolted forward down the runway. Ana's body was pushed back in the seat just before she experienced that fleeting moment of weightlessness as they climbed into the sky.

The views between Richmond, a suburban city next to Vancouver, and Tofino, the surfing capital of Canada, captivated Ana. Over the Strait of Georgia, she observed the line where the silty ochre water of the Fraser River met the briny grey Pacific, the two distinct waters resisting their union. Tugboats, sailboats, and fishing vessels dotted the ocean. They flew over outlying islands where cabins stood enshrouded by tall trees.

Ana pushed her thick, black-framed glasses up the bridge of her nose and habitually plucked at her split ends.

"You alright, honey?" the brunette lady across from her asked. Perfectly manicured eyebrows framed the wide hazel eyes she studied Ana with.

"I'm fine," Ana muttered.

The lady brushed one of her tight curls behind her ear and asked, "Fear of flying?"

"Uh, yeah," Ana lied.

Below, the city of Nanaimo was alive with traffic.

"My husband isn't very fond of planes either. He rode a motorcycle to Tofino. As if that's any safer! But, it was on his 'Bucket List.'"

Ana sighed gently, removed her headphones, and looked at the woman more closely. *She looks young, thirties maybe? Her husband probably isn't much older.* "That's wonderful, to be getting a head start on life goals so early."

The lady responded with a meek smile that didn't reach her eyes. She looked out the window for a moment, then turned back to Ana and held out her hand. "My name is Lara."

She took Lara's petite hand in her own and smiled. "I'm Diana, but everyone calls me Ana. Have you been to Tofino before?"

"Oh, yes. Mark and I used to make an annual trip to Tuff City to get a surf session in. You?"

"I lived there for three years. Haven't been home in over a year." *Is it still home?* Ana asked herself.

"Three years. Wow. Why'd you leave?"

Ana wiped a bead of sweat from her forehead and answered. "There were family matters that needed tending to."

They both turned to the window. Scars left by logging created a patchwork on the mountainous slopes between Nanaimo and Port Alberni. The plane roared over forestry blocks in various states of regrowth. The odd patch of old-growth forest lay untouched, with massive cedars that awaited their debated demise. Opportunistic alders lined unpaved roadways; from the sky they looked like broccoli florets.

"Are you moving back? To Tofino?"

"I haven't really decided. I'll see how this trip goes."

The plane passed over the Alberni Inlet next. The mill pumped sulfuric steam into the air, giving the area its characteristic rotten-egg stench.

"Mark and I can't get enough of surfing. We've travelled to Bali, Hawaii, Ireland, anywhere with a wave really. But we keep coming back to Tofino. It's always felt really special to us."

"You two sound like quite the adventurers." Ana looked over her shoulder to see the early morning light glint off Kennedy Lake.

"We've made some wonderful memories, that's for sure. Here's a picture of us on our honeymoon in Portugal. He was on the hunt for big waves." Lara pulled a leather wallet from her purse and withdrew a small portrait of herself and a red-haired man with a square jaw, high cheekbones, and bright blue eyes. The couple laughed playfully as they looked into each other's eyes.

"That's a beautiful shot." Ana returned the photo to Lara.

"It's hard to recognize him now." Lara looked down at the

picture. "Stage-four lung cancer, and he refused treatment. The diagnosis came six weeks ago. We've been travelling for over a month now and I can tell that he's getting tired. He won't admit it though, at least not to me."

"I'm so sorry, Lara."

The two women sat in silence as the plane flew over Highway 4.

They both gasped when Long Beach came in to view. Umbrellas, tents, and towels covered the sand. Surfers dotted the water where sets of waves rolled into shore at long intervals.

The plane turned away from the beach and toward the landing strip of YAZ. The descent was quick and the landing smooth. The small group of passengers applauded.

"Do you have a ride into town?" Lara asked Ana.

She shook her head. "No one knows I'm coming. My trip was pretty last minute. Hitchhiking it is." She gave Lara a thumbs-up.

"Mark is picking me up. Traded in the motorbike for a rental car. We can give you a ride, if you'd like."

"Thanks, Lara, I'd really appreciate that."

The plane taxied toward the small airport with its sage-coloured walls. To exit the aircraft, the pilots squeezed through the narrow gap between the passenger seats and made their way to the rear door. Ana and the other passengers followed.

Cool rainforest air with a hint of ocean greeted her. She inhaled deeply and looked at the tree line around the tarmac. Ana waited while Lara collected her suitcase. The sound of plastic wheels rolling across pavement escorted them to the building.

I can't believe I'm actually here, Ana thought.

Lara dropped her suitcase and ran to greet a lanky, red-haired man. She had spoken truth: it was hard to recognize the man before her as the one in the photograph. His cheeks were shallow. Dark half-moon bags cradled his eyes, which had become a dull grey rather than the sparkling blue in the picture. He appeared to have lost a lot of muscle mass. Ana noticed the drastic way his shoulders rose and fell as he took laboured breaths.

Lara and Mark embraced and kissed one another. Ana turned away and looked into the clear blue sky.

"My apologies, we're being rude. Mark, I'd like you to meet my new friend, Ana. Ana, my husband, Mark."

"Lovely to meet you." Ana extended a hand.

"Likewise." He took her hand in his own. It felt icy and boney, but he had a firm grasp.

"Hun, can we give Ana a lift into town?"

"Of course! Where are we headed?"

"Mackenzie Beach, please," Ana responded.

After waving goodbye to Mark and Lara, Ana crossed the ochre sands of Mackenzie Beach and sat on a cavernous cedar log. She ran her hand along its bark, smoothed over time by the incessant caress of the waves that had carried it there. Ana wondered where it once stood, for how long, and what path it had taken to become a frequented sunset-watching landmark on an otherwise barren beach.

Ana removed her shoes and socks, and meditatively buried her toes in the sand. Several crows flew against the cloudless sky. She watched the gentle lapping of the tide on the rocks. White spray struck the eroded coast where the small waves crashed on unseen obstacles beneath the surface. Like a metronome of the Earth, the ocean's rhythm momentarily soothed Ana.

She braided her hair and sorrow swelled within her, as she recalled the times her mother would comb and braid her hair before leaving for work in the morning. Before leaving for work for a year at a time. Before leaving her family forever for a watery grave.

A group of tourists struggled to carry massive stand-up

paddle boards to the water's edge. Tiny shore birds ran from their approach.

Ana dipped her body off the log and nestled into the sand. She leaned her head back against the cedar, pulled her legs into her chest, and took a long breath of the briny Pacific air.

The ocean mist was so light she could barely feel it on her skin, but a thin layer of moisture formed on her glasses. Ana grabbed her backpack and placed her glasses in their case next to a few pairs of contact lenses. She popped a set of lenses into her eyes and blinked away the saline solution.

She checked the time on her cell phone: it was just after 10:30 AM. There was still no word from Paul. *Well, I guess I should get this over with.* After putting her shoes back on, she stood, grabbed her backpack, and walked across the beach toward the parking lot. *Wow, it's full already. Why did I choose Canada Day long weekend to come? Shit, it's going to be busy.*

Ana placed her headphones in her ears and turned on her current favourite song to sooth her grief with: "Heart of the Sea" by Flogging Molly. She walked along the shared pedestrian-bike path, which was lined with walls of salal and blackberry bushes, while she mumbled the song's lyrics. Her destination was a fifteen-minute walk from the beach; she listened to the song on repeat nearly four times.

Familiar scents enticed her when she approached Industrial Way, the most aromatic district in Tofino. The prominent scent of roasting coffee, reminiscent of burnt toast, paired with the earthy aroma of fermenting hops, gave the air a uniquely robust tang.

She stopped walking. *This is it. Last chance to turn back.* Ana took a deep breath and headed down a gravel driveway with her heart in her throat.

HARVEY
30 JUNE 2018
10:45 PDT
HARVEY'S TRAILER
TOFINO, BC

Harvey rolled out of bed and brushed dark hair out of his eyes. *This is getting unruly... I think it's time for a trim.*

He exited his cramped bedroom and walked to the bathroom, which didn't take long in his twenty-foot trailer. He opened the bathroom cabinet to grab his toothbrush. The backside of the mirrored door featured several photographs: one of Harvey with his father, both clad in camo and sporting rifles; one of a blue heeler, Manchez, his long-departed family dog; and a photograph of a blonde woman hiking through the rainforest. He often contemplated taking that picture down, but he hadn't had the heart to yet. His focus lingered on the photo for a moment. *It's been a year, man. Get yourself together*. He closed the door on her as peppermint paste foamed in his mouth.

There was a knock at the door. *Who's here so early?* He glanced at a clock on his wall. *Okay, so maybe it's not that early.*

He spat the Colgate swill into the sink and made a short trek across his combination kitchenette-living room to peer through the peephole. There was no one in his line of sight. Harvey opened the door and walked down the trailer's steel steps. His breath caught in his throat when he saw her.

She stood in a patch of sun next to an overgrown herb garden. Her loose black curls shone with a hint of blue against a periwinkle dress that hugged her curves.

"Good morning, Kat," he said, blushing when he saw the owner of his favourite cafe, which he had been frequenting more often of late.

"Good day, Mr. O'Ryan," she said. "I made muffins for the caf. Would you like some? They're blueberry." She gestured to the contents of a woven cedar basket in her hands.

"Thanks!" Harvey reached for one as he smiled down at the beautiful woman before him.

"Please, take two. I'm sure you have a long day ahead of you."

Harvey grabbed a second muffin from the basket and said, "Actually, I'm off work today."

The corners of her lips rose, but she said nothing.

Come on, man, this is the moment. He swallowed hard, cleared his throat, and asked, "What time are you off?"

"Around noon. I'm just placing a couple orders with our suppliers and checking in with my staff."

"Wanna hit the beach after?"

"I'd like that. Here...is my number," she said, pulling a card out of the basket.

Harvey took the card and admired the heavy gothic font that read *Raven's Roost Cafe*. He pulled out his phone, tapped in her number, and sent a quick text that read *hi*. "And here is mine."

"Perfect. I'll call you when I finish. See you later, Mr. O'Ryan." She smiled and turned back up the gravel driveway.

"See you, Kat." Harvey stepped back into the trailer with a grin on his face.

ANA
30 JUNE 2018
10:45 PDT
HARVEY'S TRAILER
TOFINO, BC

Ana's steps made soft crunching sounds on the loose gravel. When she was within twenty metres of his trailer, Ana looked up and noticed he had another visitor. She ducked to the side of the driveway and out of sight.

A slender woman with cascading black curls approached Harvey's trailer. *Her* trailer.

Who's this? Ana felt her throat tighten. She hid behind a cedar and watched as the young woman knocked on Harvey's door, then stepped toward Ana's garden.

The stranger's almond-shaped eyes narrowed as she studied the garden, and a smirk crossed her face.

Yeah, laugh it up. Let's see what your garden looks like after a year of neglect, Ana thought.

She felt a pang of guilt for leaving her plants, and Harvey, and for the complete mess that the last year had been.

The aluminum door screeched open and Harvey stepped down. Ana's heart kicked up a tempo when she saw him. His dark brown hair was longer than she had ever seen it. *I always suggested he grow it.* She liked how it looked when it was shaggy, and smiled slightly, knowing this was his bedhead and he'd soon be combing it.

His voice jarred her back to reality.

"Good morning, Kat."

Ana could just make out his words from where she stood. Her cheeks burned. *What a fool I am, to have come here with no notice. Of course he's moved on. It's been a year.* She leaned her forehead against the cedar and closed her eyes.

"Wanna hit the beach after?" she heard Harvey ask his visitor.

That seals it. He has other affections. Who am I to interfere?

The other woman's footsteps headed back up the driveway. Ana sat down with her back to the cedar and nestled in amongst metre-long fern fronds. She inhaled the earthy scent of the soil beneath her and turned to her usual source of comfort. Earphones in and music blaring, Ana closed her eyes and tried to process the situation.

SKYLAR
30 JUNE 2018
10:45 PDT
SKYLAR'S TRAILER
TOFINO, BC

Ugh, my head is spinning. Looks like the damn raccoons were here again last night.

Skylar stepped out of his trailer and took in the mess around his yard. He knew the raccoons weren't to blame, but hated admitting to himself that he had gotten so drunk that he created the mess on his own.

He took a few steps to his outdoor kitchen and ignited the cookstove. Skylar grabbed a kettle, which he filled with fresh water collected from Kennedy River the week prior. He filled his French press with freshly ground coffee from the roaster up the hill. While he waited for the water to boil, Skylar picked up empty beer cans littering his plot of land.

With a steaming cup of black coffee in hand, Skylar sat in a plastic lawn chair and looked up to where the emerald-green trees met the clear blue sky. *Perfect day to get in a surf, drink some beer, hopefully meet some babes.*

Speaking of babes...

Skylar noticed a woman at his neighbour's trailer door, and another one hiding behind a tree next to the driveway. He recognized her rope of blonde hair.

Ana? What the hell? Well, Harvey, looks as though you're about to have an interesting day.

He sipped his coffee and watched Ana sink to the forest floor.

Come on, Ana, no catfight? This is Harvey O'Ryan! Surely he's worth fighting for?

Skylar's tongue flicked a broken tooth at the left side of his smile. He reached into his pocket and pulled out a pouch of tobacco. Yellow-stained fingers twisted together a couple cigarettes, one of which he tucked behind a pierced ear, the other he lit. He exhaled a cloud of pungent smoke as he saw the dark-haired woman walk away.

I should probably go scrape Ana off the forest floor. In a bit. Don't need to see her cryin' over there.

Skylar put his coffee down and butted out his smoke. He turned around, reached beneath his rusty trailer, and pulled out his surfboard: a six-and-a-half-foot funboard.

Maybe An will want to join me. I think her bike is still at Harvey's.

He heard his neighbour's truck start and watched as the matte-black Dodge Ram headed up their shared gravel drive. Harvey waved through the passenger window, and Skylar nodded back.

When the truck turned onto the highway, Skylar grabbed his walking stick and made his way into the woods where he'd seen Ana.

ANA
30 JUNE 2018
11:00 PDT
HARVEY'S TRAILER
TOFINO, BC

Ana felt something sharp jab her in the ribcage. Her eyes snapped open as she raised her arms above her head defensively.

"Skylar?" She looked up at his chipped-toothed Cheshire grin. Smile lines hugged his mahogany eyes. His sun-kissed face had a rugged handsomeness to it.

He reached forward to poke her in the ribs with his stick again.

"Hey, man, that thing is sharp!" She swatted it away.

"Gotta protect this land from transients lurking in the woods." He raised an eyebrow at her playfully. "What brings you to our driveway, Ana?"

"The city doesn't have any decent ferns to nest in."

"I can imagine." He held his hand out to her and pulled her to her feet. "Come on, then."

They walked back to his camp and sat down. Ana grabbed a roasting stick from the fire pit and began poking at charcoal within the rock circle. She let out a heavy sigh.

"I'm sorry, Skylar." She didn't look up at him when she spoke.

"For?"

"Running out on you. On everyone."

"Oh, that. Have to say, it was a shock when you disappeared, An. Then again, people come and go from this town all the time."

"It's been a rough year, Skylar. I miss it here. I miss my life."

"Why did you leave? I mean, I'm sorry your mom died. That sucks. Didn't have to turn your own life upside down though."

"I don't know... I just...wanted to be there for Paul. But he's been the one holding me together for the past year."

"And Harvey..."

"Doesn't know I'm here."

"Who was—"

"I heard him call her Kat... Do you know her?" She thrust the prongs of the roasting stick into a burnt log, and the charcoal crunched as she twisted the steel.

"Not really. She owns a new cafe that moved in near Neil's. I just go to Neil's. It's a matter of loyalty. I mean, who puts a coffee shop next to another coffee shop in such a small town?"

Ana nodded, lost in thought.

"Just call him, An. He'll be happy to see you. He's had a rough year too, you know?" Skylar ran a hand through his dark hair.

"I know. I need to clear my head first. I was pretty surprised to witness another woman at *my* door."

"Yeah... I can imagine. Hey, I'm about to check the surf, wanna come for a ride?"

"Sure. Let me grab my bike."

"Check out my new board first." He reached a lanky arm behind his chair and grabbed his turquoise funboard. "It catches *everything*, even the mushiest waves will send me flying!" He flashed his familiar grin.

Ana jumped out of her chair and grabbed the board to inspect its craftsmanship. It had an intricate airbrushed image of a trident framed between two waves.

"Wait... No way! This is Kyle's logo!"

"Yeeep! He's got a shop now, Poseidon's Pocket, and it's rockin' full production."

"Wicked. This board is amazing!"

"Yeah, she's a beaut. Go find your bike. I don't wanna miss slack tide."

HARVEY
30 JUNE 2018
11:00 PDT
HIGHWAY 4
TOFINO, BC

I'm just going to the beach with Kat. That's all. It's not like it's a date or anything. It's not like it would matter if it was. Calm down, man!

Harvey grasped the steering wheel so tightly that his knuckles were white. His turn signal pinged as he waited to turn onto Highway 4. He reached to the truck's centre console to grab a CD and knocked the case to the passenger floor.

When he leaned over to pick it up, Harvey saw strands of blonde hair woven into the passenger-side carpet. He rolled his eyes. No matter how many times he'd vacuumed his truck, those hairs wouldn't go away.

Then he noticed her favourite lipstick in the ashtray. He threw it out the window. Ana's voice popped into his head: *Don't litter, Harvey!*

When there was an opening in the traffic, he turned onto the highway.

She isn't coming back. It's time to move on. Kat is a beautiful woman. And a local. She won't be jumping ship from this town like Ana did.

He drove up Industrial Way and turned to the local deli, Smoke Show, which sold a selection of gourmet charcuterie delicacies. Harvey could smell the smoked meats as he approached the building.

The screen door's hinges let out a metallic groan and a brass bell clanged above him. He entered the small storefront and admired the cooler full of meats and cheeses.

The shop owner greeted him with a smile and a roll of the eyes. "What a day!" She wiped wiry blonde hair off her brow with her forearm.

"Rita. Busy enough for you?"

"Dude, it's never ending! Good timing, you just missed a hell of a lineup. Here, try this. Blonde ale bratwurst." She handed him a sample of beer-infused sausage. The tender morsel made his mouth water.

"Nice. Yeah, I'll take a couple of those. And the kelp sausage. Some cheeses. What are those big green olives?"

"Whoa, man, don't you hate olives? Who are you trying to impress?"

"What? No one. I'm meeting a friend."

"Right."

When she smirked, Harvey noticed a blueberry muffin on the counter behind her. "Kat was here."

"Small town. No secrets here, dude. She's pretty excited, you know."

Harvey blushed and shuffled his weight from foot to foot. "Alright, since you seem to know the situation so well, any recommendations?"

"I've got your back, bro." She selected a variety of meats and cheeses Harvey never would have considered.

"Liver pâté, really, Reet?"

"Trust me. There's nothing better than organ meat. You should really try the brain confit."

"Wait, what? You make that?" His eyes widened as he searched the display for anything resembling brains.

"Bah! No, but you should've seen your face! Don't you hunt? I didn't think brains would bother you."

"I don't *eat* them."

"Too bad; they're a great source of omega-3s."

Harvey stared at Rita blankly. "Whatever, lady. I think this lot will suffice."

"Sure! You two have fun, okay? I mean it, Harvey. It's about time. Go enjoy yourself."

"Yeah, I will." He turned and pushed the door open.

"Oh, and, Harvey? Please go change that shirt." She winked

after blatantly looking him up and down.

"We're just going to the beach!" Harvey looked down at his frayed t-shirt and grout-speckled jeans.

"Did you see what she's wearing? Step it up. You can't go like that."

"Yeah, s'pose you're right. Thanks for your help, Rita."

PAUL
30 JUNE 2018
11:03 PDT
PAUL'S APARTMENT
LADNER, BC

Paul awoke lying diagonally across his bed with a sheet tangled between his legs. He ran his fingers through his dark blond curls and smiled as he reflected on the night before.

Checking the time on his phone, he ignored the half-dozen notifications on the screen. *Eleven? Crap, how do I always sleep this late?*

He sprung out of bed and crossed the room to his bookshelf, where he scanned dozens of textbooks on genetics, microbiology, and gene splicing. *Why am I even keeping these?*

Finally, he found the cookbook he was looking for. *There's gotta be something here that'll impress her*. He flipped through the pages for inspiration.

Paul heard a vibration behind him. He doubled back to the bed to retrieve his phone. The screen displayed a picture of a young woman with dark, shoulder-length hair and amber eyes.

"Morning, babe."

"Morning? Paul, it's damn near afternoon already!"

"Err, yes, I suppose so. Joss, I was thinking, how about I cook dinner tonight?"

"Oh, you know how to cook?"

"I've survived this long, haven't I?"

"Mmm, survival grub. I love it when you talk food to me."

Paul scoffed. "You're in for a real treat, just wait. What time shall I pick you up from work?"

"That's why I'm calling. They're letting me leave early. There's a festival at the mall this afternoon. Wanna check it out?"

"Ugh, really? It's going to be so busy. Imagine the crowds, and the traffic."

"Really, Paul? Come on, it'll be fun. Cotton candy, dunk

tanks, clowns! It'd mean a lot to me. I mean, we haven't really *done* anything for a while. Other than, well, I can't say with customers around."

"We *do* stuff." He fell silent as he contemplated the past few weeks. "Alright, fine. What time should I be there?"

"Wicked! How's one?"

"13:00. Roger that."

"Shit, my boss is coming. Over and out!"

Paul opened an app subconsciously and began scrolling through images curated to entice him: photos of local rock bands, views from mountaintops, sunsets and sunrises, sports teams, beautiful women in exotic scenery. An icon appeared at the top of the screen: live feed by Rocket and the Blasters. Paul tapped the image to tune in.

A beast of a man stood before a group of lankier young men. He curled his arms to display his muscles, smirked at the camera, and gave his blond locks a playful shake.

"Yo, yo, yo! Rocket and the Blasters coming at you, live from Cox Bay, in Tofino, BC! We're cleaning this dirty, dirty beach before we ride her waves for all she's got!"

Cringy, Paul thought as he watched the athlete's broadcast.

"From the slopes to the skies to the surf, Rocket and the Blasters are givin' it our all with the performance-enhancing boost of all-natural *BullBuster Juice*, now in *Rocketfuel* flavour!" He held a can that featured a picture of himself giving the thumbs-up toward the camera and raised his other hand to display the same gesture.

I heard that's not the only thing you take for performance enhancing, Rocket. Hopefully you won't end up cracking your skull on camera again this time. Ugh, what am I doing? This is such a waste of time.

Paul pocketed his phone and exited the room, stepped past his sister's bedroom door, and entered the living room. *I wonder if I can coax Ana to go out this evening and give us some privacy.*

He rearranged the black throw pillows on the sofa, then straightened a crooked print of downtown Vancouver. Paul cleared the coffee table of an empty wine bottle, two glasses, and a pizza box.

Someone—his sister, he presumed—had left out a photo album from Paul and Ana's childhood. It was open to the last picture the Zuessen family had taken together. *Ana must have come in late last night. I didn't hear her.*

He glanced toward her bedroom, then tucked a curl behind his ear and studied the photo. The family of four stood before the *Regina Vitae*, the ship their parents would set sail on for an undetermined amount of time. Their parents, wearing white lab coats, smiled proudly at the camera.

Paul recalled that day in close detail, primarily for the pain it had caused him and his sister. That was the last time they saw their father. He never returned from the *Regina Vitae's* maiden voyage. Their mother said he had gone overboard. There was no body, no grave, and no funeral. He simply ceased to exist.

Paul snapped the album closed and tucked it back on the bookshelf before walking to the kitchen in search of provisions. *Not a lot to work with here,* he thought as he rummaged through the fridge. He flicked on the radio and drafted a shopping list.

"It's going to be a hot one, folks! Slather on that sunscreen and put on your cap! And don't forget, we're sponsoring the Maple Leaf Festival at Tsawwassen Mills. Two days to partake in the festivities, starting today at noon!"

Paul scowled at the radio. *The things I do for you, Joss.*

ANA
30 JUNE 2018
11:45 PDT
COX BAY
TOFINO, BC

The contrast of the cool wind and the warm sun caused a flurry of sensation on her skin. Ana looked out at the familiar view: a smooth, sandy beach stretched a kilometre long. Rugged rocks jutted out into the ocean on either end the bay.

Gulls and crows took turns harassing picnickers, their cacophony of calls in disharmony against the rhythm of the ocean. Hundreds of people filled the beach: strolling, surfing, stretching, or simply enjoying the view.

Saline air mixed with the smoke of a nearby fire pit, a smell that reminded Ana of summer nights she held fondly in her memory. She closed her eyes, inhaling the scents of forest and ocean, and felt an arm rest on her shoulder.

"It's good to see you, Ana."

"It's nice to be here. I didn't realize how much I missed this view."

I should send Paul a photo. She started patting herself down in search of her cell.

"What's up?"

"I think I left my phone at your place. I haven't spoken to Paul since yesterday. I don't think he knows I'm here."

"Come on, girl, get your head out of the city. Look where you are!"

"I know. I just don't want him to worry."

"You've been away, what, five hours? And he's going to worry? I know twins are close, but that's ridiculous." He poked the tattoo of antlers framing a geometric lotus on her left upper arm.

Ana gave Skylar a shove. He stumbled backward in the sand, then rebounded and grabbed her by the waist and lifted her into the air. She yelped and tried to pinch his arms in a feeble attempt at escape.

"Put me down, you brute!"

"Not until you snap out of it!"

They fell backward in the sand. Ana feigned submission, and Skylar loosened his grip enough for her to roll free.

"Finally, a smile outta you! Just needed a bit of roughing up?" He pulled himself into a cross-legged position.

"You wish you could rough me up. You're missing slack tide! Get in the water!"

"You should've brought your gear, An. Look at those waves! Perfect intervals. Even you could paddle out past the break."

"Even me? What are you saying, Skylar?"

"Well, with those little twigs of yours..."

"Twigs?! Speak for yourself!"

Skylar stood and brushed the sand off his faded denim shorts, walked to his bike, and retrieved his maroon wetsuit from a basket affixed to the handlebars. He shimmied out of his shorts and writhed his way into the dry neoprene, then lifted his surfboard from a rack connected to his bike's rear wheel. He laid it in the sand and set to work adding a coat of fresh wax to his board.

Ana watched his handiwork. *Damn, I wish I had brought my board. He's right, it is a perfect day.*

HARVEY
30 JUNE 2018
11:45 PDT
HARVEY'S TRAILER
TOFINO, BC

The hangers clicked as Harvey flipped through shirts hanging in his closet. A hunter-green golf shirt with military-style accents and brass buttons caught his eye. He swapped his grungy jeans for black cargo pants, then ran a comb through his hair. *Should've cut it, dammit.*

As he sat on the edge of his bed, about to lace up tactical leather boots that looked as though they'd outlive humankind, he noticed dirt on the carpet in the trailer's square foot of hallway. *What the hell? I just vacuumed that floor last night.*

He jumped up from the bed and walked across the trailer to discover more flecks of dirt across his tiny kitchen floor. The dirt trailed out the door, and Harvey saw footprints that led to his workshop, a converted shipping container that stood behind his trailer. Tire tracks led from his workshop up to the driveway.

Stepping back inside the trailer, he opened a cupboard where his keys hung. The shop key was there, hanging one peg over from its usual hook. Harvey grabbed the key and ran outside.

He clenched his teeth as he unlocked the deadbolt. The door let out a steely groan as it swung open. He began taking inventory of his belongings. Everything seemed in order, except for one missing item: Ana's bike.

Fucking Skylar! If you want something, just ask. Use a cell phone like a normal person.

Skylar borrowed the bike occasionally when he had female *friends* to tour around, but he had always asked permission first.

Harvey stomped back to the trailer and hung the keys in

the cupboard. A coffin-sized black steel box stood in the corner of his minuscule living room.

"Two hundred square feet to live in, and you're taking up 10% of it with that *thing?"* The memory of Ana's nagging rang through his mind.

He keyed in the password to his gun safe. Despite his certainty that Skylar didn't know the code, he had to see his collection to ease his mind.

He took inventory of his rifles and shotguns. Harvey saw Ana's Ruger 10/22 sitting in the back left corner of the safe. Would she ever come back for it? He had considered selling it. A year had passed and there it sat, waiting.

I'm getting rid of all her shit. It's time.

His finger tapped a message onto the screen of his phone. *Hi Ana. I would like to talk to you about your belongings. You know better than anyone how cramped it is in here. Please let me know what you want me to do with your stuff.* Send.

He jumped when his phone started buzzing. *It's Kat.* Harvey welcomed the distraction. He answered the call as he locked the safe.

Harvey cleared his throat. "Hullo?"

"Well, hello, Mr. O'Ryan!"

Harvey blushed when she called him that. The tone in her voice drove him crazy. She had called him by his last name for months, but lately it had a different effect on him.

"Hey, Kat. How's it going?"

"Fine and dandy. I'm finished at the cafe. When's a good time to meet?"

"Right on. I'm ready anytime!"

"Pick me up at noon?"

"Perfect. See you then!"

"See you soon, Mr. O'Ryan."

I'd better leave now. Tourist traffic will be getting heavy.

Harvey stole a quick glance in the mirror to check his hair, finished tying his laces, and exited his trailer.

LARA
30 JUNE 2018
11:45 PDT
COX BAY
TOFINO, BC

"Nice one, Stella, you throw like a—"

"Don't you dare say it, Chris! I can throw better than you with my eyes closed."

Lara nearly dropped the surfboard when a frisbee flew past her head. She caught it and manoeuvred her board back onto her hip.

The sun illuminated her cherry locks as Stella jogged over to retrieve the frisbee.

Lara handed it to the young woman with a smile.

"Nice catch!"

"Thanks. Hey, I'm looking for my husband. He's about this tall, hair is a few shades lighter than yours. Dark green wetsuit. Probably passed by here around fifteen minutes ago."

"Sorry, I've seen lots of people today, but that doesn't ring a bell." Stella shrugged nonchalantly.

"It's okay, thanks anyway."

"Stella, come on! We're going to hike up to that point!" When they called to her, Stella's friends were already walking south down the beach.

Stella nodded, then turned back to Lara. "Good luck finding him." Her heels kicked up sand as she took off after her friends.

"Yeah, thanks. Enjoy the view."

Lara turned back to the ocean and scanned the area. *Had to choose the busiest weekend of the year to visit Tofino, huh, Mark? Couldn't have waited a few days?* Lara felt ashamed after the thought crossed her mind. If her husband's dying wish was to surf a crowded beach, so be it.

The surrounding scenery mesmerized Lara. Evergreen trees

sculpted by the winds of winter storms enshrouded the coast. A rocky shoreline jutted to a point at the south end of the beach: Cox Point, where Stella was headed. To the north, hikers dotted Pettinger Point, where they enjoyed a view of surfers waiting beyond the break for their next wave. Water crashed against the rocks and threatened those nearby from getting too close. The ocean was a deep teal with glassy waves that curled perfectly before they washed out in rows of foam and bubbles.

Lara laid her board in the sand, knelt beside it, and rubbed it with wax until her forearm ached. Once it had a sufficient layer, she stretched and returned her attention to the bay.

Hordes of people attempted to catch waves in the whitewash. *Yeah, right. Mark will be farther than that.* She scanned beyond the break, knowing she was in for a tricky game of *Where's Waldo?*

Lara hoped his green suit would help her identify him amongst a school of surfers in black neoprene. Her own purple suit hung from her hips, with limp arms hanging to her knees. She finished pulling the suit on and tugged a string attached to the zipper on her back.

"Put me down, you brute!"

A familiar voice caught Lara's attention. She turned to see Ana and a tall man fall backward into the sand. *Ahh, is this the reason you came back, Ana?* Not wanting to interrupt their moment, Lara waited until they stopped play-fighting to approach.

"Hey! Ana, over here!" Lara waved.

"Lara! Hey! Where's Mark?" Ana dusted sand off herself as Lara approached.

"I'm not sure. I dropped him off at the trailhead and went to find parking... It's packed here! I'm having a hell of a time spotting him."

"I can imagine. I'll keep an eye out! Hey, this is my friend Skylar." She gestured to the man beside her, kneeling in the sand and rubbing a layer of wax on his board. "Skylar, this is

Lara. We met on the plane."

"Greetings, Lara! Pleasure!" Skylar flashed his chipped-toothed grin up at her.

"So, is this the guy you came back for?" Lara winked at Ana.

Ana's eyes widened, and she blushed when she looked at Skylar. "What? I never told you about that... You're very perceptive. No, I haven't spoken to *Harvey* yet. There was a... complication."

"Competition is more like it." Skylar made to jab Ana with his elbow.

Ana evaded him and yelled, "Skylar! Shush!"

"It's going to be a hell of a showdown. Step right up, folks, get your tickets here. In the left corner we have Ana, weighing in at a buck sixty-five and six feet in stature. To my right, Kat, standing at five-five, looking like she'll get blown away by the next gale-force wind!" He chuckled at his own joke.

Lara saw Ana take a deep breath as she looked at her feet.

"Kinda rude," Lara muttered.

Skylar shrugged.

"That's just Skylar's way of trying to make me feel better." Ana played with her braid as she defended her friend. "I think he's used to interacting with his bros."

"Funny way of comforting someone."

"Listen, ladies, I didn't mean to offend. Lara, perhaps you can have, like, girl talk or something. I'm sure you can provide a little more insight than I. Ana, the waves...they call me..."

"Yeah, yeah, get in the water, you weirdo," she said as she gestured toward the ocean.

Skylar pulled her into one of his classic bear hugs and whispered into her hair, "Sorry, kiddo."

"It's all good. Get out there!" She hugged him back before pushing him in the direction of the waves.

Skylar let out an energetic yelp and darted toward the water with his surfboard tucked under his arm.

Lara shook her head, then turned to Ana and said, "Your

friend is kind of a jerk."

Ana watched Skylar wade through the whitewash. "He means well enough."

"So, where is this Harvey?"

"On a date. Ugh, I left for too long. Do I dare interrupt his life now?"

"Your love for him clearly hasn't faded. Do you think his has?" She offered Ana an encouraging smile.

"I can't say. We haven't spoken for a while. When my... when my mom died...I had to go take care of her estate. I just... shut down. Shut everyone out and disappeared. It's understandable for him to move on. Maybe I should just let him."

"But now you're back, and won't be disappearing again. Right?"

"Right."

"So what the hell are you still doing here?" She raised her arms to emphasize the question.

"I don't know. Seeing another woman on his doorstep, it made me second-guess strutting back into his life out of the blue." Ana fidgeted with her braid as her eyes fell once again to the ochre sand.

"I can understand your hesitation, but if there's one thing my husband's illness has taught me, it's to not let life pass you by. You have to try! You've come all this way."

"You're right. I will. Thanks, Lara."

"Alright, get outta here, *kiddo*," Lara jested.

"Hah... Alright! You want a hand finding Mark first?"

"Just go!" Lara smiled at Ana.

"Okay, okay! Have fun in the surf."

"I will. Goodbye, Ana!"

Lara watched as Ana walked her bike toward the trail that led to the parking lot, its wheels carving deep grooves in the sand. *Poor thing, I hope he takes her back. If things don't work out, at least she'll have closure.*

SKYLAR
30 JUNE 2018
12:00 PDT
COX BAY
TOFINO, BC

A wall of water approached. Skylar pushed down on his board to force it beneath the surface. He executed a textbook duck dive under the wave and resurfaced after it passed.

Skylar paddled farther out, forcing his arms to cut deeply through the water to drive him away from shore. He passed the break and sat in line with the other surfers, facing open ocean in anticipation of the next big one.

Fuck, why did I crack that joke? Maybe I was a little insensitive. Ana's somehow holding herself together, and I had to go make a stupid comment like that? His board bobbed up and down as the ocean rose and fell.

"Thought that was you in that pink wetsuit, ya dummy!"

"It's not pink, you jackass!" Skylar called. He watched the man paddle toward him, his shaggy blond hair hanging in wet tendrils around his face.

"Magenta."

"Maroon!"

"Whatever, man. I still say black is best. Keeps ya warm, looks so sleek. Classic, man, classic!" He sat up on his board and lifted his arms for emphasis.

"If you say so, Kyle. How's the sesh been?"

Kyle brushed a sopping tuft of hair off his forehead. "Pretty good, man, pretty neat! Here comes another set now! Yo, here we go!"

Skylar and Kyle paddled toward shore as the next set of waves approached. When he felt the tail of his board rise, Skylar pushed harder for a few strokes, grabbed the rails of his board, and popped up into his goofy stance. Kyle popped up ten feet from Skylar. They made eye contact briefly as they rode side by side. Skylar leaned into the nose of his board, propelling himself in front of Kyle to cut him off. Kyle submitted, and dove back behind the wave as Skylar whipped his board around. He carved the face of the wave, then cut back and dove off over the backside before it broke and washed out.

"What the hell, man?! Quit being such a kook!"

Skylar laughed. "Sorry, dude, that wave was mine!"

"That's it! If you keep dropping in like that, I'm taking away your Poseidon's Pocket privileges. Your friends and family discount is revoked!"

"Hah! I've already got one of your boards. You'll have to come up with a better punishment than that!" Skylar said before he dove under an approaching wave.

Kyle made the mistake of keeping his back to the ocean, and the wave caught him off guard and swept him closer to shore. Skylar laughed at his friend's expense while he watched Kyle paddle against the waves back to the lineup.

"You're a real dick, you know that." Kyle spat a mouthful of briny saliva back into the ocean.

"Kyle, 'twas not I who unleashed that wave upon you. Poseidon's will is his own."

Kyle stared at his friend blankly.

"Anyway, man, I'm not sticking around. I said something stupid to Ana. I gotta go find her."

"Ana Zuessen? She's back?" Kyle lifted an eyebrow at Skylar.

He shrugged. "Yeah, man. Came to get Harvey back."

"Well? Now's your chance," Kyle said as he bobbed over a wave that would break closer to shore.

"Chance for what?" Their eyes met.

"C'mon, man, the electricity between you two has always been obvious."

"Huh? There's no *electricity*. We're friends."

"Deny, deny, deny. Take Harvey out of the picture, and you'd be all over that."

"Nah, man. I'm a nomad. No woman can hold this beast down." With that, Skylar paddled to catch a wave and popped up to ride its glassy face. When the wave washed out, he pulsed the board with his feet to keep his momentum and coasted to shore as he wove his way through novice surfers playing in the whitewash.

KAT
30 JUNE 2018
12:00 PDT
RAVEN'S ROOST CAFE
TOFINO, BC

"You're burning it again. Hear that shrill sound? It's the milk screaming. Ease up on the steamer," Kat instructed her mousy-looking employee from her seat on a tree stump stool beside the bar. She watched Flo's every move.

The decor in Raven's Roost Cafe was that of a gothic rainforest: the accents were dark yet earthy, with damask wallpaper and black chandeliers.

Crunching gravel caught her attention. Kat peeked out the cafe window to see a black pickup truck roll up. *He's on time. Good man. I think I'll keep him waiting a moment.*

Kat picked up two paper cups from the burl counter. "Alright, Flo, I'm off! Remember, call me if anything h—"

"For goodness' sake, Kat, get going! I'll be fine here. I usually am when you have days off. Relax!"

Kat turned, her gaze locked with the younger woman's, and a malicious glint sparkled in her eyes. "*Usually*. That's the key word."

"Kat, quit being so possessive." The young barista nervously fidgeted with her apron as she lowered her eyes from Kat's intense gaze.

"I'm what now?"

"I meant protective!" Flo's face flushed. She attempted to regain her composure.

"Possessive? What happened last time I left you in charge here, Flo?"

"I...I set the place on fire."

"You set the place on fire," they said in unison. Kat placed the cups back on the counter and walked toward a storage closet. She pulled out a small fire extinguisher and placed it behind the counter. "There. *Now* I can relax."

"Kat, that was an accident, and the chances of it happening again..." She wiped her glasses on her shirt, feigning their immediate need for a cleaning to avoid looking her boss in the eye again.

"It better not happen again."

"And how many times do I have to apologize..."

"You should be thankful you still have a job."

"I am," the younger woman whispered as she straightened her name tag.

Kat picked up the coffee cups and walked toward the door. She turned to Flo once more. "Just take care of this place. I'll see you tomorrow."

Harvey leaned against the passenger side of his truck, arms folded behind his head.

"Good day, Mr. O'Ryan."

"Hey, Kat." He opened the door for her.

She handed him a cup and stepped up into the truck. "Latte?"

"How'd you know?" He accepted it and took a long sip. "Mmm, that tastes different than usual." He closed the door and walked around to the driver's side.

"What can I say, I know my customers. It has cinnamon and cardamom extract," she said as he climbed in beside her.

"Nice touch! I never would have thought of that."

"I've been experimenting with a lot of different flavours lately." Her eyes never left him as he pulled the truck out of the driveway and drove down the hill.

"I'm curious to try the other ones."

"I bet you are."

His eyes connected with hers briefly. "Which beach?"

"South Chesterman's?"

Harvey signaled right as he waited to turn onto the highway. "It always amazes me. How busy it gets."

"More so every year."

Amid the vast number of people cruising down the pedestrian path, Kat's gaze happened upon a tall blonde woman near Harvey's driveway.

That looks like... No way. It couldn't be. Rita had filled Kat in on all the details regarding Harvey and his ex. Social media sleuthing had taken place, and this woman was unmistakable.

What the fuck is she doing here? Does he know?

Kat grabbed his arm when Harvey instinctively glanced toward his driveway as he drove past.

"Ahh! Nails!" Her attack stole his attention.

"Oh, I'm sorry, Harvey, did I scratch you? I forget how long they are sometimes. I just had an idea! Why don't we go to the mud flats instead? The beaches will be so busy! I know the sweetest little grove in the forest there. It's *very* private."

It's so private, your ex will never find us there.

"Er, sure, that sounds great." Harvey shot her a sideways look. "How are things at the cafe?"

The truck followed the twists of the winding highway as Kat filled him in on her morning. A few minutes later, Harvey pulled into the parking lot of Cox Bay Visitor Information Centre.

Kat pretended to search for something in her purse. *Let's see how chivalrous Harvey is.* She waited and watched as he walked around the truck and opened the passenger-side door for her. *Good boy.*

He gave her a hand down. The lift on his truck was high, and Kat was petite in stature. She intentionally overshot her step and fumbled her landing so her body pressed up against Harvey's. He reached out and put a steadying arm around her.

"Oops. Thank you." She could sense his nervousness when she looked up at him.

"Yer, you're welcome," Harvey stammered. He broke free from her spell, and withdrew an insulated backpack from the back seat.

"What's this?"

"I hope you're hungry. I grabbed a few things from Smoke Show. These came highly recommended."

"Ahh. Rita, a woman who knows her meats." Kat grinned mischievously.

Harvey raised his eyebrows but made no comment.

They walked down the sidewalk toward the trailhead. Despite the platform wedges she wore, Kat effortlessly navigated the cracked pavement. He admired how the periwinkle dress hugged her narrow waist. She turned, caught him staring, and gave him a wink. Harvey blushed.

"What a beautiful day, Mr. O'Ryan. It couldn't be more perfect!"

They turned right at a yellow gate that barricaded the trail. Cedar and salal on either side of the path corralled them through the forest toward the mudflats.

"I haven't been on this trail in ages. Good call," Harvey commented. They walked side by side, the contents of his backpack rustling with each step.

"Come on, I'll show you my favourite spot." Kat took his hand and pulled him down the earthen path.

"Lead the way."

ANA
30 JUNE 2018
12:20 PDT
HIGHWAY 4
TOFINO, BC

Hotels along the highway had parking lots that overflowed with temporary tenants. The pavement flew beneath Ana's wheels as she pedaled past. Her cruiser weaved between pedestrians as she warned them out of her way with a bell fixed to her handlebars.

The wind whipped her long braid behind her and a light sweat broke out on her lip and lower back. She brushed her face with the back of her arm and slowed a little.

The thoughts in her head spun like a carousal. She rehearsed what she would say to Harvey when she finally faced him.

When she approached her old home for the second time that day, Ana saw his matte-black truck driving along Highway 4. There was a dark-haired woman in the passenger seat next to Harvey.

"Fuck!" she said aloud as she stopped her bike. Ana received a glare from a passing woman pushing a stroller.

Which beach are you going to, Harvey? Mackenzie was always your favourite place to chill, but perhaps you let her decide. Damn you for being such a gentleman. Ana stood and contemplated her next move. *Ugh, it doesn't matter now. Not like I'm going to chase you down on my bike.*

She walked her bicycle down the hill toward Harvey's trailer and set it down next to his workshop, then followed the path to Skylar's plot and took a seat in one of his weathered lawn chairs.

Her backpack lay on the ground. It let out a low vibration. She grabbed her cell phone from the pack to find a text from Harvey: *Hi Ana. I would like to talk to you about your belongings. You know better than anyone how cramped it is here.*

Please let me know what you want me to do with your stuff.

Ana read the text with wide eyes. She threw her phone into the tree line and leaned back in the chair. She tried to clear her head as she gazed up at the treetops that encircled Skylar's camp. A gentle breeze shook the scaly cedar boughs, creating a kaleidoscope against the cloudless sky. Once she had calmed down, Ana got up to retrieve her phone. It took her a few minutes to locate it nestled in a bouquet of ferns.

She scrolled her social media accounts in search of a distraction. Jocelyn had commented on Paul's latest Instagram post. *Can't wait to see you after work today*, it read, followed by some rather suggestive emojis. He had already replied to her comment.

Come on, Paul. How hard is it to call me back?

She went to her contact list and tapped on her twin's name. The phone rang six times and went to voicemail. "*Hi, this is Paul. Please hang up and shoot me a text instead!*" It didn't surprise her that there was no answer. If Paul had plans with Jocelyn, he was likely manscaping or devising some way to impress her.

Ana went back to scrolling through images. She came to a clip of Rocket, a narcissistic extreme sports athlete with too much love for his own face. He was on a very familiar looking beach. *What the hell? That's Cox Bay...* Rocket held up a vial filled with a purple substance while his crew of jocks gathered around him. The hairs on the back of Ana's neck rose as a sense of deja vu flooded her mind.

An intrusive sound broke the silence. Wailing that pierced the air screamed louder than any car alarm. Ana lowered her phone and looked in the disturbance's direction: the coast.

Her heart drummed against her ribcage and a sensation tingled behind her ears. *Shit. Is that the fucking tsunami alarm? This could be a test. Or an accident. They've accidentally set it off before. Either way, I've gotta get up the hill.*

She grabbed her backpack and hurried up the path toward

the driveway. Ana felt unsteady on her feet, but forced her legs to keep moving. *Skylar. Harvey. Lara. Fuck, they're all at the beach right now.*

Ana's body felt stiff as she picked up her bike. *I don't need this. The hill is right there.* Ana dropped her bike and slammed into someone as she turned to walk up the drive. He smelled of the ocean and stale cigarette smoke. His arms encircled her.

"You were surfing," she whispered.

"I was." He released her from the embrace and held her at arm's length, his eyes searching hers.

"Why are you here?" Ana asked as she looked into Skylar's dark eyes.

"Listen, An, I'm sorry for what I said. That was a stupid joke. You know I meant nothing by it, right?"

She stared at him blankly. "You think what you said upset me? Sky, I know your sense of humour. It's fine! But now is probably not the time." She looked beyond him to the road.

"Yeah, okay. Well then. The surf was great, but I'm sorta glad I left the beach." His lips curled into a nervous smile. "Let me grab a couple things from my trailer, then we'll head up the hill to Industrial Way, okay?"

"Okay. Please be quick, Skylar."

"We'll be fine, An. It's probably a false alarm. Or a prank, some joker got access to the button and figured it'd be funny to give twenty thousand people a scare." He stepped past her and jogged up the path to his trailer.

Ana wished the alarm away. With every wail, her body tensed. Then, between chimes, the sound of smashing glass and crumpling metal added to the chaos. A second metallic crunch followed, and a third.

"Come on, Skylar, let's go!" Ana called. He emerged from his trailer, slung a backpack over his shoulder, and jogged back to her side.

"What was that? An accident?" he asked.

She nodded. "It sounded bad."

They strode up the gravel drive toward the highway.

Of all the blind corners on Highway 4, this one was exceptionally dangerous. A four-car pile-up blocked the highway near the bottom of Industrial Way. Crimson encircled a gaping hole in the windshield of one car. The smell of gasoline, antifreeze, copper, and smoke filled the air.

Ana turned away and retched, ejecting bile that burned her throat. Skylar put a hand on her back as she crouched over, coughing and sputtering the only contents of her stomach: coffee and bile.

Nearby drivers honked their horns and exited their automobiles to see what the holdup was. Bystanders ran over to help people from their wrecked vehicles.

The wailing sobs of a middle-aged woman caught Ana's attention. The woman yanked on the door handle of one of the mangled cars. The young man inside was unresponsive, his head on the steering wheel.

"Timmy! Timmy, open the door! Wake up, Timmy, open the door!" She knocked on the window so hard that her knuckles left bloody dots on the glass.

"Ana, wait here," Skylar said.

Ana wiped her mouth with the back of her arm and nodded. She watched as Skylar hustled over to the woman.

"Excuse me, ma'am? That's a real lovely scarf you're wearing. It's a nice day out, a bit warm for a scarf though. May I borrow it for a moment?"

She nearly snarled at Skylar. "What are you going on about my scarf for? That's my son in there. He's trapped. He's hurt!"

"Let me help you. Please, give me your scarf."

"Take it! Fucking take it!" She ripped her scarf off, threw it on the ground, and tugged on the locked door again.

Ana joined Skylar and the frantic woman. A crowd streamed past them up the hill; people gaped at the wreckage as they passed.

Skylar wrapped the scarf around his fist and walked to the

rear passenger door. *Oh, god, be careful, Skylar*. Ana watched, nervous for her friend, and followed his eyes to a crack in the window. Skylar punched his target. Ana flinched when the crack became a spider web. He hit it again. And again. On the fourth blow, the glass broke away enough for him to reach his arm inside the window and unlock the door. He got in the back seat and reached forward to unlock the vehicle.

"Timmy, oh, Timmy!" The distraught mother opened the door and shook her son by the shoulders.

"Skylar, I think he's..."

"Timmy!! Timmy, wake up! Come on, honey! Mama's here now!"

"An, can you distract her for a minute?" Skylar asked in a hushed tone.

Ana's head swam. *Make that alarm stop. Please, make it stop*. She nodded, shaking her head of the sensory overload, and rested her hand on the woman's shoulder to guide her away from the vehicle.

"Excuse me, ma'am? What's your name?"

"Martha. My son, Timmy..."

"Hi, Martha. Can you please step back a minute? My friend Skylar is going to try to help your son. I need you to come over here with me."

Martha looked at Skylar with pleading eyes. He nodded at her, and she backed away.

"Thank you, Martha. What brought you to Tofino this weekend?" *Keep her talking, don't let her watch this.*

"Timmy wanted to surf. He loves surfing." She turned toward the car again and let out a sob. "He dropped me off so I could grab a coffee while he went to pick up his board. We were going to go to the beach together."

Ana put her hand on the woman's shoulder again to divert her attention away from her son. "Have *you* surfed before, Martha?"

"No. No, I can't swim."

“Oh.” *Well, in that case, let’s all get the fuck up this hill before the great flood comes.* “Where are you from?”

Ana barely listened to her response as she watched Skylar. He placed a hand at the nape of Timmy’s neck, and guided his head back from the steering wheel. Timmy’s eyes were open. Blood had trickled down from a gash above his brow, pooled into his eye, and spilled back out like a crimson tear that rolled down his cheek. Skylar held his fingers under the man’s jaw and felt for a pulse. His eyes connected with Ana’s, and he shook his head as he closed Timmy’s eyelids.

HARVEY
30 JUNE 2018
12:25 PDT
MUDFLAT WILDLIFE MANAGEMENT AREA
TOFINO, BC

"Honestly, if you don't like it, you can spit it out. Try it!"

Harvey frowned. "I dunno, maybe my palate just isn't that refined."

"Castelvetranos have such a wonderful, fruity, buttery flavour though! Please, trust me?" She rolled a plump, bright green olive between her thumb and index finger.

I'd rather try Rita's brain confit. "Okay, o—" Before he could finish agreeing, she popped it in his mouth. Harvey chewed the pungent fruit. *Nasty.*

"Well?"

"It's...okay."

"You love it! I knew you would." Kat reached across the blanket to their assortment of treats and sampled one of the cheeses.

Harvey pulled a growler out of his backpack.

"Tofino Brewing Company, excellent choice. I usually crack a bottle of wine with my charcuterie platters, but I indulge in an IPA from time to time."

"You're into bold flavours then. Will blonde ale suffice?" he asked as he poured the golden brew into two glasses. A perfect layer of micro bubbles capped the surface of the liquid.

"You like blondes, don't you?"

"What?"

"Nothing. Sure, that sounds refreshing." She accepted the glass and inhaled the malty scent as she sipped deeply.

Near the mudflats, the trees grew farther apart than on other parts of the peninsula, and the underbrush grew less densely. Between boughs of cedar, they had a magnificent view of the inlet. Tide was high. Gulls flew above the water in the distance.

Their blanket lay next to a massive stump, from which sections of wood circumnavigating the trunk were missing—evidence of logging practices from a century prior. Harvey admired the handiwork that was still visible amongst the decaying fibre.

Kat offered him a chunk of cheese off the end of a knife. "Harvey, I've been waiting a long time for this."

"Well...thanks!" *Come on, you idiot! Can't think of something more charming to say?* He washed the cheese down with a sip of ale and set his glass on the stump.

"Fate favours the brave."

"What's tha—" Before he could finish, her lips were on his. Alarm bells rang in his mind. *Something's off... Wait, what the fuck? That's an actual alarm!*

Kat retreated and looked to the west toward the source of the sound. Her eyes narrowed. "Well, there goes our fun."

"Do you think it's legit?"

"Unlikely. Stupid thing is worse than the boy who cried wolf."

"It doesn't go off *that* often."

"Regardless." She ran a hand through his hair. "I was looking forward to time *alone*, to become better acquainted." Her lips were on his once more.

Huh, there's that alarm again. Harvey pulled back. Their gaze locked momentarily until he turned away and began packing up their snacks. Kat sipped her beer and watched as Harvey stood and offered her a hand. She reluctantly accepted it, and he pulled Kat to her feet, then picked up the plaid blanket they had been sitting on, shook off the debris of the forest floor, and tucked it into his backpack. "We're on pretty low ground here. We should pick it up a little."

"Oh, Harvey, are you scared? Come on. There won't *actually* be a tsunami."

"I'm just saying, haste and heels don't exactly go hand in hand. Especially on a forest trail."

"These are *wedges*. Fine. Let's do this." She kicked off

her shoes, picked them up, and jogged down the trail. When Harvey caught up, Kat shot him a sideways look. “Race ya?”

“You’re barefoot, in a dress. That’s unfair odds, I’d say.”

“Oh really? I’d say I have the advantage.” She sped off, leaving him behind.

What the hell? Well, that was unexpected. Harvey pushed himself to catch up.

When they reached the trailhead, car horns honked over the tsunami alarm. The flow of traffic into town stood still. Several vehicles turned around and headed south.

“Looks like we won’t be making it to the assembly point at Industrial Way. Mallard Lake?”

“Fancy a hike, do you, Harvey?”

“As long as the road is clear, we won’t need to hike. Besides, it’s the closest spot with a high elevation...”

She marched toward his truck, her breath steady despite their bout of cardio. “Do you think it’s high enough?”

“Yeah, I think so. The peaks surrounding the lake have to be close to a hundred metres. We have better odds there than if we try to make it out to the airport.”

Harvey unlocked his truck and climbed in. He looked through the passenger-side window and saw Kat glaring back at him.

“I guess chivalry really *is* dead,” Kat accused as she climbed into Harvey’s truck.

“Sorry? I thought we were trying to hustle. My apologies for skipping the pleasantries.” *Are you kidding me?* “You don’t think this is real yet, do you?”

“No, Harvey. I don’t think this is real. The town is likely testing their emergency response plan. What better way than the busiest weekend of the year?” Kat stepped into her wedges and smoothed her skirt.

Harvey ignored her conspiratorial comment, pulled the truck forward, and waited for an opportunity to turn onto the highway. A Volkswagen camper van heading north on the gridlocked street inched forward and blocked him from pulling out.

"What the hell, man?!" Harvey called, raising his hands to the driver. He pressed a hand on his horn and gestured that he intended to get onto the highway in the opposite direction.

The VW driver, a young man with messy locks, had no room to reverse and completely barred their path. He looked at Harvey and shrugged.

"Yeah-fuckin'-right." Harvey stepped out of the truck and approached the Volkswagen. He tapped his knuckles on the window. "Dude, let's go! You can't just block us in here!"

"We 'ave to get to zee azzemblee stasheeon," he called through the pane of glass separating him and Harvey.

"This lineup is going nowhere! We're heading up a nearby hill. Pull out and head south." Harvey pointed to the peak of the small mountain. "Move this piece of junk and follow us."

"My lovehr eez zees way." He pointed toward the dead traffic.

"Your *lovehr* is likely on high ground by now, as we should be. Come on, man!"

Harvey watched his shoulders rise and fall with a dramatic sigh. "Fine, fine, 'ave eet your way. Bring us to safety, oh fearless leadehr," he said facetiously.

A young man in board shorts and a purple speckled tank approached. "Hey, dudes, anybody have room for one more?" he asked, looking from the VW driver to Harvey.

"Whatevehr. 'Op in. Let's go."

Harvey returned to his truck.

"Oh, I do like an assertive man, Mr. O'Ryan."

He mentally rolled his eyes. "Let's get the hell outta here."

LARA
30 JUNE 2018
12:25 PDT
COX BAY
TOFINO, BC

Lara walked Cox Bay's length twice in search of Mark. The beach was packed. *We shouldn't've split up. I forgot how big this beach is. Maybe he's in the water already.*

Her arms were getting sore from toting the board up and down the bay. Sweat built up underneath the thick wetsuit she wore, and Lara realized how thirsty she was. She set her board down and walked past a family playing volleyball, toward a line of driftwood where her water bottle lay hidden next to a log.

A group of young men carrying black garbage bags shuffled around the driftwood with their eyes to the ground. The crew snapped selfies with every scrap of waste they recovered from the sand. A large tent, which appeared to be the group's home base, stood nearby, surrounded by several bags of trash. Dance music blared from within the thin polyester at an obnoxious volume.

Lara searched her hiding place to find her bottle was gone.

"Hey, I had a water bottle sitting here, have you seen it?" Lara called to the group.

"Yeah, man! We've picked up tons of plastic demons during our shoreline cleanup today. Have you seen the photos of people rippin' it out in barrels full of trash? So sick, dude. So sick, and not in the good way." The young man shook dark hair off his forehead. "That's why we're out here, Rocket and the Blasters, paying our respect to the land before we go out and rip it up!"

"I *have* seen that. It's quite sad. What I'm looking for is a *reusable* bottle. I left it right there. Hey, shouldn't you be wearing gloves?" Lara grimaced as she watched the man squat down to retrieve something wedged between two of the logs.

"That'd just create more waste, man! Whoa, what's this? Check it out, Rocket!" He held up a double-walled glass cylinder etched with a symbol of a phoenix wearing a crown. Its contents shone a vivid purple, which was leaking from the cracked inner chamber.

A mountainous, square-shouldered young man with tight blond locks strutted over. He held his hand out to his friend. "Nice find, Yu. Wicked logo. Is that a phoenix? Very cool!"

"Can I keep it, Rocket?"

"I don't really care what you do with it, as long as it's removed from this beach. Take pics for our socials, let the people know what kind of weird things we're finding!" Rocket pulled a phone from his pocket and posed with the vial before handing it back to Yu.

Lara took a step closer as she squinted at the vial. "That looks like a biohazard symbol on the back. I don't think you should handle it."

The Blasters gathered around while Yu turned the tube in his hands. His finger found a button that released the cracked inner chamber of the vial. Its contents, a thick, royal-purple fluid, flowed down Yu's hand.

"Wow! Wow...wow... Ahh! It's burning my skin!"

Lara's eyes widened. She stepped back and looked frantically for her water to rinse the substance off him.

Yu began laughing, "I'm just kiddin', dudes! You guys shoulda seen your faces!"

The Blasters joined in on his laughter.

"Really? That's not funny. We have no idea what that crap is!" Lara yelled.

"Don't even worry about it, lady. He's fine, see?"

"Incoming!"

A volleyball flew toward their crew. Yu dropped the vial to set the ball up into the air. He left ten purple smears on it. One of his buddies jumped forward to volley it. Another dove in and spiked the ball back to its owner. Upon impact, the goo sprayed little droplets over Lara, Rocket, and the Blasters.

"Ew, what is it?"

"It's a giant glow stick!"

"Lars, you know what this means?"

"Time to party!" Rocket jogged to the tent and turned the music up louder.

Lara looked with disgust at the flecks of goo that splattered her wetsuit. She inspected her hands to see that they, too, were speckled. "We should probably wash this stuff off!" Lara looked around at the crowd. They were jumping, swaying, moving to the rhythm of the beat pumping from the tent.

A loud siren cut across the beach and wailed over the music. In unison, all eyes turned toward the sound that emitted from a speaker staked forty feet in the air.

Lara covered her ears. She felt something sticky in her brunette ringlets and lowered her hand to see purple goo hanging in tendrils between her fingers. *Gross. What is this stuff?*

There was shouting as hordes of people ran toward the trail to the parking lot.

Mark, where the hell are you? Lara watched the stream of people, hoping to see his face.

"Yu! What are you doing?" one of his friends cried as Yu collapsed onto the sand and convulsed.

Three of the Blasters knelt next to Yu's twitching body.

Lara dropped to her knees beside Yu and his friends. "Is he epileptic?"

"What? No!" Lars said. "Been to enough raves together that I think we'd know."

The purple goo had oozed down Yu's forehead into the whites of his eyes. Dark circles formed around his irises. With each inhalation, he emitted sharp chirping sounds as he gasped for breath.

What's happening to him? Lara's head felt clouded. *I don't... I can't... Why...* She felt suddenly exhausted, unable to hold herself up, and fell forward onto all fours. Each breath felt increasingly laborious. Lara fell to the sand and felt her body writhe in uncontrollable tremors, just as Yu's convulsing stopped.

No one noticed when Rocket scooped up the vial, careful that its contents didn't touch his skin. After one last glance at Yu, Lara, and the remaining Blasters, he wrapped the vial in a bag and pocketed it, then fled the beach.

"Yu! It's okay, buddy, we'll get you out of here!" Lars put a hand on Yu's cheek.

Yu stirred and inhaled deeply through his nose several times. He snapped at the hand on his face and caught Lars' finger between his teeth.

"Ahh! What the fuck, man?!" Lars jerked his hand away. He gaped as his blood dripped onto the ochre sand.

Distracted by the pain, he didn't notice Yu pull himself to his feet. Yu dove at Lars and slammed him to the ground. The impact knocked the air from his lungs, and Lars struggled as Yu pinned him down.

"Get. OFF!" Lars wheezed as he thrashed.

Yu snarled at his friend, leaned down, and sunk his teeth into his shoulder.

The scream stirred her. The thoughts in her mind didn't register as words. It was an instinct. A primal survival skill without a language. The urge possessed her. *Feed.* Lara saw the prey before her and latched onto its leg. She struggled to pierce his denim shorts with her first bite. With the second bite, she found purchase on the soft skin of his inner thigh and ripped off a ribbon of Lars' flesh.

MARK
30 JUNE 2018
12:30 PDT
COX BAY
TOFINO, BC

Mark bobbed with the waves as he watched the horizon. He tugged at the neoprene that constricted his chest. He never used to feel claustrophobic in a wetsuit, not when he could breathe properly. A set of left-breaking waves rolled in, but Mark let them pass as he struggled for breath. He felt the cool ocean spray on his face and watched the surfers around him paddle to catch the waves.

Once the set passed, he turned to scan the shoreline for Lara. *"Let's get coloured wetsuits, it'll be so much easier to find each other." Yeah right. They're so trendy now, there's no way to stand out. Where are you, Lare? I told you to meet me at Land of the Lefts eons ago*. There was no sign of her amongst the crowd of surfers.

A small wave approached Mark. *I can handle that.* Despite his laboured breathing, he pushed himself to turn his board around and paddle toward shore. The wave's momentum lifted him. After climbing first to one knee and then slowly into a standing position, he enjoyed the ride for a few precious seconds before falling into the cool Pacific brine.

He reached forward and turned off the camera mounted on the nose of his board. *Here's hoping no one ever sees that pathetic attempt. Can't even do a proper pop-up anymore. What the hell am I doing out here?*

After he paddled past the break and straddled his board, Mark tried to align the rise and fall of his chest with the ebb and flow of the ocean. He felt like he was drifting. *Am I in a rip current? Okay, paddle perpendicular to it, then up to the beach. Simple.* Mark noticed the waves lapped lower than the waterline on the rocks at the south end of the bay. The tide appeared to have gone down faster than usual.

A crawling sensation shot up the back of Mark's neck when he heard the alarm. He watched as the other surfers looked around at one another with concern etched on their faces.

"Get out of the water!" a young man near Mark called.

Everyone paddled frantically for shore. Mark waited, frozen in place. He could still feel it, the tug toward open ocean.

"Come on, man! Paddle in!" the same surfer called over his shoulder to Mark.

Mark raised a hand but didn't speak. He sat in contemplation and watched the shore. He expected to see his wife standing there, holding up a hand to shield her eyes from the sun as she searched for him. But she wasn't. Everyone was fleeing for the parking lot to escape the wrath of the ocean.

He lay on his board and dipped his arms in the cool water to paddle toward shore, but another coughing fit stopped him mid-stroke. A coppery taste filled his mouth. *Lara, I can't. I'm just too tired.* He cupped some water in his hand and swished it in his mouth to rinse the blood out.

Mark forced himself to focus on the other sensations he felt: the buoyancy of his wetsuit, the feeling of the cold water trickling under the neoprene around his wrists and ankles. The warmth of the sun.

Lara, I'm sorry I let you watch me decay. I won't put you through that any longer. This is it. This is how I go. On my own terms, with nature.

He turned his board around to face open ocean and paddled out.

ANA
30 JUNE 2018
13:02 PDT
INDUSTRIAL WAY
TOFINO, BC

Ana and Skylar wove between abandoned cars that blocked the highway. They followed a stream of people heading to Industrial Way in search of higher ground. Nervous voices rang through the air. A motorbike sputtered in the distance; its roar echoed off the trees that lined Highway 4.

Ana stopped for a moment to catch her breath. She leaned over, hands on her thighs, and inhaled deeply. Skylar jogged back to her when he noticed she was no longer at his side.

"Almost there." He placed a hand on her shoulder.

"Martha..."

"She'll snap out of it and head this way."

"We just left her there! With her son's corpse!"

"Honestly, there's only two things I'm concerned about right now."

"What's that?"

"You and I. Listen, kid, it's the oxygen mask in an airplane scenario. You can't save other people if you don't save yourself first. Get up that hill! Move it!" He gave her shoulder a squeeze.

"Sir, yes, sir!" she responded facetiously, and kept moving. *I never knew you to be so protective, Skylar. Where is this coming from?*

They passed a *Tsunami Hazard Zone* sign. Skylar pointed to a sticker someone had tagged it with, which read *Tsunami survival plan: grab a beer, run like hell.* "Not a bad idea!"

Ana scoffed and made her way past it.

The bottom of Industrial Way came into sight. Ana pushed her shaking legs to make the ascent up the steep hill. Shop owners ushered customers out their doors and locked up behind them. Crowds gathered in the parking lots, babbling nervously.

Ana recognized a mousy girl with round glasses standing outside a building with a sign that read *Raven's Roost Cafe*. She stood with a young man whose curls were a faded green leftover from a bad dye job.

"Sky... Hold up a second."

"What's up?"

"I want to say hi to Flo."

"Great time to socialize."

"I'll be quick. Meet you up top?"

"Yeah, sure. But seriously, Ana, don't take long."

"I'll be right up," Ana called over her shoulder. Gravel crunched beneath her feet as she crossed the driveway.

"Ana!" Flo's eyes widened at the sight of her. She opened her arms to greet her friend with a tight embrace. "What are you doing here?"

"Honestly, I have no idea anymore. Wow, I've missed you." The two women looked one another over, their hands clasped. "Eddie, hey!" she called to Flo's boyfriend.

"Hey, An," was all he could muster as he smiled meekly. His eyes kept darting to the highway.

"Probably not the best time to grab a cappuccino. Come on, let's get to higher ground."

"Yeah, soon. There's a few things I need to finish first. If Kat finds out I left without closing properly, she'll have my head."

"Kat? You work for *her*?" Ana felt blood rush to the surface of her cheeks. "Lock the damn door and let's go!"

Flo hesitated. "Last time she left me alone, a fire started. This time it's going to flood. I'm screwed. I'll be out of the job."

"The inability to prevent a natural disaster is no reason to *fire* someone. Come *on*!"

"I'll be quick! We'll see you up there in a minute."

Ana looked at her friend imploringly. "This job isn't

worth risking your life."

"In a minute! I swear."

The roar of a motorbike rumbled across the parking lot. Ana turned as a black Harley with a surfboard rack attached to its side rolled toward them. Its rider, a muscular, shirtless man with blond locks, dismounted the bike and approached the cafe.

Wow, it's...Rocket.

"Hey, lady, can I get a water bottle?"

"I'm sorry, we're closed."

"Come on, I'm not asking for some fancy mocha-cinno. Just a water bottle. It'll take you, like, ten seconds!"

"Okay, fine. Just a second." Flo walked back into the cafe.

Eddie and Ana exchanged apprehensive looks. "Get her out of here," she whispered. Eddie nodded.

"Hey, the name's Rocket. How's it going, babe?"

Ana turned in disbelief. "Are you actually flirting with me right now?"

"What can I say, a little danger gets me going. I was out there, on the beach. When the alarm started. The highway is bunged right up. Good thing I had this beast to help me manoeuvre through it, otherwise I never would've made it out."

Would that have been so bad? Ana thought with disdain.

Flo returned and offered Rocket a water bottle. He took one sip and dumped the rest onto his hair, then crushed the empty plastic and chucked it over his shoulder. Rocket shook his head, and a purple liquid beaded off the end of his locks, splattering Eddie and Ana.

"Come on, man! What the hell is that?" Eddie wiped his face.

"To hell if I know. Some goof on the beach got it on me. Came out of this." He pulled a plastic bag containing the broken vial from his pocket. Purple goo had pooled within the bag.

Ana studied the vial in his hand. *Is that... It can't be...* "What's that symbol?"

"A phoenix wearing a crown. Pretty cool, right?"

The back of Ana's scalp tingled. *Where the hell did that come from?*

Rocket pocketed the substance and turned his attention back to Ana. "So, babe, wanna get out of here?"

"My legs work just fine, thank you. I'll see you up top, Flo, Eddie."

"Suit yourself. I'm getting the hell off this island. Heading to Vancouver."

"Wait, what? How?" Ana asked.

"This isn't the only chopper Rocket rides. I have a whirlybird waiting for me up top."

"Can my friends come? Eddie, Flo, and Skylar?" She nodded up the hill to acknowledge her absent friend.

Rocket held up a finger. "There's only room for one." He rolled his bike toward her, its engine sputtering in anticipation of being fed more fuel. "Well, what do you say?"

A ride home... I could get away from this mess? Ana only contemplated his offer momentarily. She nodded and mounted the bike behind him. Guilt washed over her as she looked back at her friends.

"Typical. Run away, Ana. That's what you do when things get tough."

Ana looked at Eddie, stunned by his comment.

"Eddie!" Flo turned to him, shocked by her partner's harsh words.

"It's okay, Flo. He's right." She wrapped her arms around Rocket as he pulled on the throttle.

HARVEY
30 JUNE 2018
12:45 PDT
MALLARD LAKE TRAIL
TOFINO, BC

Harvey rifled through a toolbox in the bed of his truck. He retrieved a set of bolt cutters and took a few strides to the yellow gate that blocked their entry up the hill. The blaring alarm echoed over the small peaks that stood between them and the ocean.

Kat poked her head out the passenger window. "Look at all these people, Harvey."

He looked over his shoulder and watched pedestrians approach the hill. "There must be an accident blocking the road."

Harvey cut the heavy steel lock. He swung the yellow gate open to clear their escape route.

The Volkswagen drove past as its driver honked several times to coax people from his path. His tires kicked up gravel when he sped up the steep road.

Harvey shook his head. *Two guys in that whole van. What a jerk. He could help others.*

"Excuse me, ma'am? Can I offer you a lift up the hill?" Harvey called to a family walking past.

The woman moved hastily at his offer and ushered her three young boys toward Harvey's truck. "Oh, bless you!" she said as she lifted her youngest son up. He looked no older than three.

Returning the bolt cutters to his toolbox, Harvey grabbed an empty milk crate, which he placed next to the tailgate for the woman to use as a step. He noticed the bulge at her belly as he gave her a hand up.

"Hoping for a girl this time." She laughed.

"That'd be nice. You seem outnumbered!" Harvey smiled at her as he helped the boys join their mother. He walked around the truck and climbed in. Harvey drove steadily up the steep hill and gave his horn a soft tap to warn a group to move over.

"Should we turn on the radio?" Kat asked.

"Good idea." Harvey turned the dial until he reached the local station.

"*—implore you all to remain calm. We have just received word that underwater seismic activity was detected not long ago. Sensors predict a tsunami will hit our coast within the hour. Again, please remain calm, and head to the muster station nearest you. They are on points of high ground: at the community centre on Arnet Road, at Long Beach Airport, and Industrial Way.*"

They had their answer. Harvey turned the radio off. He glanced in the rearview mirror and saw a line of cars following them.

The forest thinned as his truck approached the crest of the hill. Glimpses of the ocean shone through the foliage of arbutus, cedar, and pines.

"Do you have any paper?"

"Uhh, I may have an old receipt or something. Check the glovey."

Kat opened the glove box and pulled out a handful of paperwork. A picture of Ana and Harvey huddled together under an umbrella fell out of the pile. Kat looked at it, rolled her eyes, and handed Harvey the stack. "Here. I don't want to rummage through your ghosts."

"Sorry, Kat." *I have a past and I can't make it disappear in a day*. Harvey slowed down and picked out a discarded envelope from an old birthday card. "Will this suffice?"

"Thanks." Kat found a pen in one of the cup holders and scribed a quick message which she passed through the small rear window. "I wanted to let her know without alarming the children."

"That's thoughtful." His lips curled into a one-sided smile.

Harvey pulled up behind the Volkswagen, which was

parked next to a tall weathervane. A growth of alders encircled the trailing brambles and yellow grasses that dominated the terrain at the top of the hill. Lengths of rebar and wooden planks protruded from a cement slab where a building once stood.

Harvey turned to Kat. She stared straight ahead, uncharacteristically quiet. “Hey, Kat, you okay?” Harvey reached over and took her hand in his. He ran a roughly callused thumb along the top of hers and admired how soft it was. “Everything’s going to be—”

“I’m fine!” Kat shook off his hand, checked her reflection in the sun visor, and wiped her eyes. “Now what?”

“Now we wait.”

“Oh, great.”

Harvey opened his door and was greeted by the scent of exhaust mingling with ocean air. He noticed the Volkswagen still running and walked over. “Cut your engine! You’re choking us out.”

“Whatevehr. ‘Ey, man, this guy eesn’t looking so good.” He switched the ignition off and gestured to his passenger.

Harvey bent down to peer inside the vehicle. The hitchhiker looked feverish. His eyes were closed and his head swayed softly. A layer of sweat beaded on his brow. “What’s wrong with him?”

“’Eatstroke, perhaps? To ‘ell eef I know!”

Harvey walked back to his truck. “I’ll help you down in a moment,” he said, acknowledging the woman sitting in the back of his truck. She nodded. Her face looked ashen. Harvey retrieved a water bottle from the backseat, then brought it back to the Volkswagen and handed it to the driver through the open window. “Give him this, have him recline his chair and rest.”

“I ‘ave a bed in zee back. ‘E can rest there.”

“Even better.” Harvey watched the driver guide his passenger to the back of the van, then returned to his truck to help the boys and their mother down. Once they were all settled on the ground, the woman began pointing out the different plants to her sons. *Distracting them, or herself?*

Harvey climbed back into the driver's seat, sat next to Kat, and waited.

PAUL
30 JUNE 2018
12:40 PDT
TSAWWASSEN MILLS
TSAWWASSEN FIRST NATION TREATY LANDS, BC

"Check it out, check it out: Rocket and the Blasters coming to you live from Cox Bay, Tofino, BC! The waves are going off, but we're sticking to the shores today! We're celebrating Canada's birthday by giving back to this glorious land, or rather, taking away from it! Garbage, that is. Our beach cleanup is about to begin! For every bag my boys fill, I'm going to donate $1000 to—"

Paul rolled his eyes and turned off his phone. *Why the hell do I follow this virtue-signaling 'roid monkey? He's so full of himself, and his posts clog up my feed.*

Paul tucked his phone in the pocket of his black shorts and watched as people strolled down the wide corridors of the mall. *Not as busy as I anticipated. Who wants to be trapped in the mall on a summer day anyway?*

A buzz against his thigh distracted him from people watching. It was Jocelyn.

"Hey, babe, how's it going?"

"Oh, Paul, I'm so sorry. I'll be working a little later. Michelle's stuck in traffic. She shouldn't be much longer. Are you at home still?"

"Uhh, no, I'm here. That's fine. Just call me when you're done."

"Of course. Talk soon, my sweet."

He did a lap around the mall and returned to find the bench he previously occupied was vacant. Paul sat and scrolled through his social media feeds again. Another live video by Rocket popped up. *Hate to love him, love to hate him.* Paul clicked on the *View* button.

Rocket straddled a motorbike, shirtless, with a new purple

tinge to his blond locks. *Beach cleanup lasted all of a half-hour? Way to save the world, Rocket.* A young woman had her arms around his barrel chest. Paul's brow furrowed as he noticed the placement of a tattoo on her left deltoid. When her face came into view, Paul called out, "Ana! What the hell?!" A few passersby gawked at his outburst.

"Hey, dudes, Rocket coming in live from Tofino, BC. The tsunami alarm is going off and I think shit is about to get real! Somehow, someway, I escaped the beach unscathed. I even rescued this damsel in distress. It's alright, babe! I'll get you to safety."

Ana looked appalled. *"Distress? I was just fine, th—"* Rocket pulled on the throttle and the chopper drowned out her refute. The bike sped up the street and wove between pedestrians.

Paul's heart leapt. *Tsunami? Ana's in Tofino? When the hell did Ana go to Tofino? Oh, shit. Did I miss a call from her this morning?*

He tried calling her. The phone rang half a dozen times before going to voicemail. He hung up, and finally listened to her message.

"Paul. I'm going back. I'll be on the first flight this morning. Can you...please...just call me when you get this."

Paul searched the web for reports. As he read an article, he ignored a call from Jocelyn.

Breaking news: seismic activity off the coast of Vancouver Island has been detected. A tsunami is expected to reach the shores of Vancouver Island, localized around the Esowista Peninsula, within the hour...

The phone slid between his fingers to the floor. He hunched over, rested his elbows on his knees, and cupped his face in his hands. Paul stifled his urge to yell.

"Wow, are you really that bored?"

He looked up at Jocelyn between spread fingers and rubbed his hands back through his hair.

She smiled at him. “Is the mall that torturous to you?”

“Ana’s in Tofino. There’s a confirmed tsunami headed for the peninsula.”

“Wait... What? Why is she there? Have you spoken to her?”

“No, I haven’t. I don’t know—to see Harvey, I’m guessing? You won’t believe it. She was on the back of Rocket’s chopper.”

Jocelyn stared at him. “Like, *Rocket and the Blasters* Rocket?” She contemplated his words for a moment. “That isn’t funny, Paul. I’m sure it must be boring for you, waiting for me, but couldn’t you have come up with a better joke than that?”

Paul scoffed. “I wish I was joking.” He bent down and picked his phone up from the floor, unlocked it, and handed it to her with the news article open. He stood up and paced as she read.

“And Ana?”

Paul took the phone from her and pulled up Rocket’s Instagram feed. He handed it back to her, displaying the snippet of Ana on the back of his motorbike.

Jocelyn gaped. “Look! He’s playing another live stream!”

They watched as Rocket and Ana approached a small helicopter on a vacant lot at the top of Industrial Way. The propellors spun, kicking up dust and causing the nearby bushes to rustle from the disturbance. Dozens of people on the opposite side of a fence clawed at the metal, yelling, desperate to escape with them.

“*Get to the choppah!*” Rocket grinned at the camera.

“So original.” Paul glared down at his phone. He watched as his sister climbed in after Rocket.

“She’s safe then?”

“I guess so.”

“Did you call her?”

“She didn’t answer.”

“Where do you think they’ll go?”

Paul shrugged. Jocelyn put her arms around his waist. He

drew her in close, comforted by the vanilla and cinnamon scent of her shampoo.

"Paul, you're shaking!"

"That can't have been easy for her, leaving Harvey and her other friends there."

"They'll be okay. I'm sure the city has a great emergency plan. Besides, from what I've heard about all his hunting experience, this Harvey seems well-equipped to survive."

Paul didn't respond.

"You want to check out the festival still?"

"Joss, I'm really not in the mood."

"Can I at least grab a snack? I'm famished. We can kill some time until we know where Rocket lands. I'm sure he'll continue broadcasting along the way."

Paul nodded and followed her to the mall's exit.

SKYLAR
30 JUNE 2018
13:15 PDT
INDUSTRIAL WAY
TOFINO, BC

Skylar stood in the gravel next to a chain-link fence, his fingers curled around the sun-warmed steel. The yard was overtaken by brambles, broom, and salal. He watched a bumblebee as it buzzed from clover to clover, inaudible over the chatter of hundreds of voices.

Never seen Industrial Way so packed, not even during the brewery's block parties. He looked around at the crowd. Cars lined the streets and filled the businesses' parking lots.

An engine sputtered in the distance.

Where are you, Ana?

Skylar reached into his backpack and pulled out a bottle, which was nearly empty. He drank its contents and scanned the perimeter of the buildings around him for a faucet. After spotting one in a vacant lot a hundred feet away, he headed toward it, checking over his shoulder to see if Ana and her friends were nearby. *What the hell is taking her so long?*

He crouched at the tap and let the cool water run before placing his bottle beneath it. While the bottle filled, Skylar's attention was drawn to the commotion of a crowd surrounding the neighbouring lot.

A man wearing a headset stood silently inside a fenced heli-pad, his arms folded across his chest. The crowd outside the fence shouted at the pilot, pleading for a ride to safety.

The helicopter behind him had an emblem across its doors of a cartoon rocketship, with a caricature of a muscular man giving a thumbs up out the window.

Rocket? Holy shit, I didn't know he was in town. Lucky fucker has a ticket out of here.

Once the bottle was full, Skylar splashed his face to rinse off the particles of crystallized salt leftover from his surf session, which had dried around his eyebrows and facial hair. He shook his head and felt briny droplets roll down his shoulders.

The sound of the sputtering engine grew close. A black Harley rolled toward the helipad, driven by a young man with a woman seated behind him, her arms woven around his chest. When the pilot pulled the gate open, they rode through and parked the motorbike along the fence.

Who's your latest conquest, Rocket? Athletic legs. A tattoo on her upper arm. A long blonde braid. *What the hell?*

Skylar watched as dust filled the air, dancing in a whirlwind around the brambles and clovers. His chest felt heavy, from a combination of the propeller's motion reverberating through him, and the realization that Ana was leaving him behind in a cloud of dust yet again.

She'll be safe. That's what matters. I should be happy. He watched as she climbed into the chopper with Rocket, then turned to join the crowd taking refuge on the hill.

ANA
30 JUNE 2018
13:15 PDT
INDUSTRIAL WAY
TOFINO, BC

The whirring propeller was deafening. Ana shielded her eyes from the force of the wind. Through the chain links, she saw people in the crowd pleading for help.

"Please! Take my daughter!"

"You gotta get us out of here!"

"Get to the choppah!" Rocket grinned, amused by his own joke. He completely ignored the frantic crowd surrounding the helipad.

Ana rolled her eyes and stepped toward the helicopter. A hand found her waist and guided her. *Don't touch me, you pig.* Ana bit her tongue as she took a seat. The black leather felt hot against the back of her thighs.

He climbed up to the seat beside her. "What a day! We're going to have one hell of a view from the top!"

"Wait, you're going to watch?"

"Hell yah! It's a once in a lifetime shot. Imagine how many viewers I'll get. It's going to be rad!"

"You're doing it for *views*? With all these people in danger? All their homes at risk? Are you actually that shallow and selfish?" Her question went unanswered.

He ran his fingers between his locks, then pulled his phone out of his pocket with hands that had taken on a purple tinge.

The pilot made adjustments to prepare for takeoff.

Ana watched as Rocket attempted to wipe the purple stain off on his board shorts. "You said someone got that on you on the beach?"

"Oh yeah, you should've seen it. My boy Yu found this crazy vial between two logs. The vial broke, and the fricken guy got the purple goop all over us."

Ana's eyes narrowed. *How the hell did it get here?* She looked out the window at the anxious crowd around the fenced yard, then to the copilot's empty seat. "Where's *your boy* Yu now? It looks like we have room for one more." Ana nodded toward the empty seat. *So much for "There's only room for one." What a jerk.*

"Yu was having a fit or something. The rest of the crew probably carried him out."

"*Probably?* You mean you just ditched your friends there?"

"Listen, dudette, it seems to me like you're leaving people behind too."

He's right. Skylar, Flo, Eddie. Harvey… She shifted her gaze toward the window again. Ana noticed a man whose shoulders slinked from side to side as he walked away from the helipad. *Skylar!* A surge of guilt pooled in the pit of her stomach. *Shit. I can't do this.*

"Ready for takeoff?" the pilot called.

"Sorry, Captain, what was that?"

Ana caught the pilot shake his head slightly. "Ready for… blastoff?"

"Yeah, dude! Let's blow this joint!"

"Wait!" Ana unbuckled the seat belt fastened around her waist.

"What are you doing?"

"You're right. I can't leave him."

Rocket laughed and shook his head. "Self-preservation is number one, lady. Someday you'll learn that."

Ana slid the helicopter door open and climbed down from the chopper. The loud *thub-thub-thub* of the oscillating propellors drowned out Rocket's selfish preaching. She stepped as far from the chopper as she could and leaned against a chain-link fence, covering her eyes as it rose into the air. Between her fingers she saw Rocket aiming his phone toward the ground. *Documenting my foolishness, are you, Rocket?* Dust billowed around her. She turned toward the fence, catching a glimpse of a red truck and a boat before squeezing her eyelids shut.

The panicked crowd dispersed as the helicopter took off. Several people looked at her with bewilderment on their faces.

Ana approached the gate she had entered through and found that the pilot had locked it behind them. She climbed the fence and swung a leg over the top. When she hopped down, she felt her feet pulse at the impact of her landing.

A few brisk steps brought her to the road. Ana looked in the direction he was heading, but Skylar was no longer in sight. She jogged past a crowd assembled outside a brick-red building, with apartments built above workshops, garages, and other businesses. Balconies were full of people, as was the driveway. Chatter buzzed throughout the street.

A group next to the road surrounded a radio that broadcasted the news. "*An earthquake that occurred offshore this morning has, indeed, triggered a tsunami, which is set for the shores of the Esowista peninsula. We implore everyone in the area to seek high ground and follow all instructions of emergency personnel.*"

A tap on her shoulder caused Ana to turn. "Sky!"

"An, what are you doing?"

"Looking for you."

"I saw you in *The Rocketship*. You had a way out of here. Why the hell did you stay?"

I don't think I could live with myself if I just abandoned everyone. Again. "That guy was so full of himself. I couldn't bear to be around him another moment."

"Well, that was silly. You couldn't fake it for an hour? Honestly. So now what, I have to look out for you? More of a hassle than anything, really." He winked at her.

"Oh, shut up." She gave his shoulder a gentle shove.

"An? Thought you'd be a mile high by now."

Ana turned to see Eddie and Flo approaching. "I almost was. Eddie, listen—"

His gaze locked with Ana's. "I'm sorry. I was out of line."

"You weren't wrong. I'm sorry too."

Eddie scratched his forehead where the purple goo had contacted his scalp.

"What is this crap?" Flo pulled a napkin from her bag and attempted to wipe the stain from his brow.

Her hands took on a slight purple tinge where the goo transferred from the napkin to her skin.

"I'm not feeling so hot." Eddie sat down in the gravel.

"Ed? Eddie?"

"Can I please have everyone's attention?" a woman in a Coast Guard jacket asked the crowd. "We've received word that the tsunami will hit the western shores any minute. Water *will* flood the beaches and rush up the inlet. We ask that you all stay put and remain calm. We are safe here; evacuation measures will take place as soon as possible."

"*Evacuation measures?* There must be five hundred people on this hill alone. How long are we gonna be stuck here? How are you going to keep us all fed?" a robust man with a thick beard asked. His wife stood beside him, clutching her young son's shoulders with white knuckles.

"Please remain calm. For now, there are several businesses selling food in the area. No one will starve. Emergency response teams will deliver supplies via helicopter as we wait to be evacuated," the Coast Guard exclaimed with a slight quiver to her voice.

"*'Several businesses selling food.'* Maybe I shouldn't've closed shop." Flo glanced down the hill toward the cafe.

"Flo, the cafe is at too low of an elevation. It's not safe down there. And besides..." Skylar nodded toward Eddie, then looked back up at Flo. Eddie was sitting in the gravel, drawing deep breaths. "Let's get him some shade."

"Mmhm. Eddie, my love? Let's go sit under a tree, okay?"

"N-no'oh. Here is. Fine."

"No, it isn't." Ana grabbed him under one arm, Skylar under the other. Flo watched, her eyes full of concern.

They shuffled along the side of the road past the crowd.

"An, look." Skylar gestured toward the group of people. Martha was sitting on the street and staring at her shoes. Her face was pale and her eyes unblinking.

"At least she's off the highway."

Ana, Skylar, Eddie, and Flo slowly made their way through a nearby storage lot, past shipping containers, and found a young cedar at the edge of the yard to prop Eddie up against. The freight containers blocked their view of the crowd and provided privacy. Flo knelt beside Eddie and brushed the hair off his damp forehead.

Skylar stepped back a few paces. He pulled a pouch out of his pocket and rolled a cigarette. Ana watched his callused, dexterous hands twist the fine paper. "Want one?"

"Hell no. It's been almost a year since I quit."

"That's great, An. I wish I was as strong as you." He positioned himself downwind of her as he lit his smoke. They stood wordlessly for a few minutes as Skylar puffed pungent clouds into the air.

"I think Eddie needs medical attention," Ana said, breaking the silence.

"Yeah, let's find some help. It's probably stress, or the heat maybe?"

Ana and Skylar walked back toward the crowd. The Coast Guard was listening to a headset, her eyes unfocused as she stared at the ground.

"Excuse me?"

She looked up when Ana broke her trance. "What? Oh, just a sec." She held up a finger and spoke into the headset, "What about Ahousat? Opitsat? Everybody in those communities get to high ground? Good."

Ana felt a hand on her back. She turned and looked up at Skylar, sighed, and leaned into him.

He wrapped his arms around her, the lingering smell of his cigarette invading her nostrils. "Did you really come back for Harvey?"

"What? Sky. Is this really the time?" She pulled away from the comfort of her friend's arms.

"Roger that. Over and out. Okay, sorry about that, folks. What can I do for you?" the woman asked as she pulled the headset off.

"Our friend is in a bit of a state. Pale, sweaty, heavy breathing, incomplete sentences... We don't know what's wrong with him."

"Hmm. Okay, let's go check him out."

Ana and Skylar led her back between the rows of shipping containers.

Flo was lying on the ground; Eddie was kneeling over her with his back to them. He was ravishing her, pulling at her top incessantly. Flo let out a soft whimper.

"Holy shit... He was sick two seconds ago... Maybe we should give them some privacy."

"Sky... She's bleeding!"

"What's going on here?" the Coast Guard called to Eddie and Flo.

Ana ran over to her friends. Her eyes widened as she took in the pool of crimson surrounding Flo. Maroon smears melded with the purple stain on Eddie's forehead like some sick watercolour painting. His fingertips penetrated deep into the flesh of her abdomen. He inhaled a raspy, guttural breath, ground his teeth, and released a low growl.

"Eddie!"

He turned to the sound of Ana's voice. There was no humanity in the way he looked at her; his eyes glared with a predatory maliciousness.

Flo let out a tiny sob and trembled when she looked up at Ana. The scent of copper permeated through the air, along with another putrid smell Ana didn't want to identify.

Hooked by one of Eddie's curled fingers, a coil of intestine slid out of Flo's abdominal cavity as he moved away from her.

He drew another rasping breath and released it in a territorial hiss.

Eddie lunged for Ana, grabbing her by the shoe. She fell backward, and gravel pricked the backside of her body. Ana pulled her free leg back and launched a swift kick at his ribcage.

"AN!" Skylar jumped forward and knocked Eddie to the ground, buying Ana enough time to get to her feet.

The monster that was once their friend recoiled and released an agitated wail. He drooled a stream of blood, a combination of Flo's and his own.

The Coast Guard gaped. "What's going on...here."

Eddie advanced again. Skylar threw an arm in front of Ana and corralled her behind him. "Go, An! Get out of here!"

Ana hesitated and stole a glance at Flo, who convulsed in a pool of her own blood, then turned and ran back to the street.

She stopped dead in her tracks when a deafening roar filled the air, paired with a deep vibration that shook the earth. Ana looked over her shoulder to the western tree line. *Jesus. That must be the fucking tsunami.* Nausea stirred in the pit of her stomach.

"Keep running!" Skylar implored. Ana moved. She didn't turn around, even when she heard the gunshot.

STELLA
30 JUNE 2018
13:30 PDT
COX POINT
TOFINO, BC

"Jasper, move it!"

His back was to her as he stared out at the open ocean. "I don't see anything. Maybe it's a false alarm."

"Maybe we should hurry it up so we don't find out the hard way, eh, bud?" Chris clapped a hand on his shoulder when he walked past.

The alarm ushered them to move faster. Stella led the way as they climbed back along the rocky shoreline. She lost her footing and hit her leg against the side of a boulder she was traversing, scraping it on a cluster of barnacles. Stella sucked air through her teeth when crimson flowed down her shin.

"You okay?" Chris asked as he passed her.

"Yeah, it's nothing. Let's keep moving."

Jasper caught up and knelt down to check her leg. "Doesn't look too deep. Does it hurt?"

"Not as much as that will!" Stella pointed a shaky finger toward the ocean. "It took us over an hour to hike out here! We'll never make it back before the wave hits!"

Jasper's eyes followed her gesture to a blip that had risen on the previously flat horizon. It grew in size as it rushed closer to the peninsula.

"Guys, come *on*!" Chris called. "Wow, wait, do you see that?"

"Yes! The tsunami is coming. We're fucked!" Stella answered.

"No, not the wave. I think...I think there's someone in the water still!"

Stella, Jasper, and Chris looked out at the bay. There was a man straddling his surfboard and facing the approaching wave.

"Is he...waiting for it?" Stella asked.

"Guy has a death wish. I'd say we do, too, if we keep standing here!" Chris said as he turned and headed for the tree line.

"Where are you going?" Stella called after him.

"We won't make it back to the beach. Maybe the trees will protect us if we get inland a bit."

Stella looked at Jasper. He shrugged. "We don't stand a chance here."

Weathered cedars with twisted bark stood at the frontline of the forest, their branches roughly angled from years of battling harsh winds. The trio manoeuvred over logs deposited by winter storms. As they climbed farther from the shoreline, the rocky terrain transitioned to spongy soil, and the sparse foliage grew more dense.

When the ground rumbled beneath their feet, Stella looked back over her shoulder. She could no longer see the ocean between the branches.

"Over here!" Chris called from farther ahead.

Jasper and Stella ran toward him. He stood next to a cedar with a trunk wider than their arms could have collectively reached around. Chris hoisted himself up to a low-hanging branch and climbed the limbs of the tree.

The sound of roaring water overpowered the siren coming from the beach.

Jasper pulled himself up onto the branch, then turned to Stella. "Give me your hand!"

Stella reached toward him. Their fingertips grazed as the wall of water washed through the woods and dragged her away from his grasp.

Jasper clung to the branch with all his strength as cold water spewed around the sides of the tree and washed over him. A driftwood log jettisoned from the forest floor and hit Jasper hard in the back of the head. He lost his grip on the cedar and the surging water carried him away. It smashed him against the trees in its path as the water searched for more voids to fill. He held his breath until he felt a sharp pain in his torso that made him gasp, and when he opened his eyes to see what caused the pain, he found a broken branch protruding from his abdomen, skewering him in place. The constant surge of water washed the blood away.

With a sharp crack, Chris fell from the thin branches of the cedar and plunged into the rushing water. It carried him toward Jasper, who feebly held a hand up to reach for his passing friend. The distance between them was too great, and Chris drifted past. The water throttled him against a jagged rock face. He felt a crunch when his cheekbone fractured. Chris closed his eyes and lost conciousness.

Stella watched from the top of a stone ledge as the wave mangled her friends. The water rose until it was within inches of where she stood. Her drenched clothing clung to her trembling body. There was no way for her to escape. "Please! Somebody! *Help me!"* she screamed into the flooded forest.

HARVEY
30 JUNE 2018
13:25 PDT
MALLARD LAKE TRAIL
TOFINO, BC

A chickadee hopped from branch to branch on a great cedar next to Harvey. A pair of stellar jays called to one another as they lurked about the trees at the outskirts of the clearing. Harvey stood next to a dirt path where he kicked at the ground, stirring an earthy scent into the air. To his left, Kat sat against the twisted red and ochre trunk of an arbutus tree. Ferns rustled gently in the breeze.

Their sanctuary overlooked Mallard Lake, which was encircled by a ridge of hills. Its calm water was smooth and dotted with lily pads. Farther in the distance, a stretch of Cox Bay was visible. Clean summer waves lapped against its shore.

"There it is." Harvey pointed to a nearly imperceivable blip on the horizon.

"It looks so small. All this fuss for that?"

"Just wait. It'll grow." Harvey watched as the wave rolled closer to shore, building in speed and height. "Do you hear that?"

"What?"

"Exactly. It's so quiet. No birdsong. They can feel it coming." Everything was still. Kat stood up and moved to Harvey's side. Her hand found his.

The tsunami cast a shadow as it absorbed the water in its path, adding to its violent voluptuousness. Light glimmered off the peak of the wave. It reached Leonard Island, overtaking its rocky shore and consuming the lighthouse in a blast of white spray that looked like liquid fireworks.

Harvey's breath caught in his chest. As the wave washed past the island, a thunderous boom broke the silence. The ground shook as the behemoth body of water hit unseen parts of the coast.

Where the bay grew shallow, the wave finally broke. The shoreline became a mess of whitewash, which enveloped the beach. Roofs and treetops protruded from the churning surface of the flood. A helicopter circled the bay.

Harvey looked at Kat and saw a tear roll down her cheek. She wiped it away and looked up at him. "See that green metal roof, with the triple chimneys?"

Harvey scanned the roofs and treetops that were barely visible under the surface of the briny chaos until he found it. "Yes."

"That's my uncle's house."

"I'm sorry."

They stood in silence for several minutes, watching water surge across the land, until Harvey had seen enough of the destruction. "Let's go finish that growler."

They walked back to the clearing. People were sitting in groups amongst the tall grasses. At one end, a small crowd listened to a radio. At the opposite end, a few transients and backpackers had formed a circle. One had a djembe and was laying down a beat. Others clapped their hands or stomped their feet in unison.

"I 'ave a geetar, one sec, one sec." The Volkswagen driver scrambled to his feet, and cut Harvey off as he strode to his van.

"This guy is as considerate on foot as he is on the road."

Kat scoffed.

Harvey opened the tailgate and gave her a hand up. He walked to the rear door, grabbed his backpack from the back seat, then climbed up, sitting on the tailgate next to Kat. He took a swig of the tepid beer before passing her the growler.

The Volkswagen's barn doors screeched open. "Oh, sheet. I forgot about you. Ees it hot in 'ere? Eet is hot in 'ere. You're awake though, that's good!"

After Kat and Harvey exchanged a look, she drank deeply from the glass bottle. "Never imagined I'd spend the day tailgating after watching a tsunami. How long do you think we'll be up here?"

"It's difficult to say. Most likely, the *official* assembly stations will be evacuated first." Harvey answered

"What are you doing? Don't look at me like that. Qu'est-ce que fuck? 'Ey! 'Ey!"

Harvey and Kat looked toward the Volkswagen. Only the driver's legs were visible beneath the open door.

"Everything okay over there?" Harvey called.

"Aaaarrrg!" The driver fell backwards, clutching his neck; blood was seeping between his fingers.

Harvey hopped down from the tailgate and ran over to him. "Are you alright?"

A low hiss erupted from the van. Harvey peered inside. The hitchhiker squatted in an animalistic position, ready to pounce. His eyes were bloodshot and his lip curled up in a sneer. Blood dripped down his chin as he bared his teeth. He dove out of the van and knocked Harvey to the ground.

"Harvey!" Kat shrieked, drawing the attention of others taking refuge on the hill.

The hitchhiker landed on top of Harvey, lashing out at his face, screeching and snapping bloodstained teeth. Harvey grabbed one of his attacker's wrists while his other hand found his throat, keeping his bloody teeth at bay. He pulled one of his legs out from under the rabid man and wrapped it around his torso, and in one swift manoeuvre flipped his attacker over.

The man with the djembe dropped his drum and ran over. "That's enough!" He grabbed Harvey under the arms and pulled him off.

"What the hell are you doing?" Harvey shrugged the djembe player off. "*He* attacked *me*!"

"Fighting is never the ans-aaaAARRHH!" The ravenous hitchhiker sunk his teeth into the calf of the djembe player.

Harvey kicked him in the ribs, and his jaw released, but not before pulling a strip of flesh from the drummer's leg.

A tense silence filled the air as everyone at the top of the hill stared.

The driver of the VW arose; the blood from the wound on his neck had stopped flowing. His eyes didn't blink; his gaze fixed on Harvey with a predatory hunger. A child screamed as the monster lunged foward.

The growler flew, hit Harvey's assailant directly in the face, and shattered in an explosion of beer and glass. The distraction bought him enough time to move from his attacker's line of sight. He darted back to his truck and grabbed his bolt cutters, then ran back to the monster, whose attention had fallen on another man. Harvey swung the heavy tool, hitting the driver directly in the spine. A growl escaped his lips as he doubled over.

Harvey turned. He felt queasy when he saw that the hitchhiker was feasting on the entrails of the woman he'd driven up the hill. He ran over and hit the hitchhiker in the head. His stomach lurched again when he heard bone fracture under the impact of his blow.

Harvey glanced at Kat, who stood on the tailgate watching the surrounding chaos. "Kat! Get *in* the truck! Now!"

She slid down the side of the truck and climbed into the passenger seat, slamming the door shut behind her.

The djembe player rocked back and forth, hunched over his wounded leg. After a few moments, he rose, groaning as he ran toward a group of bystanders, following them into the forest. He didn't seem to notice the strands of shredded calf muscle dangling from his leg as he pursued his prey with confident strides.

"Harvey! Behind you!" Kat yelled through the passenger window, which was slightly ajar.

Harvey turned in time to see the Volkswagen driver lurch at him. He evaded the attack and hit him with the bolt cutters again, splitting the monster's cheek open.

"Mommy! Mom! Get up!" The boys ran to their mother, who lay in a pool of blood. They shook her motionless body until she stirred, and began twitching and writhing. Her eyes opened wide, then narrowed, locking on the boy closest to her. She growled and grabbed one of her sons by the wrist.

"Mommy! Let go! You're hurting me!"

Her nails dug into his skin. She rolled over and pulled her eldest son to the ground, biting into his shoulder, as his brothers ran.

"Kids! To the truck!"

They stopped to look at Harvey, their eyes full of terror.

Harvey nodded in encouragement, then turned to the VW driver, who was climbing to his feet. Harvey gave him another swift blow, causing him to fall forward. He hit him again, this time on the back of his skull. He hit him in the same spot again and again until his skull caved in. And again, because the adrenaline that coursed through his veins told Harvey one thing: survive. The driver lay still.

"Come on, Patrick!"

"No! Dis way!" The youngest boy tried to pull his brother toward the forest.

"No. Pat, we're getting in the truck!" He pulled his reluctant brother to the rear passenger-side door and pushed him in.

Harvey closed the door behind the boys and ran around the truck, stepping up to sit in the driver's seat. He looked around. Their sanctuary was compromised. Everyone had fled, save for those who lay on the ground bleeding, and those consuming the ones who were bleeding. Dozens of people had run off into the forest.

The sound of the truck's doors closing distracted the boys' mother from her meal. She left her eldest son sobbing in the dirt, his white shirt soaked crimson. She rose shakily to her feet and laid a bloody hand on the window between her and her boys. Kat rolled up the windows to block out the sound of her feral snarling.

"Stop, Mommy! Please, stop!" The boys wailed as she lay blow after blow on the glass barrier between them.

SKYLAR
30 JUNE 2018
13:45 PDT
INDUSTRIAL WAY
TOFINO, BC

Skylar followed Ana through the panicked crowd. Sunlight glimmered off a rope of golden hair that trailed behind her as she ran. It seemed shinier than before. Everything seemed brighter. Despite the ringing in his ears, he heard snippets of concerned conversation when he passed.

"What was that?"

"Was that a gunshot?"

"Who's lighting firecrackers at a time like this?" People scanned the area for the source of the sound.

"It's not safe!" Skylar called between breaths. "Find shelter!"

The people nearby looked at him with eyes full of concern, intrigue, anger, and fear.

A groan resonated from the direction Skylar and Ana had run from. Three figures stumbled around the corner and toward the refugees of Industrial Way. Eddie snapped at the air, eager to sink his teeth into his next meal.

His chest bore a gaping gunshot wound encircled with coagulated blood. Flo nearly tripped on her trailing intestines as she shuffled forward. The Coast Guard's blood stained her red jacket a deeper shade of crimson. They advanced on the crowd.

A young girl screamed when she saw the monsters approach. Her father plucked her from the ground and ran with her in his arms.

"This is great! We're on one of those prank shows, right? Like, with the dude from *That '70s Show*? Come on, who's in on it? Where are the cameras?" a young man called as the infected trio moved toward him.

"Run, you idiot!" Skylar yelled.

Bystanders tripped over one another as they retreated from the infected and fled the area.

The skeptical young man lingered too long as he laughed at the fleeing crowd. “Come on, guys, it’s coloured corn syrup.” Flo grabbed him by the arm and Eddie knocked him to the ground. The pavement muffled his screams as they feasted on him.

Skylar caught up to Ana and grabbed her above the elbow. She turned and looked through him with dilated pupils.

“Hey, An, you okay?”

“Am I...okay?”

“Right, stupid question. We need to find shelter somewhere safe.”

“This *was* somewhere safe! Flo and Eddie... Did they just turn into fucking *zombies*?!”

“We don’t need to make sense of things right now. We just need to find shelter before—” Another shrill scream filled the air, followed by more gunshots.

“That’s it,” Ana stated.

“What?”

“Guns. We need to arm ourselves. Harvey has rifles in his trailer. I bet you he hasn’t changed the code to his safe since... well, last year.”

“Now we’re talking. Let’s go!”

She stepped past him and took steady strides, bracing herself as she jogged down the hill.

As they made their descent, Skylar heard deep bass notes that reverberated from within Tofino Brewing Company. The garage doors, which were usually wide open and welcoming, were closed. *Perhaps we can find shelter there... Seems pretty secure.*

They passed a group of stragglers heading up the hill from the abandoned, gridlocked highway. “It’s not safe up there!” Ana called to them.

“It’s not safe down here either!” one of them responded, wide-eyed and wary. “Where are we supposed to go?”

"Try to get into one of these buildings. People up there are getting...*violent*," Ana warned. "Our friends...they turned into...I think they turned into *zombies*!"

There was a moment of silence as the group looked at one another and then back at Ana skeptically. One of them began to laugh.

"It's not a joke! Didn't you hear those shots? That was someone firing at one of them." She looked at Skylar, her eyes imploring him to say something.

"It's true," was all he could muster, shrugging.

"I thought that was fireworks, or maybe a flare gun," one of them said, looking up the hill.

"There's no way! No way in hell that's true," the man beside her said.

"I'd rather not find out," the young woman retorted.

"An, come on," Skylar said, stepping away from the group. "You can't save everyone."

"One of those doors has to be unlocked. Just go take shelter!" Ana gestured at an apartment building up the hill from the brewery. She turned and followed Skylar across the highway, past the four-car pile-up they'd encountered earlier.

They jogged down Harvey and Skylar's shared driveway. Below the tree line, they could see water surging. "It hasn't reached the trailers. We better make this quick though. There could be a second surge."

"Alright!" Ana called back. A lock of purple hair fell from behind her ear. She wiped it away with the back of her forearm. The purple transferred to her skin, moistened by the sweat on her forehead.

"An, what the hell?! That's that same purple crap Eddie had on him."

"It's nothing. Don't worry about it." She grabbed a bit of moss from a tree trunk and tried to scrub the stain away with it.

"Actually, I *am* pretty worried about it."

"If...if *that* happens to me, you have my permission to...put me down. Okay? *'We don't need to make sense of things right now,'* right? Let's grab the guns and get out of here! Watch the waterline for me, will you?" She opened the trailer door and stepped inside. Faint beeps emitted from within the trailer.

Fuck, if she turns into one of them... She sounds pretty coherent though. But if I hear her thrashing around in there... Skylar cut off the thought and angled himself to watch the rising water. *Shit, Mr. Robinson's house is fucked up. Still about ten metres between us and the inlet. If it reaches the tree with the birdhouse, we're outta here.* "How's it going in there, An?"

"It was something stupid, like 0000 or 1234... Ugh. I thought I had it. If I try too many times..."

"It'll lock you out. You know what I'd make it?"

"What's that?"

"007."

"It takes 4 digits."

"Okay, 0007."

Ana scoffed. After four more beeps, she exclaimed, "Seriously? That was it!"

"Great minds think alike."

"Fools seldom differ!" she called.

"Huh? Come on now, I'm the genius who cracked the code!"

"Here." She handed a shotgun through the trailer door, along with several boxes of buckshot. She stepped out with a .22 slung over her shoulder.

"That's it? Doesn't he have, like, twelve guns in there?"

"I'm not looting him! He'll need some too. Besides, these things are damn heavy. These two will be enough for us."

"Well, perhaps we *should* loot him. Think he has any granola bars?" *She still seems coherent...*

Ana stepped back inside.

He loaded a couple rounds into the shotgun, placed a few in his pocket, dropped the rest into his backpack, then slung the gun's strap over his shoulder.

Returning his attention to the water, Skylar saw that it had risen several feet beyond his marker with the birdhouse. "An, water's rising. Let's move it!"

"Okay!" She emerged from the trailer with an addition to her firearm.

"What the hell is that?"

"A drum magazine. Holds a hundred rounds. Pretty badass, huh?"

"You're insane. Why do you even own that?"

Ana shrugged. "Harvey bought it. Nice of him to have it pre-loaded for such an occasion."

"And you think you know your neighbours..." Skylar shook his head. "Find any snacks?"

"All sorts. Jerky. Granola. Should keep us going for a while. Where to now?"

"The brewery should be high enough of an elevation. We can take refuge there."

"Skylar, this is not the time to sit down for an ale!"

"I'm not planning on *indulging*. It's a secure building. We know the staff. There's water and facilities. Offices to hide in, should the doors be compromised."

Ana considered his suggestion and nodded.

They jogged up the hill in silence until they arrived at the brewery. The rolling garage door was locked. Loud music blared from within the building. Ana knocked several times. There was no answer. She kicked the door, and the metal clanged against its tracks. After a few moments, a chain clattered as the steel door rolled up.

Ana and Skylar followed a beam of sunlight in through the open door. The brewery was dark, aside from emergency lighting that shone down from the offices above. Skylar looked to the loft where he saw a dozen faces peering down at them.

"Hey, thanks for letting us in. Where's Justin?" Skylar asked. He scanned the group for familiar faces, for the brewmaster and bartenders, but he didn't recognize anyone.

"Who?" someone called back.

"Uhh, the bartender, Justin? How'd you guys get in here?" Ana called up.

Skylar looked at Ana and noticed a piece of paper on the floor beside her, crumpled and covered in dirt.

"Don't know a Justin, but the door was open when we got here," one of the strangers said.

"What's this?" Ana said, following Skylar's eyes to the note on the floor. She picked up the paper and read it out loud: "Closed due to tsunami. *Grab a beer, run like hell.*"

"We were just following instructions, see?"

"Hey, what's that in your hand? You two packing heat?"

Skylar began to explain, "Listen, someone attacked—"

"One little emergency and you two decide it's time to loot, is that it?" someone else shouted from the crowd.

"Speak for yourselves!" Ana scoffed.

"You shouldn't show up toting a gun like that. Someone might get the wrong idea," one of the men said. His fierce eyes glazed over in an inebriated glare as he moved down the stairs. His friends followed until the group stood before Ana and Skylar.

"It's not just the tsunami! There's another danger out there. People are becoming violent, attacking one another. Our friends turned into..." Skylar trailed off when he heard a sound outside.

Two men from the fish plant, located across the street from the brewery, limped toward the open door, dressed in blood-drenched rubber aprons and gumboots. It wasn't unusual for them to be coated in a little gore in that line of work, but as they approached, Skylar noticed blood also speckled their faces and hair, and that they walked unsteadily. *Shit. When Ana kicked the door, the sound must have attracted them. That, or this awful music.* Skylar made eye contact with Ana and nodded toward them. He pumped the shotgun, loading a round into the chamber.

"How dare you threaten our sanctuary!" one of the

inebriated men shouted.

Ana ignored him. Her focus was on the two infected outside the door. She fumbled with her magazine and it fell to the floor.

The group, blind to the approaching threat, charged foward. Ana felt a hand grab hold of her braid. Blinding pain seared across the back of her scalp as her assailant yanked her down by her hair, pulling her to the ground. The force of the impact left her winded and fighting for breath. The man placed a grimy boot on her chest and picked up her .22.

Skylar yelled as three of the drunks detained and disarmed him. Two of them held him under the arms, while the third pried the shotgun from his grasp.

Screams erupted within the brewery when the two infected stepped through the open door. Their flesh bore deep lacerations, with bite marks covering their arms. One of the infected, who had a gaping wound on his cheek, grabbed the young man constraining Skylar, and before he could pull away, the monster bit down on his arm.

When the boot lifted from Ana's chest, she gasped hungrily for air. She grabbed the magazine that lay on the floor beside her. The man pointed her empty .22 at the monster biting his friend and pulled the trigger uselessly several times. "What the hell is wrong with it?!"

Ana rolled over and jumped to her feet. "Give me that!" she sputtered as she grabbed the gun from him. She inserted the magazine into the chamber and aimed the barrel at the infected's head, then tapped the trigger lightly. The monster fell to the ground and didn't make another sound.

Skylar backed away from the man holding his shotgun. *I need that back. How can I disarm him?*

He looked around for a weapon. A broom leaning against the wall caught his eye. He reached over the bar and grabbed it.

A shot reverberated through the air. Skylar turned and saw the second infected, with a gaping hole in his forehead, fall to the ground. The man holding the shotgun gawked at the corpse. Skylar swung the broom into the back of his knees and grabbed the firearm as the man fell forward.

"An! Let's go!" Skylar called as he exited the brewery.

She retreated with her gun pointed at the group of men. "Your friend who was bitten is in real trouble. I'd isolate him, if I were you guys," she warned them.

They exchanged panicked looks, then turned to their bleeding friend.

"Guys, come on. Seriously, guys, that won't happen to me..."

Poor fucker. Better lock him up or put him down. Skylar could hear him whimpering as they ran toward the road.

"Well, that was a bust." Ana winced as she rubbed the back of her head. "New plan: there's that water reservoir at the top of the hill."

"Where we watched the meteor shower a couple summers back? There's no shelter up there. We'd be exposed to the elements."

"Forecast didn't call for rain this week. I don't think these monsters could climb the ladder. They seem pretty clumsy."

"Hah, have you ever trusted that forecast? We live in a rainforest, Ana. Well...*I* do."

"*We* do. Come on. If another opportunity presents itself, we'll take it."

The streets were eerily empty, aside from the occasional pool of blood and a few infected who lurched about unsteadily.

"Where did everyone go?" Ana asked.

"Broke into apartments? Ran into the woods? Who knows."

Over the crest of the hill, the road became a winding gravel path. They followed it toward the water reservoir.

A disturbance in the bushes stopped Skylar in his tracks. He held an arm up, signalling Ana to stop. Skylar raised his shotgun as a woman darted out of the woods in front of them. He lowered it when he saw she was one of the living.

"Help me!" she shrieked, looking over her shoulder. Two

infected were in pursuit of the woman. Ana raised her gun and fired a round into each of their heads.

The woman watched the infected fall to the ground. Recognition replaced the fear in her eyes when she looked up at her rescuers. "Oh, it's you! You...you tried to help my son... Timmy..."

"It's Martha, right?" Ana called. "Come on, we're headed up to the water reservoir!"

"Don't go that way!" she implored. "They're everywhere. Simone was climbing the ladder... They were pulling at her, so many of them, pulling at her legs until she... We can't go there!"

Ana looked up at Skylar. "Those shots will bring them here. We gotta move!"

"The fire station," he said. "Around the corner. Let's go!"

PAUL
30 JUNE 2018
14:00 PDT
TSAWWASSEN MILLS
TFN TREATY LANDS, BC

Paul checked his phone for the third time in five minutes.

"She'll call when she can," Jocelyn tried to reassure him. She offered him a mini donut from the oil-blotched paper bag in her hand. The scent of cinnamon wafted toward him with her gesture.

"I'm not hungry." A sound in the sky caught his attention. Paul's heart skipped a beat when a black chopper came into view. "Do you think...?"

"It could be. Slim chance though, don't get too excited."

"It's weird that Rocket hasn't posted online for a while. That goof displays his whole life for the world to see."

"Maybe he had to turn his phone on airplane mode?"

"He was broadcasting before, during the tsunami." The aerial view of the monstrous wave that flowed across his cell phone's screen was imprinted in Paul's mind. The shadow it cast before it broke. The way it swallowed the beach Paul had walked with his sister countless times. He shuddered and snapped himself back to the present.

The chopper lurched sideways in the air. "Whoa! Steady!" Paul yelled.

It moved erratically and fell nose first. The helicopter descended beyond Paul's line of sight behind the mall. A thunderous crash halted the festival-goers from their merriment. They looked around to see what caused the disturbance.

"ANA!" Paul bellowed and sprinted through the crowd. People scattered out of his way.

"Paul!" Jocelyn dropped her donuts and tried to keep up, but fell behind when she became tangled in the crowd.

Paul could feel his heartbeat pounding in his ears as he

ran across the parking lot.

Don't be her. Please, for the love of—

A firetruck's siren wailed in the distance.

Be someone else. Be someone else. Paul pushed himself as a surge of adrenaline ran through him. Black smoke billowed into the sky. When he turned around the corner of the mall, the wreckage came into view. The propellors still turned slowly as flames licked the side of the black machine, caressing the sooty emblem of a rocket ship.

"FUCK! No, no, NO*!*"

As the sirens grew closer, his legs moved faster. The firetruck arrived at the crash site before he did.

Paul saw a figure emerge from the burning helicopter, his clothes aflame. A firefighter leapt forward and wrapped the man in a fire blanket. The flames were smothered, but the man's screams did not subside. His moans were so full of anguish that they seemed inhuman.

"Sir, you're going to be alright. We're here to help you. Can you tell me your name?"

His only response was a snarling wail. His blond and purple hair was singed, his skin charred and cracked. He bore third-degree burns that marred his once perfect body.

The firefighter patted down his patient in search of further injuries. He felt something in the man's pocket. "Is this your wallet? I'm going to pull it out. I just want to know your name, sir." He reached into the pocket with a gloved hand, and pulled out a sticky mess of melted plastic, broken glass, and purple goo. "What the hell..."

Paul's attention was drawn from the flaming vehicle to the fireman assisting the man who ran from the wreckage. *Rocket.* He caught a brief glimpse of the broken vial in the fireman's hand. The glass was cracked but Paul could just make out the logo etched into the glass: a phoenix wearing a crown. *What the fuck... Where did that come from?* Paul shook the image from his head and turned back to the helicopter.

Several firefighters held a limp hose the thickness of a python at the ready. The one at the front gave a verbal cue, and water surged through the tube and sprayed the smouldering chopper.

Paul moved closer to the wreckage.

"Get BACK!" one of the firemen yelled at him. He turned to see a man with a roll of yellow caution tape coaxing onlookers farther from the crash site.

"My sister is in there! Please!"

"I need you to stand back, son. Let us do our job."

He didn't argue. Paul could feel the warmth of the wreckage from where he stood a dozen metres away. The firefighters were suited to withstand the heat. He was not.

Paul heard a yell. He turned and gaped when Rocket lashed out at the fireman assisting him, grabbed his arm, pulled it toward his face, and bit down. *Holy shit, did he just bite that guy?*

The fireman released his grasp on the broken vial and was spattered with purple droplets as he attempted to detain his patient. "Whoa! What the hell, man?"

Rocket crawled away and pulled himself unsteadily to his feet.

Paul turned back to the chopper. Once the flames were extinguished, a firefighter approached the helicopter and opened the pilot's door. A loud hiss greeted him.

"Sir, it's okay, I'm here to help!" He reached in and assessed the man's wounds. "He has a broken leg! Johnson, Stevens! Grab the stretcher." He turned his focus to the passenger door. "There's no one else here!" he called.

"You're sure?" Paul asked, his scalp tingling. The man nodded.

Paul furrowed his brow as Jocelyn approached. She looked at him imploringly and placed a hand on his forearm. "Ana?"

"She's not there."

"Whoa, what the f—"

Paul followed Jocelyn's line of sight. Her eyes were fixed

on Rocket. Hunched over, like a cat backed into a corner, his attention darted from one bystander to the next. He rose and stepped toward the group of leering onlookers. His movements quickened. With each step, fluid oozed from his cracked skin. He charged the crowd. Screams broke out. Rocket, burnt and bleeding, was on top of a little girl. He screeched and bit her shoulder.

"My baby! Get off my baby!" a woman pleaded. She pummeled Rocket with her purse. He grabbed her arm, pulled her down, and bit her too.

A couple of men wrestled Rocket off the little girl and her mother. The bloodied woman rose, baring her teeth in a cruel sneer. Someone reached out to her, and she knocked him to the ground.

Two squad cars pulled up. The officers exited their vehicles and assessed the scene. One of them ran to the firefighter kneeling on the ground, put a hand on his shoulder, and asked, "Sir, what's going on here? Are you okay?"

The firefighter swayed erratically. His eyes were unfocused. He inhaled deeply and snapped his teeth at the officer who held him steady. A shrill scream summoned the other officers to pull the two apart.

People scattered as gunshots filled the air.

"Let's get out of here!" Paul said to Jocelyn. They fled as the parking lot erupted into chaos.

HARVEY
30 JUNE 2018
14:30 PDT
MALLARD LAKE TRAIL
TOFINO, BC

"Maybe, if we stay really still, they'll forget we're in here. Just like a T-Rex in *Jurassic Park*, right, kids?" Kat said to the two sobbing boys. Bloody handprints painted the truck's windows where their mother pounded on the glass between her and her sons.

Harvey leaned his head back against his seat and closed his eyes. *Think, man, think. How do we get out of here?* He looked over his shoulder at the only road down the hill, which was lined with parked vehicles. *I think I could fit along the shoulder. It'll be sketchy, though.*

The boys suppressed their sobbing until only an occasional sniffle was heard.

"What are your names, boys?" Kat asked to distract them.

The youngest child remained silent.

"Th-th-th-the one outside is Tyler. This is Patrick, and I'm Mikey."

"Hello, Patrick and Mikey. It's nice to meet you both. I'm Kat, and this is Harvey."

If I just had a gun... Ugh, why don't I keep one under the back seat for emergencies like this? Like this? What even is this? What the hell just happened? Harvey's eyes were still closed. Kat nudged him with her elbow.

"Hmm? Hi, Mikey and Pat."

"Harvey..."

"I'm sorry." He kept his voice low. "But I just bashed someone's skull in; forgive me if I'm not quite myself right now. I'm trying to figure out how to get the hell out of here."

"Do you have a map?"

Harvey reached under his seat and pulled out a back road

map book. He flipped through it and found the Esowista Peninsula. "The topographies aren't very detailed." He laid it on the centre console and Kat leaned over it.

"Only one road in. The wave didn't reach Mallard Lake. That's around 30 metres in elevation, see?" Kat pointed to a spot on the map.

Harvey nodded. "We should assume water has come up the inlet as well. The highway is jammed, so that's no use as it is."

"Unless we take it on foot."

Harvey looked out the window when he realized it was quiet. "Where did they go?"

Kat looked over her shoulder. "Still there. Waiting." She turned back to the map. "There's the memorial at the top of Radar Hill."

"We would be in the same position there. One road in, and no shelter."

"Maybe we wouldn't need the shelter. Maybe there aren't any creepers up there."

"Creepers?"

Kat shrugged. "Do you know what they are? What's going on here?"

"People were bitten. Then they turned violent. Damage to the brain takes them down. I think it's safe to say—"

"Okay, okay. Please don't say it. Not in front of the kids."

"Radar Hill is too risky. The rainforest is far too dense to get there without a path. If one of those *creepers* follows us in, it'd be pretty hard to keep ahead of it, especially with the boys." Harvey mouthed the last part.

"We can't drive into town. The road between Cox Bay to Chesterman's Beach could have washed out."

"Town would be another dead end anyway. We need to head inland, to Port Alberni," Harvey suggested.

"Hah! Now that's a long walk."

"There's a gas station at the junction. We could get food and water there. Maybe take shelter overnight in one of those cabins at the campground."

"No, we won't make it past Long Beach. Look, it's totally flat." Kat pointed to a narrow stretch of land where the map bore no elevation lines.

Harvey sighed. He reached into the back, grabbed a couple water bottles, and handed one to each of the boys. Their eyes were puffy and red. He leaned back against the headrest and watched a stellar jay fly across the carnage to land on the Volkswagen, where a storage unit rested on the roof rack. Two paddles were tied to it with bungee cords.

"I have an idea," Harvey said.

ANA
30 JUNE 2018
14:00 PDT
FIRE HALL, INDUSTRIAL WAY
TOFINO, BC

"Let us in! Come on, man!" Skylar called as he beat his fists on the fire hall's door. "I saw you through the window! I know you're there, Dion!"

They stood on a small deck, just large enough to hold the trio. Six stairs separated them from an infected person in Canadiana flannel, who bared bloody teeth and hissed up at them. When he climbed the first step, Ana raised her .22, lined her sights with his forehead, and tapped the trigger. *Fuck, that one was too close.* When he dropped, more monsters stepped clumsily over him toward their prey.

"Come on, Dion, it's Skylar! Open the door!"

Ana fired round after round, and the pile of corpses grew. "There's too many! I can't keep up!"

Skylar turned around and unloaded a round from his shotgun at the approaching horde. Martha yelped when their blood rained through the air. *Thank god we're upwind of that,* Ana thought. The buckshot stalled the horde momentarily, but they advanced toward the stairs again, ignoring the gaping holes the pellets tore into their flesh.

Ana could see dozens of infected lurching in the distance toward them, drawn by the sound of their only defence. *Just focus on the ones in front of you,* she told herself when she became aware of the monsters in the distance. She kept firing, and tried not to look too closely at their faces as she exterminated them.

Something—someone—beneath them groaned, causing Martha to cry out. An infected reached up from beneath the platform and grabbed hold of her ankle. Skylar stomped hard on its wrist and the monster recoiled, letting Martha go.

"Has anyone been bit?" a muffled voice finally called through the door.

"No!" they yelled in unison.

The door swung open. *Fuck, finally!* Ana fired three more rounds and then ducked inside.

Skylar slammed the door closed once Martha and Ana were through, and Dion bolted the lock. The knocking of the infected rang through the metal door.

It took a moment for her eyes to adjust to the dimly lit room. Ana could just make out Dion's features in the shadows: his round cheeks, pointed chin, and dark hair that hung in loose waves to his shoulders. She took in their surroundings: they were in a narrow room with a kitchenette, couch, table, and chairs. A hallway lined with several doors led to the back of the building.

"Thanks, Dion. Took you long enough, though!" Skylar exhaled heavily.

"Sorry, Sky. Can't be too careful."

"Where's the rest of your crew?" he asked.

"They drove out to Long Beach for a house call before the alarm went off. Been nothing but dead air for the last hour," Dion said as he gestured to a radio at his hip. "Here, take a seat. Sorry I didn't open the door sooner—"

"It's okay to be cautious; we're all scared," Ana muttered without meeting his eyes. She sat at the table, planted her elbows on its surface, and cupped her face with her hands. *Why the fuck is this happening?*

Skylar paced.

Martha went to the couch and sat alone.

Dion walked to the kitchenette and poured water for everyone, distributed it, then found a candle and joined Ana at the table. He pulled a lighter out of his pocket and lit the wick. The flame flickered, and the light danced gently across his face.

"What the hell is going on?" Skylar asked as he crossed the room for the fourth time.

"End of Days," Dion said as he stroked a pendant that lay under his shirt.

"Revelation doesn't mention zombies," Skylar said.

"It isn't the *End of Days,*" Ana said. "Can you stop pacing? You're making me nervous."

"Alright, girlie. What's your theory?" Skylar grabbed a chair, turned it around, and straddled it with his chest leaning against the backrest.

Could it be connected…? Ana ran her hand over her tattoo and exhaled. "I…I don't know. It's some kind of outbreak, obviously. Tofino is small, isolated. Maybe this *disease,* or whatever it is, is only spreading locally?"

Martha sobbed softly on the couch. Dion walked over and offered her a blanket.

"You need to go wash that purple goo off," Skylar said through gritted teeth, though not quietly enough.

"Sky, it's nothing! I'm okay!"

"What's up with the purple goo?" Dion asked as he returned to the seat next to Ana.

Tension filled the air as Skylar and Ana stared each other down. *Thanks, Sky, for throwing me under the bus.*

Dion looked apprehensively at his rifle leaning up against the counter. "You said no one was bitten. Is there something else I should be concerned about?" He touched the pendant through his thin cotton shirt again.

Ana studied him. *I can't risk getting tossed outta here. Even if it is what I think it is… But it can't be. This is nothing like what they were developing…*

The room was silent, aside from the infected pawing at the door and an occasional sniffle from Martha.

"I said, what's up with the goo?" Dion asked, more sharply this time, as he rose from his chair.

"I have no idea! It leaked out of a vial found on the beach. My friend came into contact with it too, and they turned. It's probably a coincidence! We don't know *what's* turning these people into monsters, or if the purple goo had *anything* to do with it! It's been over an hour since I came into contact with it, and I'm *fine*!"

Martha repositioned herself on the couch, looking more alert. "How could that be?" she asked. "If others who've come into contact with it turned, why haven't you?"

Dion looked troubled as he considered the situation. "Go take a shower. There's a washroom down the hall to the left."

"Thanks, Dion. I'd appreciate that." As she stood, Ana noticed Martha was glaring at her. *If looks could kill... Jesus, lady.*

"You'll find bleach under the counter. Sanitize the area when you're done," Dion called after her.

Ana nodded and walked down the hall. She found the washroom, removed her grimy clothes, and stepped into a white-tiled shower. The hot water soothed her tense muscles.

Why the fuck did I come today of all days? Ana's exhaustion left her too tired to cry. She scrubbed her skin and watched the tainted water, murky with dirt, blood, and a tinge of purple, as it spiraled the drain. Once the water ran clear, she got out of the shower, dried herself off, and sanitized everything she had touched.

She looked at her clothing in a heap on the floor. *Gross, I can't put those on. They're probably contaminated.* Ana wrapped herself in a towel and opened the door, surprised to see Dion's fist knocking the air where the door had been.

"Sorry, I didn't mean to startle you. Do you, uh, want some clothes?" he asked, and handed her a bundle of folded laundry. His eyes flicked up and down before he averted them.

"Thank you." *Keep your eyes to yourself, pervert.* She blushed and quickly closed the door. When Ana unfolded the basketball shorts and muscle shirt, a piece of paper drifted to the floor. She picked it up. It read: *Don't trust Martha.*

SKYLAR
30 JUNE 2018
14:15 PDT
FIRE HALL, INDUSTRIAL WAY
TOFINO, BC

"Kill her," she said.

"Excuse me?" Skylar turned to Martha with a look of fury on his face.

"*Kill her*. She has that purple shit on her skin. God only knows when she'll become *one of them*. She's a ticking time bomb."

"Listen, lady, we just saved your ass. *Twice*. I think you owe her a debt of gratitude. Stop trying to be judge and jury. No one is killing anyone here."

"Come on, don't you watch movies? My Timmy was big into those monster flicks, I could never figure out why. There's always that one person in the group that everyone will make an exception for, and then, when everyone thinks they're safe, the person turns into one of those fucking zombies and starts eating them."

"If she turns, we're equipped to deal with it. We will not execute a living person," Dion reaffirmed.

Martha let out a heavy sigh. "They'll break through the door soon. She'll attack from the hallway, and they'll storm the door. Then we're all dead. Dead like Timmy. Dead like everyone."

"That door is solid steel. We're safe in here. There's enough food to survive a while. Dry food in the cupboards. The crew's lunches are in the fridge... I don't imagine they'll be back for those anytime soon." Dion walked to the fridge and opened it.

"Turkey sandwich?" He held it up in Martha's direction. She shook her head and rolled over on the couch.

Dion held the sandwich up in offering to Skylar, who nodded and cupped his hands to catch the saran-wrapped meal.

"It's so dark in here. Don't you have a generator?" Skylar asked.

"Yeah, but it's not worth it to use it yet. Don't want to waste gas or draw more of *them* in with a bunch of unnecessary noise," Dion said as he crossed the room to a set of lockers.

Skylar bit into the sandwich and watched Dion as he gathered some clothing, went to the counter, scribbled on a piece of paper, and walked down the hall.

Dion returned to the kitchen, retrieved two more sandwiches from the fridge, and sat down at the table.

"Sky, can you come here a second?" Ana called from the washroom.

He got up and followed her voice. The door was open a crack and one green eye peered out. When she saw him, Ana opened the door, grabbed him by the shirt, and pulled him into the cramped washroom. They were nose to nose.

"Well, hello. No, those shorts don't make you look fat."

Ana stared up at him.

"Okay, so you don't have time for my humour right now. What's up?"

"What the fuck is this?" She handed him the note from Dion. *Don't trust Martha.*

"Oh. Well, he's being a bit alarmist, perhaps. But she may have mentioned something about executing you since you might be a danger to us all."

"WHAT?!" Ana yelled.

"Don't worry! We talked her out of it. And we'll watch out for you."

"Don't worry? Easy for you to say. You don't have a target on your head!"

"Do you honestly think that boomer is going to kill you in cold blood? She's lying on the couch mourning her dead son."

Ana crossed her arms and absently ran a finger over her tattoo. Skylar put his hand over hers, and their eyes met. She sighed and shrugged his hand off.

"This whole situation is so fucked up, Skylar."

"Yeah, it is. But you know what? We're going to get

through this."

She nodded silently.

"Dion has sandwiches, you hungry?"

"Starving."

"Come on."

Ana followed Skylar back to the common room. Martha was facing the couch's backrest and didn't acknowledge their return. Skylar turned to Ana, who glared in the older woman's direction. He gestured to a sandwich that had been laid out for her on the table.

"Thanks. I need to make a call first." Ana rummaged through her bag and pulled out her phone.

Skylar watched as she walked down the hall and stood by what little light shone through the back door's narrow window. He frowned. *Checking in with Paul, or still pining after Harvey?*

STELLA
30 JUNE 2018
14:30 PDT
COX BAY LOOKOUT
TOFINO, BC

Her tongue felt like sandpaper against the inside of her cheeks. Stella cursed. Her backpack, and with it her water bottle, had washed away when the wave tore her from her friends.

She looked across the water at Jasper's limp body and grimaced. A branch protruded from his midsection. Straps hung from his shoulders, and Stella noticed he still had his bag, which was secured by the tree limb that held his corpse in place. *He has water.*

Stella peered through the trees. She saw glints of cerulean through their boughs, but she couldn't determine the state of the beach or whether the tsunami had subsided. Beneath her slate platform, the water level had dropped somewhat, but she was still surrounded.

Thirst finally overtook her, so Stella knelt at the rock's edge, slowly swung her legs over, and toed the rock's face for small indentations to climb down. The frigid water made her gasp when she slid into it. She waded against its pull.

Stella's stomach churned as she approached her friend's corpse. Skewered in place by the cedar bough, crimson stained his shirt where the branch pierced through cotton and flesh. Jasper's lifeless eyes gazed past Stella. A tear rolled down her cheek as she placed a hand on her friend's face and guided his eyelids closed.

She grabbed the backpack's straps and unclasped the buckles under his arms. A sob escaped her lips. *Hold it together*. She gave herself a shake and opened the pack. Stella rummaged through Jasper's belongings and found a reusable glass bottle at the bottom of his bag. She sipped deeply from it before expelling the pungent fluid between parted lips.

"Vodka! What the hell, Jasper?" She sighed and considered the bottle. "Fuck it." Stella raised it to her lips once more and took a long swig. She shuddered after swallowing it. "At least this will take the edge off the chill, eh, Jasp?" *Okay, now I'm talking to a corpse. Time to go.* She clipped the buckles back together and slung the pack over her shoulders.

Stella waded through the water back toward the platform. To the left, where the surge had carried Chris, the elevation fell. Water rushed rapidly in that direction. *He's dead. I heard his skull crack. There's no way he survived that. It's too risky... I'm sorry, Chris. I can't follow you.* To the right of the platform, the elevation rose farther in the distance, and Stella walked through the water toward higher ground.

The tips of sword ferns and salal pierced the water's surface. Cedar scales and humus swirled around her as Stella manoeuvred through the murky water. An unseen root caught her foot, and Stella fell to her knees. Submerged to her chin, her lips trembled. She grabbed a nearby tree and pulled herself back up. She continued, drenched and dripping, through dense undergrowth, lifting her knees high with each step to avoid tripping again. Though her feet were numb, she pushed on.

After nearly an hour of wading through the swampy rainforest, Stella reached dry land. She sank to her knees and rolled onto her back. Dappled sunlight filtered through the trees. Stella was thankful for the little warmth it provided, but it wasn't enough to take away the chill that had seeped deep into her bones.

Blisters pulsed on her heels where her skin rubbed against the backs of her soggy shoes. She removed them, clapped them together to knock off forest debris, and placed them in Jasper's backpack. She took another swig of vodka and continued her ascent.

Another forty minutes passed as Stella trekked up the hill. *There's the peak. Maybe I can catch a glimpse of the highway from up there. Fuck, wait, is that...another survivor?*

He sat on a bowed tree trunk overlooking a flooded Cox Bay. She took a couple more steps toward him.

"Hello?" Stella called out to the figure, who wore a black wetsuit rolled down to his hips.

He slowly turned to the sound of her voice. The man stared at Stella with a blank gaze before he snapped out of his stupor.

"Holy shit, are you okay?" He stood up from his perch on the tree and walked toward her. "You're covered in blood!"

Stella looked at her shin, which was still bleeding from the barnacles she bashed her leg on before the wave hit.

"I, uh, yeah, that's nothing really. It doesn't hurt. I'm just really cold."

"No, not your leg! Your arms, your face… What happened to you?"

She raised her arms to inspect herself and found her skin covered in lacerations. "Oh, I didn't even notice those. I'm fine, really."

"Your eyebrow looks like it'll need stitches. You really don't feel that?"

She sighed. "Okay, I get it. I look like shit. I got taken for a ride by a freaking tsunami and watched my friends die. My eyebrow is the least of my concerns."

"I'm not trying to give you a hard time, I'm trying to see if you're okay." He held his hands up defensively and took a step toward her. "I'm sorry about your friends. Where did you just come from?"

"Cox Point."

"Oh, shit."

"You were surfing?" Stella asked.

"Yeah, I was catching some sick waves. It was a perfect day, glassy, clean. Never heard that siren go off while I was in the water. Really freaked me out. When I saw everyone running for the parking lot, I had this feeling that I wouldn't get through to the road in time. Ran straight up here. Ditched my board down below, poor thing. It was her maiden voyage. I just put the last layer of fibreglass on her a few days ago."

Stella didn't respond as she gazed out over the bay.

"I guess my surfboard isn't anything to complain about when you just lost your friends. I'm sorry. Hey, my name's Kyle."

"Stella."

"Stella. Nice to meet you, despite the circumstances."

Stella wiped a fresh trickle of blood off her arm with her damp t-shirt. "Do you...have a plan? Or were you going to stay here until the water subsides?"

"No plan. I've never witnessed something like this before." He gestured toward the flooded beach. "Figured this was as good a place to wait it out as any."

"Do you have any water?"

Kyle looked down at his second skin of black neoprene. He gave her a lopsided smile and shrugged. "What you see is what you get."

Stella sighed. She reached into the backpack and pulled out Jasper's bottle, took a swig, cringed, and offered it to Kyle.

"I take it that isn't water."

She sucked air through her teeth as she shook her head. Kyle accepted the bottle and drank deeply, then coughed.

"I don't think we should stay here. It could be days before it's safe to go down that way," Stella said.

"You're right." Kyle sat back down on the bowed tree. "There's a trail over Vargas Cone, over there, that leads to Mallard Lake. At the top of that peak," Kyle pointed, "is a road that connects to the highway. Could be others taking refuge up there."

"Lead the way."

Kyle's eyes returned to the view of a flooded Cox Bay before he turned and led Stella down a path into the woods.

PAUL
30 JUNE 2018
14:15 PDT
TSAWWASSEN MILLS
TFN TREATY LANDS, BC

"Joss, this way!" Paul guided her against the flow of the fleeing crowd.

"What?! Why? I thought you parked on the west side?"

"The hunting store is right there! We may need to defend ourselves."

"Are you kidding me? I'm not *shooting* anyone!"

"We witnessed the same scene back there, right? Would you rather face one of those monsters unarmed?" Paul ran to the store entrance. Once inside, he looked at the staff near the front counter. They chatted with customers, ignorant of the chaos outside. Paul locked the set of glass doors behind them and ventured into the shop.

The vast store had tall, arched ceilings with displays of taxidermy animals posing in faux forest scenery. Paul scanned the signs at the end of each aisle until he located the hunting section. He grabbed Jocelyn's hand and led her across the store. Shoppers stared as they bolted past aisles of camping gear and fishing rods until they reached the firearms display.

"Whoa, cowboy. We have some great sales on, but you've got all weekend. No need to rush." A weathered man in a camouflage uniform greeted them from behind a glass display counter. "What's your hustle?"

"It's an emergency! Outside... People are turning...*violent*. They're attacking each other!"

"What's this now?"

"Please, hurry! Something light for her. Not too much kick-back. I'll take a shotgun, something that holds a lot of rounds, and a handgun as well." Paul eyed several models beneath the glass display.

"Listen, son, I'm not sure I'm comfortable selling you something today with you talking like that. Are you even licensed?"

Paul pulled his wallet from his back pocket and threw his firearms license on the counter. "Ammo too. Lots of it."

The man grabbed his card, inspected it, and nodded. "Ammo is on the shelves behind you. I need more specifics. What kind of calibre are we talking for the missus?"

"That .22 should do it. We'll need a hefty magazine, though." Paul turned to the ammunition shelves. He grabbed boxes of slugs and buckshot, .22s and .9mms. "Joss, find a bag for these. Quickly."

Jocelyn moved toward a display of backpacks.

The man backed away, feigning consideration for the firearms under the glass display. He reached for a phone that was affixed to the wall. "Soloman? Yeah, it's Bill. Listen, I think we've got a situation on our hands over at firearms. Yeah, following protocol. Roger that."

When Paul returned to the counter, arms full of ammunition boxes, sirens blared through the store.

"What is that? What did you do?" Paul asked. "Don't send people outside!"

The man grimaced at the phone in his hand. "Wasn't me. That's the fire alarm, son. Looks like we gotta split."

"No! Please, just help us finish this transaction."

"Company policy says—"

"Screw company policy! I can guarantee you there's no fire. We're in danger from what's *outside*! Don't go out there!"

Jocelyn returned with a backpack as Paul felt his pocket vibrate. "Here," he said as he handed her his wallet and pulled out his cell phone. *Ana!*

"Ana! what the hell is going on?"

"Paul! Oh thank god. Paul, I'm in Tof—"

"I know! I saw you on Rocket's Insta! We just watched his fucking chopper crash at the mall! An... I thought you were in it!" Paul watched as a crowd rushed in from the mall, making their way to the parking lot through the store.

"I got out before he took off. Why the hell didn't you call me back earlier? Paul, listen. The tsunami isn't the only...emergency here. People are...turning on one another. They're like monsters..."

"Here too, An. Rocket went crazy and started... He started biting people! If you had been on that flight... Ana, listen. I saw the first responder pull something out of Rocket's pocket. A vial, with a logo of—"

"Yeah. I saw it too."

"What the fuck did they do?" The siblings fell silent for a moment. "Where are you? Are you safe?" Paul asked.

"Yes! Well, relatively. We're in the fire hall at the top of Industrial Way. There's a lot of *them* outside, but we're pretty secure. We have food and water and firearms."

"We? Are you with Harvey?"

She was silent for a moment. "No, I'm with Skylar. You remember my old neighbour? Where are you? What's that sound?"

"We're at the hunting store trying to arm ourselves. The fire alarm is going off. They're driving people outside toward those *things!*" He looked at Jocelyn, who was negotiating with the man behind the counter.

"Sir, what's your name? Bill? Do you work on commission? Look at this lot. You'll get a nice one off this, I'm sure!" Jocelyn tried to coax the man into the sale.

"Ana, I'm so sorry. I gotta fly. I'll check in soon, okay?"

"Okay."

"Paul?"

"Yeah?"

"I'm scared."

"Me too. I'll talk to you soon, Okay? Ana...I love you."

"I love you too."

Screams cut through the air as a group attempting to exit through the main doors darted back inside the store.

"What in tarnation?!" the man behind the counter exclaimed when he heard the commotion.

Paul looked around for another exit, hiding place, or anywhere to keep them safe. *Bingo.* "Joss. Grab that backpack." He reached over the counter and grabbed the firearms.

"Come on now, that's looting!" the man yelled.

"You have my credit card. The code is 5-4-4-0. Charge me when you can. Joss, this way!" Paul led her to some scaffolding next to a display beneath the vaulted ceiling. "Go!" he yelled.

As she climbed the ladder up to the platform, he shoved a few bags of trail snacks from the display beside him into their new backpack. Once she reached the top, he handed her the shotgun and .22 and climbed up after her.

"Outta my store! Out! Out! There'll be no fighting in here!" Bill yelled at the chaotic crowd.

Paul was halfway up the ladder when he turned to see the infected lurching toward the man. "Arm yourself!" Paul called out to him. "They won't listen!" He hustled up the last few steps.

Once he was on the platform, Paul loaded rounds into the pistol first, then the shotgun. "Do you know how to use it?" he asked Jocelyn as he nodded to the .22 in her hands.

"It's been years since I fired a gun."

"The safety is here. Red means ready to fire. There's no scope, so you'll use this notch on the end of the barrel as your sight. Line it up with these two bumps. Aim for the head. This is your magazine. Load it up."

"Paul, I don't want to shoot anyone!"

"Joss, those aren't people anymore. Don't you see what's happening down there?"

She scanned the gruesome scene below them. People were on the floor, twitching, screaming, writhing in pain in pools of their own blood while the infected feasted on them. Jocelyn closed her eyes and nodded.

A thunderous boom reverberated through the air. The man behind the counter pumped another round into his shotgun's chamber as more infected lurched toward him. He waited, letting them draw closer, and fired once they were within range. Bits of skull and brain sprayed the shelves behind the monsters as they collapsed to the ground.

Paul set the shotgun down and took the pistol in hand. He aimed it at a monster feasting on a man fifteen yards away, fired, and missed. He steadied himself and tried again. This time, he hit his target. His ears rang, and a surge of adrenaline ran through him, along with a pang of guilt. *No. This is how we survive. It has to be done.*

The .22 fired next to him. Paul followed the direction of Jocelyn's barrel. She'd taken down an infected man whose soggy socks and sandals left a trail of bloody footprints across the store. Paul raised his eyebrows. "Nice shot."

"Beginner's luck?"

"Natural talent."

The screams of a woman down below caught their attention, as she ran from an infected child with blonde pigtails that were slick with gore. The child was gaining on her. Paul aimed and fired. She dropped. The woman turned to the fallen child and fell to her knees.

"Move! Lady, move!" Paul called out. He grimaced when he saw the beast that approached her. Its charred flesh oozed some sort of bodily fluid. Singed locks hung sporadically from its black and red scalp. It moved with the inhuman speed of a feral Olympian. *Rocket.* Paul tried to line up a shot. His target moved too quickly.

The woman scrambled to her feet and followed the sound of Paul's voice. She was halfway up the scaffolding when Rocket grabbed her foot. She wiggled out of her shoe and continued climbing. Rocket bit into the leather and cast it aside, unsatisfied. He followed her up the ladder. *Oh fuck, wasn't expecting that.*

"Joss, get back! Move into the display!"

Jocelyn grabbed the .22, shotgun, and backpack and set

them down next to a cluster of faux ferns. She pulled herself onto the platform, then turned and reached a hand down to the other woman, helping her up. They nestled in next to a stuffed fawn, skunk, and rabbit.

The monster reached the top of the scaffolding and sneered at Paul. The whites of his eyes stood out in stark contrast to his burnt and bubbled flesh. Paul lined up his sights, aiming at the center of Rocket's forehead. He tapped the trigger, and the force of the bullet whipped Rocket's head back, but his grasp on the ladder held strong. Blood sputtered out of his mouth as a growl escaped his lips and grew into a roar.

"What the fuck!" Paul yelled. Silver glinted on the beast's forehead where the bullet had struck. Paul held up his pistol and tapped the trigger again. *Click.* The round jammed. He scurried back and pulled himself up into the taxidermy display.

As Rocket climbed atop the scaffolding, Paul pressed his legs against the edge of the steel structure. Rocket reached out, his fingers grazing Paul's foot as the platform tipped. He screeched and growled as he fell, then went silent when he hit the ground.

Is he...? Rocket was still for a moment, then sprung to his feet. A dislocated arm hung from its socket. He let out one last snarl, then ran off to find easier prey.

Paul scooted farther into the display and leaned into the artificial greenery. He closed his eyes and inhaled deeply.

Jocelyn turned to Paul. "What the hell just happened? Why didn't he die? You hit him clear in the forehead."

"Bastard has a metal plate."

STELLA
30 JUNE 2018
15:10 PDT
MALLARD LAKE
TOFINO, BC

The overgrown trail wove between trees in all stages of growth, from saplings to decaying nurse logs blanketed in moss. Sheets of old man's beard hung in tendrils from their branches and bracket fungi clung to their trunks. Kyle and Stella passed salmonberry bushes, skunk cabbage, and red huckleberries.

The rainforest's dense underbrush grazed Stella's bare legs as she followed the winding trail down the backside of the cone. Her head swam as she took a swig of vodka.

"We're making headway." Kyle turned to see Stella squinting into the neck of the empty bottle. She hiccupped as she placed the vessel in her backpack. "Do you want to take a break? You don't look so good."

She held a hand up to her forehead. "I just need water. Let's keep moving."

"Didn't do yourself any favours by finishing that off," Kyle muttered.

"Mind your own business, man."

A branch snapped in the bushes behind them.

"Hullo, is someone there?" Stella called into the shrubs.

The forest was silent.

Kyle shrugged and continued along the rough path. "Probably a bird or something. Come on."

Stella followed him with aching feet and thighs chafed from damp shorts. *Some vacation. Shoulda stayed home.*

Thick roots latticed the path, forming a natural ladder down the sloping hill. Kyle traversed a steep section, his hands gripping the tree's exposed anchors tightly. Stella followed him. She fumbled and slid a few feet before slamming into Kyle.

"Oh, sorry." She gave her head a shake as she steadied

herself. Kyle grabbed the handle of her backpack and guided the teetering woman to lean closer to the roots.

"Watch it! Stella, be more careful. You could have taken us both out! Try to keep your centre of gravity lower so you don't topple over."

"Mhmm," she mumbled under her breath.

A scream echoed through the forest.

"What the hell..." Stella whispered.

"That sounded like it came from the lake. Let's move." Kyle hastened down the path toward Mallard Lake. "Hello? Hello, is someone there?" he called through the bushes. "We heard screaming. Does someone need help?"

The slope levelled out, and the trees grew sparse when the lake came into view. Its glassy sheen reflected the surrounding foliage. Lily pads floated on the surface of the water and cattails protruded from the shallows. Kyle scanned the area. No one else was in sight.

"Hello!" he called through cupped hands, his voice echoing over the water. He turned to Stella and shrugged.

Bubbles tickled the surface of the lake near the shore. Something rose from its depths. *Is that...a person?* Stella's gaze fell on a set of wide, bloodshot eyes that locked on Kyle from underwater. A man's face broke through the lake's surface; he sputtered and hissed as he emerged. Blood stained his drenched clothing and permeated into the surrounding water. His arms bore crescent-shaped wounds and his hands held something. Someone. He let go of the lifeless body.

The woman floated to the surface and stirred. Hunched over, she slowly rolled her shoulders forward and her spine straightened as she stood. She lashed her teeth and shook her head back and forth. Her eyes flicked open and locked on her target: Kyle. The infected sloshed through the muddy bank toward him. Stella felt the hairs on the back of her neck rise.

"What the f—"

"Kyle! RUN!" Stella darted forward and grabbed him by the

arm. They ran along the path past the lake and ascended the next hill. The trail was steep. Clumsy footsteps followed them.

Another scream filled the air, this one from the top of the hill they were climbing. Kyle hesitated and turned to Stella.

"Keep going!" she pleaded as she nudged him toward another exposed root lattice. Footsteps closed in behind her, and Stella pulled the empty bottle from her bag. She turned and swung it at the infected man. Glass shattered in her hand, slicing her palm, but she managed to stop their stalker momentarily before he snarled and continued his pursuit, incensed by the coppery scent drifting through the air. Stella grabbed a branch to steady herself and kicked the monster in the chest. He keeled over backward and knocked down the bloodthirsty woman behind him.

Stella turned and saw Kyle's hand reaching for her. She grabbed it and clambered up the roots. When she made it past the particularly steep section, she turned back to see the monsters climbing shakily to their feet.

A rustling in the bushes ahead caused them to pause. Kyle cursed when an infected child emerged, lifting claw-like hands up in hungry desperation, his tiny fingers caked with dry blood and smeared with dirt.

Stella grabbed a rock from the side of the dirt path. She pushed past Kyle and swung it at the child's head. It hissed as it fell to the ground. Two more blows and the child stopped moving.

Hunched over the lifeless body, she didn't have a chance to react when more of the monsters descended the hill, didn't have time to run before they were on her. Their fingers clawed at her flesh. Stella screamed as teeth pierced her skin. Her eyes met Kyle's as the two monsters from the lake grabbed him from behind. She wept, calling out for her mother, as the infected tore bite after bite from her flesh until finally, mercifully, she fell unconscious.

HARVEY
30 JUNE 2018
14:45 PDT
MALLARD LAKE TRAIL
TOFINO, BC

"Distract the boys," Harvey whispered to Kat. "I don't want them to see this." He gestured toward their infected family members. Kat nodded, and Harvey exited the truck. He scrambled around the side of the vehicle, luring the infected away from his target. They followed him. Once they were around the side of his truck opposite the Volkswagen, he dashed to the other automobile.

Bloody hands reached for Harvey as he climbed the ladder up the back of the VW. The infected hissed and screeched as he scrambled onto the roof and grabbed a paddle, which was tied onto the outside of a plastic cargo carrier.

Harvey turned and swung at the monster nearest the ladder. One blow to the head stopped the reanimated woman—the woman Harvey had driven to safety just hours before. She fell, stirring a cloud of dust that drifted until it settled upon the blood that flowed from her fractured skull.

Her infected son approached, stepping over his mother's corpse without any comprehension of her death. Only one thing drove the boy: hunger. Harvey watched the small monster for a moment, until he was sure that he wouldn't be able to climb the ladder. He turned and unlatched the storage container beside him.

A buzzing in his pocket stole his attention. Harvey pulled his phone out. His finger slipped and pressed the answer button before he had a chance to register the name on the screen.

"Hello?"

"Harvey, hi." Her voice sounded hushed.

Harvey sat down. "Ana. This isn't the best time." He watched blood drip down the end of the paddle toward the little boy.

"Are you safe?" she asked.

"Relatively. I guess the tsunami was all over the news in the big city?"

"Ladner isn't a *big city*. And I'm...well, I'm *here*, Harvey."

He felt his chest tighten. *The tire tracks... Skylar didn't lend out her bike. It was actually her who took it.* Moments passed before he could find any words to say to her. "Why?"

"Haven't been sleeping well. I'm so sorry, Harvey, I don't like the way things ended between us. I needed to see you. I got on a plane this morning."

"Where are you?"

"Industrial Way. I'm in the fire hall."

He glanced at the truck. Kat watched him intently. Harvey frowned and shook his head to convey *there's no help on the way*.

"Harvey, have you seen anything...strange?"

"Yes, there are zombies here too."

"Oh. Where are you?"

"Up the hill by Mallard Lake. There are two children with us."

"Us?"

Harvey didn't answer.

"Right. Harvey, those things, they've made it to the mainland already."

"What? How do you know?"

"I just spoke with Paul."

"So we're on our own. No one will come to help us."

"Unlikely."

A few more moments of silence passed. "So now what?" Harvey asked her.

"Can you get home?"

"I'm working on it. Really wish I had a rifle in the truck right about now."

"I grabbed mine. We're safe in here...for now, but I think we should go inland..."

"We?"

"I'm with Skylar. And Dion, you know, the fireman? And a tourist named Martha. Listen, Harvey... Can we work together?"

Harvey held the phone away from his ear. The battery was low. "Industrial Way? I'll get there. My phone is about to die though. What's your plan?"

"I was thinking we could head up the inlet, to Port Alberni? We'd need to find a boat."

"Water's probably surging up that way too. It'd be a mess right now. We'll figure something out."

"Harvey, thank you..."

"I'm not doing this for you. I happen to know you're a good shot, being that I taught you myself. Strength in numbers, alright? Just because I'm willing to work together doesn't mean I want to discuss...whatever it is you came here for."

"Understood."

"If I don't make it there in a few hours, I'm probably not coming."

"Okay. Harvey, be safe."

"Yeah, you too." He ended the call and stared at his phone, contemplating the conversation.

Kat's head popped out the sunroof. "Who was that?" she called.

The infected boy shuffled from the Volkswagen to the truck, drawn to her voice.

"Survivors. A group we can try to join. They have guns and shelter."

The infected boy turned to Harvey's voice and shuffled back to the Volkswagen.

"Where?"

"Industrial Way."

"That's miles from here! Harvey, I thought you wanted to go the opposite way?"

"I really would feel more comfortable if we were armed first."

"Fine. So, how do we get there?"

Harvey waved a bloody paddle at her.

"You have got to be kidding me."

"Why do you think I climbed up here?"

"To check what supplies are in that tote? I don't know!"

Harvey opened the storage container and found a six-person inflatable river raft. *Bingo.*

"Do you realize how loud inflating that thing will be?"

"Do you have any other ideas? Kat, listen. Ana just told me that this outbreak, or whatever it is, is spreading on the mainland as well. I don't think we have much hope of being rescued."

"Ana? As in, your *ex,* Ana?"

"That was your takeaway?"

"Was that her on the phone?"

"Yes."

Kat sat back down in the truck and closed the sunroof.

Harvey rolled his eyes and dropped the raft from the roof. The impact drew the little monster to the other side of the Volkswagen. Harvey waited to see if the sound drew more infected from the bushes. Satisfied that the boy was the only threat in the immediate vicinity, he hustled down the ladder and readied the paddle. The tiny predator approached him with teeth bared. Harvey swung at him, aiming for the base of his skull. The boy fell next to his mother's lifeless body. He didn't get back up.

Harvey knelt in the Volkswagen and rummaged through the carelessly packed camping gear. *Aha! Knew I'd find one.* He grabbed the compressor, climbed into the front seat, turned the ignition, and plugged it into the cigarette lighter socket. *Shit, she's right. That's a lot louder than I anticipated.* He stepped out of the vehicle and inserted the compressor's hose into the raft's valve. The limp PVC slowly began to take form. Harvey paced around the vehicles and monitored the edge of the woods while the raft inflated.

SKYLAR
30 JUNE 2018
14:25 PDT
FIRE HALL, INDUSTRIAL WAY
TOFINO, BC

Ana joined Dion and Skylar at the table, taking an empty seat. She unwrapped the sandwich and bit into it ravenously.

"So, is your brother coming to our rescue?" Skylar asked.

Ana looked up at him and swallowed. She shook her head. "These...things...are there."

Dion turned to her. "What was that?"

"The infected are in Tsawwassen. On the mainland."

"Shit," Dion and Skylar said in unison. Martha didn't move from where she lay curled in a fetal position on the couch.

"It was Rocket. His helicopter went down, and he started attacking people. Paul saw the whole thing."

"Holy shit." Skylar put a hand on her shoulder. "An, if you had been there..."

"I wasn't. That's what matters. I'm just thankful that jerk put me off enough that I chose a tsunami over sitting next to him."

"Put you off? Here I thought you ditched the helicopter to stay with me." Skylar wagged his dark eyebrows at her.

Ana rolled her eyes. "I also called Harvey. He'll be heading this way."

Skylar's eyes didn't meet hers when he nodded. He stood up and walked down the hall to the washroom.

The sterile scent of bleach invaded his nostrils. He removed his clothing and stepped onto the damp floor of the shower stall. Warm water crept down his scalp, and Skylar let out a sigh. *Of course he's coming here. What did I expect? The apocalypse hits and suddenly she chooses me?* He ran his fingers through his wet hair. His muscles ached.

When he turned the water off, he heard raised voices. Skylar wrapped himself in a towel and inched the door open.

"Come on, babe. Great way to blow off some steam."

Dion, what are you up to?

"I said *no*. I'm not interested, so keep it to yourself," Ana retorted.

"What's holding you back? Loosen up. We've got time to kill until your *boyfriend* gets here. Or is it your *other* boyfriend in the shower you're concerned about?"

"Neither of them is my *boyfriend*. Keep your hands off me!"

"Get over yourself, girl."

Skylar felt blood burn at the surface his cheeks. He stormed into the common room and yelled, "What the hell do you think you're doing?" His nails dug into the skin of his palms when he clenched his fists. Dion had Ana backed into the corner of the kitchenette.

"Come on, man, I didn't mean any harm." Dion sniffed. His dilated pupils bore into Skylar as he ran the back of his hand over his nose, failing to wipe away the white powder that encircled his nostrils.

"She said not to touch her. Step back."

Dion sneered and bent over the counter for another dose. He snorted and coughed when the powder entered his sinuses.

Ana retreated and grabbed her .22 from the table. She moved toward the sofa, as far from Dion as she could get. Martha scowled at her.

"What the hell did I do to you, Martha?"

"I still don't trust that you won't become one of them!"

"That's ridiculous! I haven't been bitten!"

"Sky, you want one?" Dion taunted.

"Is this really the time, Dion?"

"Haven't seen you turn it down before."

Skylar glanced at Ana. "Sure, at parties. This is different."

"Doesn't have to be, man!" Dion sauntered over to a radio at the other end of the counter and mashed its buttons until death metal blared through the room. "Come on, man! Let's make the best of this!" Dion bounced around the dark kitchen, emulating a one-man mosh pit.

"Dude. Chill." *This is getting out of hand.*

"Fuck it," Martha said. "It's been years. Lay one out for me."

Dion laughed, intoxicated by his hedonistic revelry.

Skylar and Ana's eyes met. "Let's get out of here," Ana mouthed.

HARVEY
30 JUNE 2018
15:00 PDT
MALLARD LAKE TRAIL
TOFINO, BC

"Harvey, stop! You've got about three inches before we roll down the side of the damn hill."

Metal screeched on metal as Harvey tried to squeeze his truck past a car blocking the road.

"Well, if we had walked down like I suggested..."

"Those *creepers* are following us! We can't walk down this hill carrying a freakin' boat!"

Kat looked back at the predator lurking behind the truck. It reached over the tailgate with arms flailing in their direction.

"Lure it to the side."

"What?"

"Open your window and call it over."

Kat groaned. "Hey! Hey, over here!"

The infected leered at her with bloodshot eyes. It followed her voice and shuffled around the side of the truck. The monster lost its footing on the uneven ground, and stumbled with a loud hiss, rolling out of sight.

"Hah!" Harvey laughed with relief. He inched the truck farther and passed another car.

The two boys, pale and exhausted, sat arm in arm in the back seat.

Harvey noticed two figures sitting in the next vehicle they approached. He rolled down his window and signalled the other driver to do the same.

"Hi, sir, ma'am. Are you...doing okay?" Harvey asked.

The older man nodded. The woman leaned over her husband and said, "We saw demons chasing people down the hill."

Harvey furrowed his brow and nodded.

"Some vacation. There's a tsunami *and* demons running

amok. Bet we woulda been fine if we'd gone to Barkerville, like I suggested." He looked at his wife with narrow eyes.

"It's been a hell of a day, that's for sure," Harvey said.

"Where are you headed?" the man asked when his eyes fell upon the raft in the back of Harvey's truck.

"Back into town to join some friends who are hiding out. You should come with us."

The old man chuckled. "No, no, I don't think we'll be riding the tsunami today. Betty here has a bad hip."

"It holds six people. There are only four of us."

"Listen, son, we aren't as young and spry as you lot. You go on now. We'll be just fine."

"Sir, I don't think there's going to be any rescue teams coming anytime soon. These...*demons*... They're popping up in other places. On the mainland, too."

"Mmmhm." The man considered this and shook his head.

"Oh, Nigel, let the kids pass."

"Yes, yes, of course. You need to get through. Here, hold on a sec."

"Sir, are you sure you won't come with us?" Paul offered one last time.

"Yeah, yeah. Go on now. Wild kids, I tell ya. Got the fight of a survivor!" He reversed his car as an infected approached. "Hold on, Betty!" Nigel moved forward, knocking the monster down, and pinned it under his front bumper. Its arms flailed while it snarled and hissed.

"I don't think we should leave them here," Kat whispered.

"I can't force them to come, Kat."

She called across Harvey, "Sir, please, will you reconsider?"

He stuck his head out the driver's window. "I said go on now! Don't you worry about us."

Kat nodded and leaned back in her seat. Harvey continued inching down the narrow shoulder of the gravel road.

"There! Oh, what a mess!" Kat groaned when what should have been Highway 4 came into view.

Water seeped across the pavement from beyond the tree line and flowed down the highway, carrying forest debris and lost belongings. A bicycle helmet, a broken surfboard, and a life jacket drifted past them on the surface of the waist-deep water.

"Wish we had a few of those," Kat said as they watched the life jacket float past.

They sat silently and surveyed the water.

"Think we can paddle against it?" Kat asked.

"Only one way to find out. Okay, boys! Ready for an adventure?"

"I don't want to," Mikey whined. Patrick said nothing.

"I know. It's okay to be scared. We're going to be alright though. It's just a short ride, that's all."

"I'm not *scared*, I just don't want toooooo."

"But we're going to, and it's going to help us get to safety, alright? Now, listen, boys. I want you both to stay right in the middle of the raft, got it? Kat and I will paddle, so you don't have to worry about anything except holding on."

Kat peered through the sunroof and checked the perimeter of the truck and surrounding area for signs of infected. "We're clear!"

Harvey scanned the area to confirm, exited the vehicle, and unloaded the raft. He carried it to the water's edge, then retrieved the paddles.

"Alright, boys, let's do this!" Harvey opened the rear door and offered Mikey a hand down. His lip trembled, but he took Harvey's hand and followed him.

Patrick sat in the truck with his head down and whispered, "I want my mommy."

Kat appeared at the door. "Hey, buddy, it's okay. After we take this raft, we'll go somewhere safe, and then we can work on contacting the rest of your family, alright?" She reached in toward the reluctant child. He grumbled before crawling across the seat and into her arms. She lifted him out of the truck and carried him over to the raft.

Once the boys were settled, Harvey held a hand out for Kat. She accepted it and stepped onto the raft. Harvey handed her a paddle, then started pushing them into the newly formed river.

Crisp water seeped into his boots as he waded into the surging depths. He hoisted himself onto the float and immediately felt the current carry them southeast, in the opposite direction of town. Harvey paddled vigorously against the rushing water.

"Kat, let's go!" he urged.

"Right, sorry! It's just... a lot to take in." She joined in and they began inching forward.

The path was winding, and the abandoned vehicles that blocked the road made it difficult to navigate.

Harvey grimaced when they bounced off the side of a black Volvo. "Let's try not to bump into too much shit." He felt a pang of guilt after swearing in front of the young boys. *Fuck it, they've seen and heard worse than that today.*

"Isn't this thing designed for river rapids? With lots of rocks?"

"Do you want to test its durability?"

"No."

Kat and Harvey paddled in silence through the coniferous bayou that was once Highway 4.

The raft approached the stretch of highway that passed the turnoff to Cox Bay's parking lot.

"There! We can follow the bike path and avoid this mess of vehicles," Harvey called.

"Bet they never thought someone would paddle down it," Kat said.

"No kidding. How are your arms, Kat?"

"Screaming."

Harvey paddled toward a tree at the road's edge and tethered the raft to it. When he finished the knot, he realized that they were near the entrance to the forest they had picnicked at hours before. *Some date this has become.*

Kat sighed with relief and drank some water.

Something floated down the path directly toward the raft.

"What is that? Push it away, Kat."

She readied herself as the mound of soggy material drifted toward them. When it was within reach, she used her paddle to guide it around the raft. With a shriek, it rolled over, revealing itself as one of the infected, carried by the current. He grabbed hold of her paddle. Kat yelped as he pulled her into the water.

The boys cried out in unison.

"Kat!" Harvey called. *Shit, shit, shit.*

The water carried them away. Kat clung to the paddle, thrusting it to push the clammy-skinned infected out of arm's reach.

Harvey untied the knot holding them to the tree and the raft drifted after Kat and her assailant. He paddled hard to close the distance between them.

"Kat! Here!" He threw her the rope. Kat pulled herself toward the raft. The monster flailed, his nails inches from her face. When they were within reach, Harvey swung his paddle into the back of the infected's head. With a sickening crunch it went limp, and sanguine water carried it away. Harvey offered Kat a hand and pulled her into the raft, then anchored onto another tree.

"Are you okay? You're shivering."

Kat nodded and attempted to steady her breathing. She looked down at her drenched dress and frowned.

"Here." Harvey took his shirt off and handed it to her. "You'll warm up more quickly."

She shimmied out of the wet dress and put on his shirt. "Th-th-this shirt is wet t-t-too!"

"Oh, sorry. Paddling is hard work!"

"N-n-no kidding."

"Were you bitten? Scratched?" He grabbed her arms and inspected her, but found no trace of blood.

"N-n-no."

"Thank God. Come here." Harvey wrapped his arms around her and rubbed his hands on hers.

"W-w-we lost ground. W-we should keep moving."

"Just relax a moment. Catch your breath."

"I can paddle," Mikey said quietly.

Kat smiled at him. "Th-thank you, Mikey. I-I'll be okay in a minute th-though."

Harvey looked up at the cerulean sky. He felt the raft trembling, bound against the current, and the sporadic rise and fall of Kat's breaths against his chest. He looked out along their path. *At this rate, it'll take us hours to get there.*

After a few minutes, Kat's breathing levelled out. Harvey looked down at her. "You ready?"

She nodded and took up her paddle. "Let's d-do this."

PAUL
30 JUNE 2018
15:00 PDT
TSAWWASSEN MILLS
TFN TREATY LANDS, BC

A mound of corpses lay beneath their perch. The fire alarm stopped blaring, and the hunting store was eerily quiet.

"We'll need to grab more ammo on our way out," Paul said as he loaded rounds into the empty pistol.

"Is that all of them?" Jocelyn asked as she scanned the floor.

"Looks like it. No sign of Rocket either. He must have gone into the mall."

"How do we get down?" the lady with one shoe asked.

Paul looked around for something useful amongst the fake foliage and preserved animals that surrounded them.

A whistle caught their attention. It was the salesman that Paul and Joss had bickered with earlier. "Well, son, I'm sorry I doubted you! Never imagined I'd see anything like this in my lifetime, but here we are," he said as he toed a lifeless body on the floor.

"Call it even if you help us down?"

"Yeah, well, let's just see now," he muttered as he attempted to lift the scaffolding. The bodies surrounding it blocked him from erecting the steel platform. "No, well, that's not gon' work. We have a ladder in the back, jus' a minute now." He walked behind the counter and through a door with a sign that read *Staff Only*.

Paul grabbed some snacks from the backpack and handed one to each of the women. "Better fuel up. Who knows when we'll get another opportunity."

"I'm a vegetarian," the one-shoed woman said as she frowned at the jerky in his hand. He looked in the backpack again and offered her a bag of nuts.

"Thanks... Well, for saving my life, mostly. I'm Amy, by the way."

"Of course. Amy, this is Jocelyn, and I'm Paul. Was that your..." Paul trailed off. His eyes lingered on the lifeless body of the infected child he had shot.

"My boss's kid. Somehow I got roped into nannying. It was definitely not part of the job description."

Paul watched as the older man struggled through the door with a tall ladder. He dragged it across the floor and set it down away from the corpses and scaffolding. Jocelyn, Paul, and Amy crawled through the wilderness scenes toward the ladder. "Sir, we can't thank you enough."

"It's nothin'," the man said as he caught his breath. He steadied the ladder as they climbed down.

"Sir—"

"The name's Bill."

Amy scanned the floor and found her shoe.

"Bill, do you, uhh, mind if we grab some more ammo on our way out?"

"You take whatever it is you need. Let's get ya'll equipped. Come on over here now." He led them through the store. "You don't want to weigh yourself down so much that you can't run, but you don't want to run out either. What's your name, miss? Amy? Step on over here and we'll find you a firearm."

Paul loaded several boxes of ammunition into his backpack and tested the weight before adding two more. Jocelyn grabbed a bag and did the same.

Bill turned to a locked cabinet and retrieved a semi-automatic rifle. "I'll be staying right here, for now. You see any more *normal* folks out there, you send them my way. I'll get 'em ready for battle."

Paul nodded. "Thank you, Bill."

"Of course. Ya'll be safe out there, eh?"

"We'll try," Jocelyn answered.

Amy, Paul, and Jocelyn walked to the exit, passing dozens

of mutilated bodies along the way.

"My car is on the other side of the mall. Who knows what we'll find out there, but we'll try to get to it. You with us, Amy?"

Amy nodded, grasping her firearm tightly.

Paul took a deep breath and opened the door. There were bodies strewn across the parking lot, with the infected crouched over many of them, feasting upon their prey. Paul shielded his eyes from the sun as he looked west at the grid-locked highway. "Ferry traffic. It isn't moving. Look, most of those vehicles were abandoned. There's no way we're driving out along the highway."

A moan echoed across the pavement. Paul turned to see dozens of infected shuffling toward them.

"Come on!" he called and headed the other way, back toward the helicopter's remains.

The trio approached the smouldering wreckage. Wisps of black smoke still curled into the air. Half-eaten bodies littered the scene and a sickly sweet, coppery smell permeated the area. Red and blue lights from a police car still flashed, but the officers were nowhere in sight.

Two squad cars blocked access to 52nd Street, which led into Ladner. Paul squinted down the road. He could just make out orange pylons and yellow police tape in the distance, and the flashing lights of another police cruiser.

"I don't think it's worth the risk of facing a horde to get to my car. Hold up a sec." He jogged over to one of the patrol cars and peered in the window. The keys were in the ignition. "Ladies, get in." Paul pulled the door open and sat in the driver's seat.

Jocelyn ran around to the passenger's side.

"Are we seriously considering stealing a cop car?" Amy hesitated before climbing into the back seat.

"I don't think they'll mind, given the circumstances. Or would you rather run?" Paul turned the key in the ignition. Once she had closed her door, he reversed, turned the car around, and sped down the farm road. The field on the east side of the road, to their right, housed golden sprigs of barley that gently swayed in the summer breeze.

Paul's heart quickened when a group appeared at the end of the road. *No way*. A horde of the infected was limping toward them, coming from the north end of 52nd Street. He slowed the vehicle.

"I don't think the officers on that end would've just let those zombies walk right past them. Let's take shelter and wait this out a bit," Paul suggested. He turned into the driveway of one of the few houses on the street: a three-story heritage house with boarded windows and chipped white paint. "Come on, let's get inside before *anything* joins us." He exited the car, leaving the keys in the ignition.

Jocelyn got out and stared up at the boarded windows. "It's creepy," she said.

"Creepier than out here?" As if to emphasize Paul's point, the wind rustled through the leaves of several plum trees that stood in front of the house.

"Fair. Let's go."

"Hey, let me outta here!" Amy's muffled cry summoned them back. She was locked in the back of the cruiser.

"Oh shit!" Paul turned back to the car. "Sorry, Amy."

"Don't you watch movies? It's a cop car! For goodness' sake!" She stomped past Paul toward the house.

The wooden stairs creaked as they walked up to the front entrance. Plywood boards sealed every door and window. Paul attempted to pry one off, to no avail. "There's gotta be a way." He walked along the porch that wrapped around the house. All the windows were secure. Paul descended the back stairs and circled the lower perimeter. On the western side of the house, he found an entrance: an open window at ground level leading into the basement. *Bingo*. "Over here!" he called.

"I am not crawling through that," Amy said stubbornly.

"Have any better ideas?" Paul asked.

They stood in silence for a moment.

"Alright then." Paul lowered himself through the window into the dark basement.

HARVEY
30 JUNE 2018
15:30 PDT
HIGHWAY 4
TOFINO, BC

"We're going to have to get out and walk!" Harvey called to Kat. The road's elevation had risen.

Never thought asphalt could look so beautiful. He paddled to the edge of the pavement and clambered off the raft, then offered Kat a hand. She took it, slid down the edge of the raft, and inhaled sharply when her feet touched the cool water.

Kat turned to the boys. "Come on, Mikey." She lifted him to the road. "Your turn, Pat." Once both boys were on land, Harvey dragged the raft onto the pavement.

"Can't drag this over the hill... It could get damaged."

"I can help you carry it."

"I'd rather you had a hand free for the boys. Let's check these cars, maybe we'll find something useful."

Kat and Harvey searched several abandoned vehicles.

"How about this?" Kat asked. She held up a skateboard.

"Going to shred some hills?"

"No, we can pull the raft on it!"

Harvey smiled and nodded at her. He continued rummaging through the car, but found nothing useful. He moved on to a large van with an emblem of a surfer riding a wave. Checking the back hatch, he found it unlocked and full of wetsuits and longboards.

"Hey! Come over here."

Kat and the boys looked at the wetsuit in Harvey's hand.

"Here, this should fit. Put this on." Harvey handed Mikey and Pat each a petite black neoprene suit. He handed Kat a lilac-coloured one.

"Wish I had this, like, an hour ago," she said as she accepted the suit from him. She shimmied the tight neoprene onto her legs and wiggled it up around her torso. "It's...so...tight!"

"That's good. That's how it should be. Kat, have you never surfed before?"

"Not once."

"Didn't you grow up here?"

"Mhm."

"Damn. Well, I'll have to take you sometime."

"Honestly, after watching *that* wave, I don't think I have much interest in getting in the water."

"There goes my idea for our second date." Harvey smirked at her. He grabbed a navy-blue suit and pulled it on, then handed out booties and gloves.

"How do people pee in these things?" Kat asked as she helped the boys into their suits. Harvey raised an eyebrow at her.

"You just...go."

"Eww!" Kat and the boys said in unison.

"When you're in the water you can rinse it out! Not on dry land!" He removed leashes from several surfboards that were piled in the back of the van, and he used them to harness the raft to the skateboard. He gave his knot of leashes a tug, and the raft rolled after him. *Perfect.*

Kat found a duffle bag in the back of the van and packed everyone's clothing into it.

Harvey studied the route ahead. The path veered away from the highway, separated by a row of shrubs and trees. *Can't go that way. It's narrow, and the view is too obstructed.*

"Alright, let's move. We're taking the road. Everybody stays close. Kat, take this paddle and cover our rear. Let's keep quiet. Who knows what's on the other side of the hill." He towed the raft with one hand, rested a paddle on his opposite shoulder and marched onward.

They climbed the hill wordlessly. When they reached the top, they came upon a view of the same haunting scenery: abandoned cars, no survivors in sight, and swift water churning through the forest and into the street.

Harvey allowed gravity to pull the raft down to the surging water. He looked over at the junction where the path rejoined the road, ensuring it was clear, then untied the leashes and removed the makeshift dolly.

Once the raft was in the water, Kat placed the duffle bag on it and lifted the boys in. A rustling caught her attention. “Harvey, behind you!” she called.

Three infected sporting board shorts, thickly padded shoes, and helmets emerged from the concealed pathway. Bloody teeth snapped and gnashed in his direction.

Guess I know whose skateboard that was. Shit!

“Get in!” he yelled at Kat.

The boys whimpered as Kat climbed in with them. She turned and held the paddle in a defensive stance.

Harvey swung his paddle at the infected nearest him. It fell back as another lurched forward and caught his arm. Harvey screamed when it bit down. He shoved it with all his strength, jumped back onto the raft, and used the paddle to push them farther into the water as the third monster waded in after them.

“GO, KAT! PADDLE!”

She did, and the current began to lift them, but not quickly enough. The infected skaters clung to the edge of the raft.

Harvey struck their clutching fingers until, one by one, they lost their grip and were carried away by the rushing water. He lay back in the raft, exhaled deeply, and cradled his arm. Coagulated blood coated the navy-blue neoprene of his wetsuit.

“Did they...” Kat hesitated.

“No, this isn’t my blood. The neoprene is too thick. Hurt like a bitch though.” He flexed his fingers and shook his hand before rinsing the contaminated blood off his arm.

PAUL
30 JUNE 2018
15:30 PDT
HERITAGE HOUSE
TFN TREATY LANDS, BC

Cold sludge splashed up Paul's calves when his feet hit the basement floor. His nostrils filled with the musty scent of black mould and stagnant water. As his eyes adjusted to the darkness, he inspected the dim room. Soggy boxes lined the walls. Across the room stood a rough staircase that was missing several steps.

Jocelyn lowered herself through the narrow window. "Gross!" She cringed at the murky water. "Why is it so wet? We haven't had rain in weeks."

"Guess that's what happens when you build a basement below sea level on the coast."

"Umm, Paul, can you please help me?" Amy asked as she peered in the window. "I'm not as agile as you two..."

"Of course. Turn around. Yeah, you've got it. Feet against the wall. There you go." Paul coached Amy as she climbed down.

He stole one more glance out the window. The infected had reached the squad car. He looked around for something to cover the window with, but all he could find was water-logged cardboard. He placed a few strips outside to cover their entrance, then headed up the stairs. The boards groaned under his weight. Even at his stature, Paul had a hard time clearing the three missing steps. He turned back to offer Jocelyn a hand, and continued upward as she helped Amy.

Something thudded above them. Paul held a finger to his lips as they stopped to listen. There were no further sounds.

"They condemned this building a long time ago. Could be nesting animals. Raccoons or birds or something," Paul whispered. He moved toward the door and turned its antique brass knob. The hinges creaked as the door opened. The deteriorating wood of the staircase groaned under their combined weight. Paul grabbed Jocelyn by the wrist and hastily stepped through the doorway.

A mud-stained Persian runner ran the length of the entrance hall. A large painting hung crooked on the buttery-yellow wall. Someone had taken the liberty of adding their own décor: foul words and gaunt characters were hastily sprayed, with drips of paint dribbling down the wall. To the left was the boarded entry door and a walnut staircase; to their right stood three solid oak doors.

Paul walked toward the three doors. His heart thumped heavily as he turned the handle of the first door, inching it open. Narrow beams of light shone through the gaps in the boarded windows, illuminating dust particles that floated in the air of the abandoned kitchen. Empty beer bottles were strewn about the counter.

He checked the other doors: both rooms were vacant, save for a few pieces of run-down furniture. Satisfied that the area was clear, he entered the kitchen and turned on the faucet. Nothing came out.

Jocelyn grabbed a crumpled piece of receipt paper from the counter and unfolded it. "Liquor Mart. June 30th. Paul, these are from today!" she exclaimed.

Another thud sounded above them.

"We have to warn whoever is up there," Paul said.

He checked his firearms before heading back into the hallway and up the staircase. Each step squeaked with his ascent. Paul heard faint music through the wall. A skunky odour greeted him at the top of the stairs.

Paul sniffed, smirked, and knocked swiftly on the door. "I don't want to startle you, but you have company! We're coming in," he called before entering.

Smoke drifted out of the room and revealed three teenagers sitting cross-legged on the floor. A curly haired boy tried to hide a brightly coloured glass bong behind his back.

"Blane! I told you it wasn't safe here!" the girl hissed at the boy holding the bong.

"Listen, Occifer, technically, we aren't trespassing... This was my Gramma's house. So we didn't really do anything *that* wrong, did we? I mean, it's legal now, and we didn't break anything. That basement window has been missing for years."

Paul's face broke into a smile. "I'm not a cop."

"Then why do you have guns?" the boy next to Blane asked. "Listen, we don't want any trouble."

"There's trouble whether you want it or not, but not from us. Have you looked outside lately?"

"Nah, man, the windows are all boarded up, duh."

Paul walked across the room and tested a board. One was loose enough that he managed to pry it off. "Come here."

Blane hesitated, looked from one of his friends to the other, and rose to his feet.

The window overlooked the front yard. Groups of infected slowly staggered down the road, and several of them were in the driveway. Blane looked down at the scene, silent for a few moments, until he broke into laughter.

"Where's Brian? He put you up to this?"

"Who's Brian?"

"Oh, come on, my brother, Brian? Obviously this is another one of his pranks. Him and his film buddies are always up to something. This is much more elaborate than his previous tricks, I'll give him that. How much is he paying these actors? Ridiculous. Shawn, Leah, you've gotta see this."

Blane's friends joined him at the window.

"I don't know your brother," Paul said, "but this isn't a prank. Those aren't actors. This is *happening*."

"I want to go home," the girl said. Her eyes were bloodshot and glazed over.

"I wouldn't advise that right now," Jocelyn chimed in from the doorway.

A shriek pierced the silence outside. Paul leaned over the

teens and peered out the window to see a figure climbing one of the plum trees in the front yard. *Oh shit, he isn't a zombie.* The man chucked his cell phone at an infected reaching up for him. It bounced off the monster and fell to the ground.

Paul raised the stock of his gun and smashed the window, then turned the firearm around and pointed its barrel through the shattered opening.

"You just gave away our hiding spot!" Amy whispered sharply.

"We have to help him!" Paul retorted.

It was too late. The monsters had ahold of the man's foot and dragged him down from the tree. He fell to the ground, and three infected were ravishing him before Paul could fire. He screamed as they feasted upon his flesh. More infected joined in, reaching for entrails and spreading his still-warm organs across the lawn.

Shawn hurled. Leah started sobbing. Blane continued to stare out the window with no further mention of his brother's alleged pranks.

Paul watched as dozens of infected joined the feast, and several peered up at them. *Shit.*

"Can they get in here?" Shawn asked.

"The doors and windows are boarded pretty tight. The weak spot would be the basement window we came in through."

"So we barricade the basement door," Blane said.

"With what?" Paul asked.

"There's a cabinet down there. Gotta be a hundred years old. It's heavy."

"Let's move."

Paul and Blane made their way down the creaky staircase. The teen opened the door beside the kitchen.

The room was empty aside from one piece of antique furniture, a solidly built credenza. They inched it down the hallway and in front of the basement door. A thud and a splash sounded below. *Jesus, how's that for timing.* Paul held a finger to his rounded lips, then pointed to his ear and down to the basement.

Blane's red eyes followed the direction of Paul's finger. He nodded. There were several more splashes, and the basement stairs creaked. Another splash. *Dummy fell through the missing steps.* Its attempts looped: creaking boards, splash, groan. Creaking boards, splash, groan.

ANA
30 JUNE 2018
15:45 PDT
FIRE HALL, INDUSTRIAL WAY
TOFINO, BC

The sound of pounding fists reverberated through the steel door. Every thud added to the tension in her chest and the lump in her throat as Ana tried to ignore the infected cannibals attempting to paw their way in. A similar thud echoed from the washroom, where Martha and Dion had disappeared to enjoy their intoxicated state a little more intimately.

Ana sat with her .22 in hand and reflected on the chaotic day. She tried to make sense of the outbreak of monsters inhabiting the peninsula. The image of a phoenix wearing a crown popped into her mind. *That vial... How the hell did it get here?* She shook the image from her head. Ana closed her eyes and remembered the feeling of the wind against her skin as she raced from the beach to Skylar's trailer. Another memory took its place: the feeling of the wind from the helicopter's propellors tugging at wisps of hair that had fallen loose from her braid. She recalled catching a glimpse of a red truck and a boat when she abandoned her seat on the helicopter. *That's it! That's how we get out of this mess.*

Ana looked at Skylar, who was pacing again. "Sky, I want to go. We should slip out the back door while they're distracted."

"What?"

"We can't stay on this hill. On this peninsula. We gotta go."

"Go where? We're safe from the zombies in *here*."

"Safe from them, yes... But how long until those other two turn on us? Or until we run out of food? There was a boat next to the helipad..."

"Do you even know how to operate a boat?"

"No. Harvey does though. Can you hot-wire a truck?"

"Come on, Ana, is it because I live in a trailer, you think

I'm some ruffian?"

"Hey, I lived in a trailer too. I didn't mean it like—"

"I'm pulling your leg. I do know how to. I know a little about boats, too. I just don't think this is the best idea."

"I don't feel safe here. Martha is probably seducing Dion into joining team 'Put Down Ana' right now."

"Everyone reacts to stress in their own way. They're processing the situation a little...*differently* than we are. And trust me, I've known Dion a long time. He wouldn't *put you down*."

"I trust *you*. It's *them* I don't trust. Did you see his eyes? He looks mean. Evil."

"That's from the drugs."

"Do you actually do that stuff?"

"Been a while."

She grabbed her backpack, checked that her rifle's magazine was loaded, and walked across the common room. "I'm out. Join me if you want. I won't force you."

Skylar rubbed his chin. His tongue glided over his broken incisor as he contemplated.

"Fine. I don't like it though. Give me a minute to find some tools."

Skylar rummaged through several lockers and cabinets until he found what he was looking for: a hammer, various screwdrivers, and some wire cutters.

"Let's go, then."

Ana tiptoed down the hallway to peer through the back door's narrow window, and saw that their path was clear. She turned the deadbolt and pulled the handle open.

An alarm system beeped several times. The beep turned into a chime. The chime grew louder.

"Fuck it," she said and stepped through the door.

The washroom door swung open, and a naked Dion walked into the hallway. White powder crusted his nostrils. "The fuck is this? Some kind of sabotage?" He punched a sequence of numbers into the alarm's control panel fixed on the wall beside the door.

Ana descended the steps without turning back. Skylar followed. “See ya, man.”

“Once you’re out, you don’t come back,” Dion yelled after him.

Skylar nodded, and the door slammed closed behind him. He jogged a couple paces to catch up to Ana, who watched the group of monsters at the front door. They looked at Ana and Skylar with hungry, soulless eyes, drawn by the sound of footsteps crunching through the gravel, and began staggering toward them.

“This was a terrible idea,” Skylar said under his breath.

“Come on, this way.” Ana pointed to a storage lot at the corner of the road, past the helicopter pad. Beyond the chain-link fence and shrubs of Scotch broom, a glimpse of the red truck was visible, and beyond that, a boat.

Skylar smirked. “Old man Greg’s rig. He brought it in from the docks for cleaning the other day.”

“Well, that’s nice. We have company! Let’s move!”

They ran down the gravel road until they entered the storage yard. Ana pulled the gate closed moments before the horde reached it. Bloody fingers grasped the barrier between the monsters and their meal. She raised her .22 and laid out a few rounds into the nearest infected.

“I’ll get to work with the wires. Hollar if we’re in trouble!” Skylar called.

Ana fired at the monsters that pushed against the fence. Their bodies piled up. *Friggin’ zombies’ corpses are going to block us in.*

She followed the perimeter of the fence away from the gate, dragging the barrel of her gun along the steel links to lead the infected away from the yard’s only exit. The monsters followed her. Several lost their footing and tumbled into the ditch.

Behind her, Ana heard the engine roar to life.

Skylar reversed the truck toward the boat’s trailer to hitch up.

Ana felt a vibration coming from her backpack. She reached for the side pocket and pulled out her phone. *Paul.*

"Hey, bro, it's not the best time. I left the fire hall. The situation became a little...uncomfortable there. So we're commandeering a boat," she said.

"What?! Tsunamis can come in sets! Stay out of the water!"

"We're running out of options. There's too many of those *things* here."

After a moment of silence, Paul said, "Okay. Just stay safe, got it?"

"Yeah... Where are you?"

"You remember that boarded-up old farmhouse on 52nd?"

"That place is creepy as hell."

"Well, now it's our hideout. There're some biters locked in the basement though."

"Gross."

Skylar climbed back into the truck. He tested the gas pedal; the boat and trailer followed. "An! Let's go!"

"I'll check in when we're on the water. I gotta run, Paul. Over and out."

"See ya, sis."

Ana ran back across the yard and swung the gate open. She dragged a few limp corpses out of their path, ran back to the truck, and climbed into the passenger seat. Skylar pulled out of the yard as quickly as the boat trailer would allow and drove down the hill.

Not a single survivor was in sight, but waves of infected lurched along the road, drawn to the sound of their vehicle.

When they reached the bottom of the hill, they saw the highway was gridlocked with abandoned vehicles that blocked their path down to the water.

"Shit. I forgot about that," Ana said.

Skylar looked at her and raised an eyebrow. "I guess we'll have to move them."

FREDDIE
30 JUNE 2018
16:00 PDT
STRAIT OF GEORGIA, BC

Freddie's footsteps were nearly soundless against the steel floor. He strolled through rows of RVs, large trucks towing boats and trailers, and tall semis delivering goods to the island. Satisfied with his inspection, he paused by the railing at the starboard side of the ferry and watched as they sailed through the strait toward their destination: Swartz Bay, Vancouver Island. *Fifteen knots, give or take. Come on, Cap'n, we can give it more than that.*

A refreshing mist splashed up from the wake. After a while, Freddie broke away from the ocean's spell and continued his patrol. He approached a horse trailer, and a thrashing within caught his attention. *Poor beast probably has anxiety. Not used to being on the water, eh, Seabiscuit?*

He stepped toward the trailer and noticed a dark liquid pooled beneath it. Freddie bent down and poked it. Crimson dripped from his index finger as he reached for the radio at his hip.

"This is Freddie, Cargo Deck 3. We've got a serious problem down here. Blood is seeping from this horse trailer, and I hear struggling. Send the owner down. Now!"

"License plate number?"

How many horse trailers do you think are down here?

"555-LFE! Over!"

Freddie paced the length of the truck and trailer, trying to ignore the strange sounds coming from within.

"Would the owner of license plate number 555-LFE please make your way to the vehicle deck? I repeat, license plate 555-LFE. Please make your way to the vehicle deck. Thank you."

Kelly sounded calm through her announcement. *She's always calm, whether it's a lost child, a man overboard...*

Come on, let's make haste here.

Freddie checked his watch several times. *Come on, where are you?* As if on cue, hurried footsteps rang from the stairwell. A man and young girl trotted over.

"What's the problem here?" the moustached man asked.

His daughter's face was tight with concern.

Freddie pointed an unsteady finger at the pool of blood.

The young girl gasped and cried, "Ladybug! Daddy, do something!"

Three of Freddie's colleagues, Angie, Luis, and Kevin, emerged from the stairwell.

Angie called, "Kevin knows first aid. He's no vet, but we'll help in any way we can."

The father's eyebrows furrowed. "Suzy, stay back. Ladybug will be fine."

"How do you know that?" she cried.

"Just stay back!" He pulled Freddie aside and whispered, "I don't want her to see this. Can you distract her a moment?"

"Of course." He took a step toward Suzy and said, "Do you want to see the channel where orcas swim? Come on, I'll show you, there's been a lot of sightings lately!"

"No! I need to make sure Ladybug's okay!"

"Suzy, go with him. I'll take care of Ladybug, alright, sweetie?"

Suzy followed Freddie reluctantly, looking over her shoulder as they walked toward the railing. Freddie guided her to the opening overlooking the ocean. "See that island over there? That's Arbutus Island. The orcas swim all around here," Freddie told her. He pointed to the small island whose shores were lined with the curling, peeling trunks of winding arbutus trees.

Suzy's father opened the lock. A rumbling hiss escaped the trailer.

Never knew a horse could make that sound, Freddie thought with alarm.

"Whoa, Ladybug. Whoa. I'm coming." Suzy's father swung the trailer door open.

Suzy wasn't looking for orcas when the burnt monster leapt onto her father and knocked him to the ground. Crimson spattered its silver forehead as the monster sank its teeth deep into her father's flesh.

"Daddy!" Suzy shrieked. Freddie caught her wrist as she tried to run toward her father.

"Angie, come on!" Angie and Luis ran forward and attempted to pull the two men apart. Kevin stood frozen and gaped at the altercation.

The monster thrashed, its arm flailing wildly despite being limp in its socket. Angie recoiled when his hand struck her face. After touching her cheek, Angie looked at her hand to find her fingers wet with blood. She bolted.

Luis, a gangly boy who looked no older than eighteen, was Rocket's next target. The monster knocked him down and sat on his chest, pummeling the fist he still had control of at the boy's forehead until he stopped struggling.

The beast drove his fingers deep into the boy's eye socket. He pinched the gelatinous ball, stretching the optical nerve until it snapped, and the monster popped the morsel into its mouth.

Kevin vomited as his colleague twitched beneath the monster.

Freddie pulled the screaming girl away. He grabbed the radio at his hip and yelled into it, "Code Charlie! Code Charlie! Cargo deck 3!"

As he made the call, the speaker announced their arrival. *"We have now arrived at Swartz Bay Ferry Terminal. Would all passengers please return to the vehicle deck? Please do not start your engines until we have made berth. We thank you for travelling with Coastal Connector Ferries."*

"No! Don't send more people down here!" Freddie called into the radio. He heard muffled screaming from the level above.

Suzy's father climbed unsteadily to his feet and shuffled toward Freddie and his daughter. Freddie dragged the girl to the stairwell.

If we go up, we lead him to crowds of people. If we go down, we'll be trapped. Shit!

"Can you swim?" he asked Suzy.

"Y-yes," she answered, tears streaming down her cheeks.

"Come on." He pulled her toward the ship's stern. *Shit, propellors.* They ran to the port side. *It's gotta be deep enough...*

He looked over his shoulder; Suzy's father was gaining on them with every hesitation Freddie made.

They reached the railing. "Suzy, we need to jump. We're very close to shore, you gotta swim for it. Are you ready?"

"No! No, please, I'm scared. I want my daddy!"

"Your daddy won't help you. Trust me, we need to jump now!"

"No!" Her nails dug into the skin of his forearms as he lifted her over the railing. He dangled her over the edge just as her father tackled Freddie, pinning him against the steel bar. Before she let go, her father's nails grazed her cheek, cutting into her soft skin. Suzy shrieked as she fell toward the water.

HARVEY
30 JUNE 2018
16:00 PDT
HIGHWAY 4
TOFINO, BC

"I think I'm going to move inland when all this is over," Kat said.

Harvey noticed her strokes had grown wearier. He tried to pick up the slack, though the muscles in his shoulders protested as he rowed. They paddled through the flooded stretch of highway that passed Mackenzie Beach. "I bet they're from the prairies," Harvey said, nodding at the boys.

Mikey and Pat were curled up in the middle of the raft. Their eyes were closed. "First time seeing the ocean? Great experience," Kat said sarcastically.

Ahead, the pavement rose and broke through the shallow water. "Boys, we'll be on foot in a minute. Ready yourselves," Harvey whispered.

Mikey blinked and rubbed his eyes. Patrick looked around, startled, as if he had forgotten where they were and woke up only to return to a bad dream.

Harvey stepped off the raft. Cool water seeped between his booties and wetsuit. Kat followed and lifted the boys down. They dragged the raft up the hill a few metres from the water's edge.

"My trailer is just around a couple more corners," Harvey said. "Watch out, Kat. Ready yourself."

Harvey pointed to an infected woman heading in their direction. Her damp hair fell over her face as she staggered toward them. When she drew closer, he saw dark veins that protruded from the pale skin around her eyes. Dried blood stained the skin around her mouth like smeared lipstick.

He took a few steps toward her and swung the paddle at her head. His aim was off by a few inches. The monster's jaw became dislocated with a sickening crack. She continued to snap at him with a crooked, mangled mandible. He swung again, this time hitting her in the temple. The monster fell to the ground. Harvey continued swinging. Two more blows stopped her twitching.

He cringed when he saw coagulated blood and bits of gore speckling his wetsuit. Harvey turned to see the two boys clinging to Kat's legs, their eyes wide and lips trembling.

"Come on." Harvey turned and led them away, leaving the monster's corpse lying lifelessly on the ground.

They were about to round the last corner when gunshots filled the air. *Ana.* Harvey swallowed hard. *This is not how I imagined we would reunite.*

He turned to Kat, stopping her and the boys. "It sounds like they've run into trouble. We're going to head down to my trailer. Kat, I want you and the boys to hunker down there, alright? Eat something, and pack some food. Grab whatever you think we'll need. I'll set you up with a rifle. Then you stay put until I return. You got it?"

"I can help you. I'm a good shot."

"No. Help them." He nodded at the boys. "Come on."

Around the corner from his driveway, Harvey led them into the woods. They crossed a section of forest until they reached gravel. Farther down the driveway, past the trailers, the inlet had risen significantly above its usual high-tide line. Harvey's home stood out of harm's way, but the same couldn't be said for the main house on the property, which stood in water a metre deep.

A few infected shuffled past Skylar's place. "Keep an eye out." Harvey pointed to the monsters making their way up the hill, following the sound of the gunshots.

He slowly opened the door and peered inside. Satisfied that it was unoccupied, Harvey climbed in and went straight to his gun cabinet. A shotgun and the .22 were missing, as well as several boxes of corresponding ammunition.

Kat and the boys stepped inside.

"Take a seat on the couch, boys. Here's a blanket. Get comfy and have a rest, okay? I'll be right back."

They nodded, and Kat tucked them in.

Harvey handed Kat a rifle and a box of ammunition. He loaded his .308 and slung the strap over his shoulder.

"Harvey?"

"Yes, Kat?"

"Please...be careful."

"Always." He smiled and left.

With his heart in his throat, Harvey jogged up the driveway. He walked along the highway, following the echoing sound of gunshots.

Jesus. What a mess. Four mangled cars blocked much of the road, and many other abandoned vehicles lined the street. He stood beside one of the wrecked cars and peered within. There were dots of blood on the outside of the driver's window, and the corpse of a young man sat in the driver's seat. *He's dead. Dead-dead. Lucky, in a way. Didn't turn into a monster or become a meal.*

He looked up when more shots filled the air. Infected emerged from the forest and lurched onto the highway. Harvey resisted the urge to fire at them. *Gotta get closer, get a visual of Ana and Skylar before I give my position away to those beasts.*

A driverless car rolled across the street and bowled down two ravenous infected, who snarled as the car dragged them across the pavement. Harvey looked up the hill where the vehicle had come from. He saw Skylar running toward a truck towing a large fishing boat.

His heart skipped when he saw her. Ana stood in the back of the truck. Her long braid fell across her shoulder as she rested the .22 against the vehicle's roof. She scanned the area, assessing which threat to take out next, lowered her cheek to the stock, tapped the trigger twice, and called, "The hatchback is clear!"

Skylar scampered across the street to the vehicle. He opened the door, reached inside, put it in neutral, and backed away as it rolled into the ditch.

The infected closed in on Skylar and Ana from all directions. Ana continued to pick them off one by one, covering her companion as he cleared their path. Harvey admired her stance. *I taught her well.* Then the barrel of the gun pointed in his direction. The shot reverberated through the air. Warm blood trickled down his cheek. He fell to his knees, his eyes never leaving her, until the world went dark.

ANA
30 JUNE 2018
16:20 PDT
HIGHWAY 4
TOFINO, BC

Blood dripped from a wave of dark brown hair that fell across his forehead. It wasn't until she pulled the trigger that she registered his face. The layer of gore on his wetsuit made her think he was one of them. Harvey fell to his knees and slumped over.

Ana's lip trembled. "Harvey?" She climbed off the tailgate and ran to him. Ana threw herself to the ground, hardly noticing the pavement that tore at her knees. She took his head in her arms and screamed. Ana shook Harvey by the shoulders, but the only answer she received was a fresh surge of blood that wept from the bullet hole in his forehead. Harvey was dead.

SKYLAR
30 JUNE 2018
16:20 PDT
HIGHWAY 4
TOFINO, BC

"An!" Skylar called. "An, we're clear! Get in the truck!"

"Harvey?"

Skylar turned in time to see her run toward a body sprawled on the ground. Several infected were in her pursuit.

Oh, no fucking way... Did she just...? No... Is he... Skylar ran across the road to Ana, who was sobbing over Harvey's corpse. He let out a heavy sigh. *Fuck, my dude.*

Ana looked up at Skylar with bloodshot eyes and wiped a tear from her cheek, leaving behind a smear of Harvey's blood.

"He's... He's..."

The infected drew closer. Skylar lifted the shotgun's muzzle and fired at the approaching monsters. *There's too many. We've gotta get out of here.*

Skylar grabbed Ana by the elbow and pulled her to her feet.

"An, we need to go."

"No!" she howled. "I can't leave him here!"

Skylar half-dragged, half-carried her to the truck. He guided Ana to the passenger seat, then turned and fired another round of buckshot into the nearest infected. Skylar climbed in over Ana and slammed the door shut, then rolled into the driver's seat.

"Where's your gun?"

She sobbed into her hands without answering.

He turned around and saw her .22 in the truck's bed. *Oh, thank fuck you didn't lose it.*

"Harvey was with others. Didn't you say there were kids? Where are they?"

Still no response.

Bloody fingers clawed at the windows. Skylar put the truck

in drive, and sped down the stretch of road they'd cleared, right past Harvey's corpse.

Don't look up, An, please don't look up.

She continued to sob into her hands.

Skylar drove onto the highway shoulder to skirt around the accident, then turned down his driveway.

A dark-haired woman popped her head out of Harvey's door. Her brow furrowed, and she disappeared again. Skylar hopped out of the truck and darted to the trailer, letting himself in.

MIKEY
30 JUNE 2018
16:30 PDT
HARVEY'S TRAILER
TOFINO, BC

Mikey jumped when a man he never met burst into the trailer: a stranger. *Mum always said not to talk to strangers unless she was around. Now there are only strangers around. Strangers and Patrick.* He felt some reassurance when his little brother's hand found his beneath their blanket.

"Hi, uh, Kat, is it? Let's go, before those things catch up. They'll be following us."

"Where's Harvey?" Her grip tightened on the rifle Harvey had left her with.

The man looked at his feet as he tried to find the words. "Harvey has fallen. We need to go *now*."

"What do you mean, he's *fallen*?"

He glanced at the children, and then his eyes met hers. "He's dead. We're launching a boat and getting the hell outta here. I suggest you come with us." The man turned toward the door and muttered, "I'm sorry."

Mikey hadn't known Harvey for very long, but he felt sad losing another person. Patrick let out a whimper.

Kat turned to the boys. "Come on." Mikey saw a tear roll down her cheek. Kat pulled the blanket off the boys, balled it up, and grabbed the duffle bag containing their snacks and clothing. They followed the man out the door.

"He kinda looks like a pirate," Mikey whispered to Patrick. "Did you see his broken tooth? I wonder what happened."

Kat shushed him and ushered them to move more quickly.

Patrick froze when he saw monsters hobbling down the driveway in their direction. The man lifted him into the truck, and Mikey and Kat climbed in after. There was a lady sobbing in the front seat.

The man drove down the gravel driveway to the water's edge. "Mr. Robinson's yard should be flat enough to launch from."

No one responded.

He turned the truck around and reversed, directing the boat into the water. "I'm going to need some cover while I launch this thing." He was met with silence again.

"Hey! An! Please don't shut down. I need your help!" The man turned to Kat. "You too. Let's go, ladies!"

The woman he called An stopped covering her face. Tear stains streaked through a red smudge on her cheek. She exited the truck without saying anything. Mikey watched her climb into the truck's bed and pick up a gun.

Kat steadied her feet on the driver's and passenger's seats and stood up through the sunroof. She looked down at Mikey. "Cover your ears, boys. This will be loud."

Mikey nodded and pushed his fingers in his ears. It didn't stop him from flinching every time she fired a round.

The man fastened one end of a rope to the boat's bow, and the other end to the trailer, then pushed the boat into the water.

"Look, Pat, he *is* a pirate!" Mikey nudged his brother.

The boys watched him return to the truck, gathering the bags and blanket, and depositing them onboard. He opened the truck's rear door. "Come here, little dude." The pirate carried Mikey to his ship.

He stood on the deck and watched as the two women shot at a group of monsters heading toward them. A couple emerged from the trees and staggered to the truck with outstretched arms.

"That's Flo and Eddie..." The sad lady lowered her gun.

"What are you doing? Shoot them!" Kat shouted.

"They were my friends."

"They aren't anymore!" Kat put a bullet in each of their heads. Mikey saw Ana's shoulders slouch as the two monsters fell to the ground.

The man carried Patrick to the boat as he called out, "Let's get the hell out of here!"

Kat disappeared into the truck and then stepped out of the vehicle.

Ana started firing at the horde again.

"Ana! That's enough!" Kat yelled. "Save your ammo."

After firing several more rounds, Ana jumped from the tailgate of the truck. Both women waded through the water to the stern of the boat. They climbed the short ladder and joined the boys on deck.

The man untied the rope that tethered them to the trailer. He pushed the boat away from shore, clambered up the ladder, and dripped water on the deck as he walked to the captain's seat.

The tips of ferns and rhododendrons pierced the surface of the water. The boat glided silently over the flooded yard, past a small house. Monsters staggered into the water after them, but the boat drifted faster than they could wade.

Skylar played with the controls, flicking switches and cursing.

"There we go!" he called. The motor descended and then revved to life.

"Mikey, why don't you check the cabin to see if there are any life jackets." Kat pointed to a small door between Skylar and Ana's seats.

Mikey nodded and walked over to the door. He looked up at Ana as he passed. She sat with her legs tucked up to her chest and her face buried in her knees. Mikey shimmied the latch open and peered into the dark cabin. He held tight to the railing as he descended the steps.

"What the hell happened?" he heard Kat ask the man.

"They got him," Skylar said stiffly.

"How? He was so careful."

"Accidents happen."

"*Accidents*?"

Mikey had a hard time seeing in the depths of the cabin. "It's too dark!" he called up. He heard rummaging in a compartment above.

Skylar poked his head through the cabin door. "Hey, kid, do you know why pirates wore eye patches?"

"Umm, they lost one?"

"Usually not. It was so they could see below deck. Their eyes wouldn't have to adjust to the darkness, since one eye was already immersed in it. They'd just swap which eye was covered when they went below deck. Pretty cool, huh?" Skylar smiled and handed him a flashlight, then went back to operating the boat.

"Wow!" Mikey whispered back. *I knew he was a pirate!*

Mikey turned on the flashlight and shone it around the cabin, illuminating dust particles that drifted around him. To his right was a narrow door. To his left was a counter with a tiny sink. At the front of the boat, a tangle of blankets and pillows lay atop a bed. Cabinets lined the walls. *Maybe in there?*

Mikey climbed onto the bed. His knees hit something beneath the quilts. It began to stir. A hand clamped on Mikey's wrist and he let out a shrill scream.

PAUL
30 JUNE 2018
16:30 PDT
HERITAGE HOUSE
TFN TREATY LANDS, BC

The infected staggered past the farmhouse in search of their next meal. Paul shuddered as he watched them from the window. He reflected on the things he had witnessed that day: oozing, cracked, burnt flesh. A fleeing crowd. Teeth ripping into the skin of another human being. A broken vial leaking purple fluid. *Could that vial really have been... No...there's no way...*

A whirling sound broke his train of thought. Paul's attention shifted to the sky as a helicopter came into view on the horizon: a CH-147 Chinook with a camouflage paint job.

"Wow. Guys, the military is here," Paul said. Everyone gathered around the window.

Barley swayed and submitted to the disturbance the machine created as it crossed the field, making its way toward the herd of infected.

"There's a small deck connected to the roof. It'll have a better view," Blane said, and turned to the door.

"What the hell? Why haven't you ever taken us up there before?" Leah asked him.

Blane shrugged. "It's visible from the road. Didn't want to get caught."

"Now we probably *do* want to get caught. Think they'll rescue us?" Shawn asked.

"Doubt it, man. They'll be cleansing first," Blane said.

Shawn frowned. "Don't like the sound of that."

Paul followed Blane and his friends through the hall and into another bedroom. Inside the closet was a ladder leading to the attic. As they waited for the teens to climb up, Paul put his arm around Jocelyn. "You okay?"

She leaned into him. “Does that word have context in this situation? I don’t think any of us are *okay.*”

He leaned down to kiss her forehead. Then it was his turn to ascend the ladder. The attic was dark, the floor unfinished.

“Gotta balance,” Blane called as he walked across a beam of wood. “Don’t put your foot through the ceiling.” He pointed to a gaping hole that implied he was speaking from experience.

Paul followed his lead and walked across the beams. They reached a window and Blane pried it open, then climbed out onto the narrow platform. Paul, Jocelyn, and Amy followed.

They watched as the extermination began. The Chinook fired at the army of infected and dozens of monsters fell, their limbs fragmented by the heavy artillery that rained down on them.

“Should we help them?” Blane gestured to Paul’s pistol.

“I think they have it covered. Best to save our ammo,” Paul said.

Once most of the infected had fallen, three drones emerged from the chopper. They hovered close to the ground and spewed streams of flames with bright blue cores.

“Flame thrower drones? Are you serious? That’s badass!” Shane cheered. The mass cremation filled the air with the scent of charred flesh.

“I think I’m going to be sick,” Amy said.

Flames crawled across the barley field. Dark smoke billowed skyward as the dry grass in the front yard of the abandoned house ignited. The fire was heading toward them.

“That doesn’t look good,” Blane said.

“Time to go!” Paul urged. Being closest to the window, he quickly climbed through and followed the wooden beams to the ladder. He ducked back into the first bedroom, grabbed their pack, and led everyone down the staircase.

Paul weighed their options. Fire crackled audibly through the heavily boarded front door. *We’ll never pry those boards off in time.* He looked at the basement door. The moans of its trapped tenants could be heard from the basement's depths. *Not ideal, but it seems to be our only option.*

"Blane!" Paul called as he grabbed one end of the credenza.

"On it!" Blane hurried to help Paul. They moved their barricade away from the basement door. Paul looked at the teen and nodded. Blane twisted the brass knob and pulled the door open.

The moaning grew into a desperate hiss. Paul raised his shotgun and fired two rounds into the darkness, briefly illuminating a figure on the stairs. They heard a splash.

He set the shotgun aside and drew his pistol, then inched toward the door frame to get a view of his targets.

Cold, claw-like fingers latched onto his ankle and pulled him down into the basement. His finger hit the trigger as he fell through the missing stairs, wasting one of his bullets.

"Paul!" Jocelyn screamed. She leaned through the doorway with her .22 in hand. It was too dark to fire blindly with Paul somewhere below.

His pupils dilated as they adjusted to the darkness. He could feel hands groping him, trying to find a tender spot to dig into his flesh. He pulled the pistol's trigger and the hands recoiled.

"Get your phones!" Blane shouted.

Flashlights of three cell phones shone down on him, and Paul could see an infected woman move toward him in the haunting blue light. One of her eyes protruded from its socket and rested on her cheek. He raised his gun and fired. Paul felt her blood spatter his face, and she fell backward. His eyes darted around the dim room. Two more monsters crawled through the murky water toward him. He fired two more rounds, and the hissing, moaning, and splashing subsided. *Fuck. That was too close.*

Paul scanned the dingy room. Satisfied that it was safe, he called up, "We're clear!" Soaked in putrid water and speckled with blood, he climbed to his feet. "Come on, let's get outta here!"

As the rest of the group made their way down the stairs, he peered out the window. The fire devoured the vegetation along the side of the house and caught onto its wooden panels.

"Where do we go? Back to the squad car?" Amy asked as she approached the window.

"Too many corpses on the road. We should cut through the farms."

Amy placed her foot in his cupped hands and pulled herself through the window as Paul hoisted her up.

Leah went next, followed by Jocelyn, and then Shawn. Smoke wafted in the window as Blane approached. "I got it. Thanks, man." He gripped either side of the window frame and pulled himself through. Paul climbed out after Blane.

The group was ahead of him, running through the adjacent farm field. He saw Jocelyn look back several times to be sure he was following. Paul ran past flaming clumps of grass and brush. He tried to breathe shallowly until he was past the smoke. When the air was clearer, Paul sprinted to catch up. Jocelyn turned at his approach. He took the backpack and shotgun, lightening her load.

A whirring approached from behind. Paul turned to see a drone advancing on the fleeing group. *What the hell?* He waved both arms in the air as if to signal *"It's okay, we're human and you don't need to exterminate us."*

The machine continued its pursuit. A flame sputtered beneath it.

That's how it's going to be, huh? Paul raised his shotgun, fired at the drone, and watched as it fell from the sky in a ball of fire.

KAT
30 JUNE 2018
17:00 PDT
BROWNING PASSAGE
TOFINO, BC

A shrill scream escaped the cabin.

Mikey! Fuck, I don't really wanna risk my life for this kid, but we're all done for if that's a fucking zombie down there.

Kat grabbed her rifle from its resting place against the bench and jumped down the steps. She peered into the dim cabin and lifted the gun's muzzle.

Mikey's flashlight rolled off the bed, briefly illuminating a man's face.

"You...you aren't infected."

"What in the heck is going on here? Who are you people? You stole my boat!" a weathered voice responded.

She lowered the firearm. "Sir, can you come up on deck? Perhaps we can discuss this with the group...in the light."

"Yes, yes. My goodness!"

Kat ushered Mikey up the steps before her.

The old man stepped out, removed the round glasses that sat at the end of his nose, and rubbed his eyes. He squinted in the bright afternoon light. His lip housed a thick, bristling moustache.

"Mr. Peters!" Skylar smiled when he saw the cause of the commotion. He slowed the boat, now safely in the inlet and away from the wading monsters. "I...uh... Sorry?"

"Skylar! You know you can call me Greg. I didn't realize it was you out here. Gave me a start!"

"Greg. Did you see the—"

"The zombies? Yes, yes. I had just begun scrubbing the hull when the alarm went off. Right place to be when there's a tsunami coming, at the top of the hill there. Next thing I know, people are getting violent! I took shelter below deck to bide my time. I have some canned goods, you know, some water. Coulda made it for a few days. Guess I'll be sharing those provisions with you lot now. Gotta tell ya, I was pretty startled when ol' *Bertha* started moving!" He patted the boat's dash.

"My apologies, Greg, but it really was the only way to get away from those monsters..."

"Oh, I was just giving you a hard time. Truth of it is, I'm thankful to be out of that mess! Water still has a strong current to it, hmm? Well, where are we off to then?"

"Hadn't really thought that far. We just needed an exit."

"We were thinking Port Alberni," Kat interjected. "We, me and Harvey..." She looked directly at Ana when she said it. Ana tugged on her messy braid and looked away.

"Mm-hmm. Hmm. The inlet could be a right mess as well, what with the tsunami and all. Well, my sister lives in Sidney. We could head that way if it suits you lot... I suppose the rest of you will be looking to get in touch with your families as well."

"Our mom is dead," Mikey squeaked out.

Kat gave his shoulder a squeeze. "Mr. Peters, do you mind if the boys rest in the cabin? They've had a long day."

"Of course, of course. What is it you were looking for down there?" he addressed Mikey.

"Life jackets."

"Under the bed. You were almost there! I'm sorry for startling you." He pushed his glasses up the bridge of his nose. "Those wetsuits are pretty buoyant too. You lot weren't surfing today, were you?"

Kat looked down at the lilac wetsuit she wore. "No. We found these in a van along the highway. They were great protection actually. Harvey was bitten, but the monster's teeth couldn't penetrate the neoprene."

"You don't say. How's that for a second skin?"

Kat twisted uncomfortably. Her skin felt clammy beneath the neoprene. She scanned the deck of the boat. *Did I leave the damn clothes in the truck? Where is that bag?*

Patrick yawned audibly and rubbed his eyes.

"Ah yes, the boys. Go on, go get some rest." He patted Mikey's head as he passed, and watched the younger boy follow.

Kat walked past the elderly man and tailed the boys into the cabin.

From below deck, Kat heard Mr. Peters say, "Quite a crew you have, Skylar!"

"Yeah. That was Kat, a local who owns one of the cafes on Industrial. This is my friend Ana. Not sure who the boys belong to. Tourists, I suppose."

Kat closed the small cabin door. She picked the flashlight off the floor and shone it around. There were tiny curtains covering the portholes. She pulled one aside to allow some light in and sat on the bed next to the boys, lifting the blanket to their chins. "Rest, little ones. You're safe now."

The boys cuddled up to one another.

Pulling the booties from her feet, Kat flexed her clammy toes. They were wrinkled from their time spent in the wet confines of the neoprene.

A sorrow filled Kat. She lay down and wrapped her arms tightly around herself. *My home. My cafe. My crush. In one day...everything's gone. What the hell do I do now?* She suppressed the urge to cry.

When her eyes fluttered open, Kat felt the unsettling confusion of waking up somewhere unfamiliar. She hadn't intended to fall asleep. She swung her legs off the bed, gently, so as not to disturb the sleeping boys. Their breathing rose and fell in unison. *At least they still have each other. More than I can say for myself.* Kat walked to the cabin door and climbed up onto the deck.

Mr. Peters had taken over at the wheel. Skylar was sitting in the passenger seat and attempting to roll a cigarette in a cubby sheltered from the wind. Kat took a seat in the chair behind him. The sun reflected off the cerulean depths of the open ocean. Ana was on her cell phone at the back of the boat. Curiosity got the better of her as Kat listened in on the other woman's conversation.

"Sorry, no, I'm having a hard time hearing you. Paul... Yeah, we made it out... Harvey?" She was silent a moment. "He didn't make it. Paul. It was all my fault. There were so many of them." She sobbed between her words. "I shot him, Paul. I...I didn't mean to. He was covered in blood... I thought he was one of them. It all happened so fast. We were surrounded. I just kept firing! I didn't know it was him!"

There was a moment of silence.

"Paul? Paul! Please say something!" Ana stood and waved her phone in the air, attempting to regain the signal.

Kat felt a burning between her ears. Her heart pounded heavily within her ribcage. She got to her feet, took a few steps, and pushed the other woman overboard.

SUZY
30 JUNE 2018
17:00 PDT
SWARTZ BAY, BC

With a spluttering cough, water gushed from Suzy's lungs, spilling out of her mouth, and she gasped for air. Applause broke out, and when Suzy opened her eyes, she saw the blur of a small crowd gathered around her. Suzy glimpsed the woman who cradled her before being rolled onto her side and gently patted on the back.

"That's it, girl, let it all out."

"You're a hero! Linda, here, turn around so we can snap a quick picture!"

"Now, now. That won't be necessary. Let's give the girl some privacy."

"What's all the commotion up there? Must be something serious for them to have missed the poor child going over."

"You hear that? Sirens are approaching. I think you're right, Linda."

Suzy coughed some more and rubbed her chest. Her lungs burned, and her head swam. "Ladybug, Daddy… Please, they need help."

"Ladybug? Who's that, sweetheart?" Linda leaned over Suzy and tried to make eye contact.

"My horse."

"Well! Where are Ladybug and your daddy now?"

"On board, where the monsters are." She lifted a shaky finger and pointed it toward the ferry. As if on cue, screaming broke out on the ferry's deck.

"Good god, what is happening up there?" someone commented.

"Ya know what's weird? They haven't lowered the pedestrian walkway. No cars have exited the ferry either."

The people in the crowd gasped as a figure plummeted overboard.

"I guess that's one way off. Child, what is happening? Why did you jump overboard?"

"I didn't jump. I was thrown. The monster was coming... and my daddy... He became one of them."

Linda grasped Suzy by the shoulders. "What monsters, child? Whatever do you mean?"

Everyone was silent until another splash stole the crowd's attention. They looked up in time to see several more figures hurtle themselves over the ferry's railing. Linda and her friends gasped in unison.

Suzy pushed the woman away and climbed to her feet.

"Oh, thank goodness! Look, there's the police. No, wait... Is that the military? What the hell is going on?" the woman asked.

The young girl held a hand up to shield her eyes and squinted at the people in the water. One of the figures was swimming for shore, the others were thrashing nonsensically. "I think those are the monsters. But look, they can't swim." Suzy pointed.

She looked behind her, seeking confirmation from the adults. Several of them had taken off and were running to the parking lot.

Linda gaped as she stared at the figures in the water. She shook off her stupor and ran for shore. Her friend called after her, "Don't go! Linda, please, I think something's really wrong here!"

"They need help! I can't just leave them!" She was already knee-deep in the water. Linda waded in a little farther, and then dove through the surface.

Her friend shook her head and took off toward the parking lot.

Suzy looked around frantically. Daddy was usually there

for her. Now she had no one. They were all strangers, and running away.

Then she saw the man in the armoured uniform. He carried an enormous gun. She walked slowly toward him, shivering slightly.

He spoke into a radio clipped to his chest. "Five in the water. One on land. One of the fish is the metalhead we've been hearing so much about. How do we proceed?"

"Take the one with the plate and cleanse the rest."

"One's a child."

"This situation needs to be contained, Charles. Do your job."

"Yes, sir."

When the barrel of his gun pointed at her, Suzy tried to scamper away and lost her footing. She fell backward and held her small hand up to the stranger, as if it could stop the bullet intended for her head, and said one word, softly: "Please."

Charles looked around to make sure none of his comrades were watching. "Were you bitten or scratched by something? How'd you get that wound on your cheek?"

Suzy shook her head as a rattling sob escaped her lips. "No. I scratched myself on accident..." she lied.

He held his breath as he looked back over his shoulder once more. "Fuck, I'm going to regret this. Follow the rocks, over there. There's a path between the trees. Go!"

Suzy pulled herself up and ran. Her wet shoes squelched with each step. She didn't look back until she reached the tree line. Piercing gunfire rang through the air, and Suzy turned in time to see a fountain of blood spray from Linda's head. The woman who had saved her just minutes before bobbed in the water lifelessly. Suzy stepped farther into the cover of the trees, but stayed close enough that she could watch the situation she had escaped. Her bottom lip quivered, and she trembled from a combination of adrenaline and the chill from her damp clothing.

More men arrived at the shoreline. They wore shielded

helmets and carried a strange net covered in metallic discs.

One of the figures in the water still moved. As he neared shore, Suzy could see the glint of silver on his forehead and recognized him as the monster that attacked her father. *Shoot him*, she thought as she watched the men approach him, carrying their strange net.

Shoot him! He hurt my daddy! And my Ladybug!

She watched them throw the net over the monster and drag him to shore. Once he was out of the water, one of the men pressed a button on a remote in his hand. The monster twitched as the net sparked around him, and then he lay still.

"We've got him, bring in the bird," the man with the remote called into a radio strapped to his chest.

Propellers whirred, and a helicopter appeared dangling a long cable. The men below connected it to the net containing the monster that attacked her daddy and her Ladybug. It flew the monster away, back over the water, toward the mainland.

Suzy turned up the path. Her head spun and her vision began to blur.

ANA
30 JUNE 2018
18:22 PDT
BARKLEY SOUND, BC

Her lungs protested, hungry for air. Ana's hands flailed, attempting to grab onto something, anything. The frigid saline water burned her eyes when she opened them, but for a brief moment, Ana saw light. *That way.* She kicked harder than she ever had in her life. The pressure in her head eased as she floated upward. When she breached the surface, Ana gulped in a desperate breath. The churning water pulled her farther from the boat, which continued to cruise steadily away.

"Sky!" she choked out, but her cry went unheard. She screamed until a small wave crashed over her and salty water filled her mouth.

This is it. How fitting. Mom is lying in the ocean's depths, and now it's my turn.

Ana's legs were tired, so tired. She stopped kicking as the chorus of the last song she had listened to flooded her mind. She closed her eyes and leaned her head back, submitting to the movement of the surrounding water.

The sound of the engine replaced the song. She opened her eyes and saw the bow of the boat heading in her direction.

Skylar stood on deck with a life ring at the ready. When they were within range, he threw it in her direction. She exerted the last of her energy until her fingers clutched the cold plastic. She feebly looped her arm through the ring, and Skylar reeled her in.

The engine cut as she drifted toward the boat's stern. Her hands felt useless when she pawed at the ladder. Skylar leaned over and pulled her out of the water.

SKYLAR
30 JUNE 2018
18:38 PDT
BARKLEY SOUND, BC

"Ana! Jesus, what happened?"

Ana tried to recall. Her head swam. "I'm feeling...warm now."

"Your lips are blue! Come on, we gotta get you inside."

Skylar carried her to the cabin.

"Kat! We have an emergency. I'm going to need you and the boys to vacate!" he called. The sleepy boys walked past him, guided by Kat, whose eyes boiled with malice when she saw Ana. *What the hell was that about?* Skylar thought as they passed.

He brought Ana to the edge of the bed. A dim flashlight hung from the ceiling, swaying as it illuminated the inside of the cabin.

"Ana, we need to take off these wet clothes, okay?"

She didn't respond.

Skylar pulled the dripping basketball shorts from her hips, sat her down, then grabbed the sopping hem of her muscle shirt and pulled it over her head. He gently guided her toward the mattress and lifted her legs up to lay her on the bed, then quickly stripped his own clothes off and climbed in next to her, cocooning them both within a thick quilt. Her skin felt like ice against his.

This is not how I imagined getting into bed with Ana Zuessen.

He listened to her breathing: it was shallow and shaky.

"Ana? I need you to stay awake, got it?"

"Thanks, Dundee."

"Huh?"

"The way you threw me...that boomerang."

Skylar scoffed. She turned toward him and nestled closer.

"Can you try taking deeper breaths, Ana?"

She made a noise of acknowledgement, but her breathing remained shallow.

"How the hell did you fall in?"

Her head shook ever so slightly.

Greg poked his head in after a knock on the cabin door. "How is she?"

"Delirious. Cold, but she's thawing out."

"Good. Just keep doing what you're doing." Greg reached into a cupboard and pulled out more blankets. "For Kat and the kids. We'll let you two have the cabin tonight. Let me know if I can get you anything. I'm going to set anchor near Salmon Beach. We'll travel down the coast in the morning."

"Thank you, Greg."

The older man nodded and left.

The boat swayed, and the engine chugged back to life. Skylar rubbed Ana's arms and continued monitering her breathing.

"I love you, Harvey," she said.

PAUL
30 JUNE 2018
18:18 PDT
FARMLAND
TFN TREATY LANDS, BC

The phone went silent. *Come on, you piece of shit.* Paul stood and walked away from their hiding place behind a greenhouse.

The group had taken refuge on a farm northwest of the burning heritage house, which was completely engulfed in flames. Rows of flowers, various brassicas, and carrots stood between them and the next road.

Distant gunshots resonated through the smoky air. The helicopter circled the mall, culling the monsters that roamed the area.

Paul paced along a row of cabbages. He waved the phone around, attempting and failing to find a signal. He kicked at a large weed, dispersing its seeds into the air.

Jocelyn walked toward him. "Did you speak with Ana?"

"Briefly, but the call dropped, and now I can't get a signal. I hate being in limbo like this. If I could just get to her..."

"You want to go to the island?"

"What else can I do? My sister's heartbroken and in danger. I have to help her."

"Heartbroken? So Harvey refused her?"

"He's dead, Joss. Ana was defending herself from a group of these *monsters* and...and she got confused..."

Her jaw dropped. "No, she didn't..."

"It was an accident. She was trying to protect herself."

Jocelyn looked at her feet. "Poor Ana. I can't imagine the pain she's going through. If it had been me, us, I don't think I could live with myself."

Paul lowered himself to the ground, defeated. He ran his fingers through his hair and sighed heavily. "I just feel so helpless."

Jocelyn sat next to him and rested her head on his shoulder. "We all do. But we'll get through this. Let's just focus on surviving this mess, and we'll go from there, alright?"

"Alright," Paul said. "So, what's our next step?"

"Go home? Take shelter? Wait to hear what the authorities say?"

"The authorities just tried to burn us to a crisp."

"The drones are probably automated to follow motion."

"Doesn't make it any better. If it can't tell man from monster, that's some scary technology."

"Let's just keep moving."

Paul scanned the farm. "There's a truck over there." He pointed north toward the barn.

"I think you're developing an affinity for stealing vehicles," Jocelyn jested. She got to her feet and offered him a hand. Paul took it and grunted as he rose. They walked back to the rest of the group.

"We're heading into Ladner. Join us, if you like."

Exhausted, sweaty, and dirty, the group rose and brushed themselves off as Paul doubled back and grabbed his pack and shotgun. He led them along a dirt path riddled with pineapple weed and plantain. Dragonflies darted across the field, zigzagging in search of their afternoon meal. Paul smacked a mosquito off his calf.

When they reached the truck, Paul peered in through the driver's side window. The keys were dangling from the ignition. "I love small towns," he said as he opened the door.

"Shotgun!" Jocelyn called and winked at the boys.

Amy, Shawn, Blane, and Leah climbed into the bed of the two-seater truck. Once everyone was seated, Blane gave the truck's side a pat, signaling to Paul that they were ready to go. Paul revved the engine to life and drove slowly down the dirt path until he reached the road, then drove east along 28th Avenue, passing the abandoned squad cars they had seen in the distance earlier that afternoon.

Paul did his best to drive around the lifeless bodies and carnage that marred the road. His jaw dropped when he got to the next intersection.

"Whoa, looks like help is here!" Jocelyn said.

Paul observed the path ahead. Along 53rd St, the military occupied the overpass that led to Ladner Village. A tall barricade blocked the way, and behind it stood soldiers armed with heavy artillery. Shawn's words about the monsters being *cleansed* echoed through Paul's mind. His chest tightened when he noticed the guns that followed their movement as they approached the blockade.

"They *are* here to help, right?" Jocelyn asked with less enthusiasm.

"Only one way to find out." Paul stopped the truck when they were a hundred feet from the blockade. He exited the vehicle with his arms in the air.

"Was anyone in your party bitten?" a voice boomed through a megaphone. "Is anyone injured or scratched?"

"No, we're all fine!" Paul called back.

"Pull your vehicle to the side of the road, then slowly approach the wall. Hands in the air. Leave any weapons behind."

Paul inched the truck to the shoulder of the road and parked. He removed the pistol from his belt and placed it on the driver's seat. "Come on, Joss."

"Guys, I'm scared. Why do they keep pointing their guns at us?" Leah asked.

Blane gave her a hand down from the truck. "We'll be fine," he said. "If they were going to fire at us, they would have done it already."

The group approached the blockade. A gate opened, and a dozen officers in armoured tactical gear jogged toward them.

The voice on the megaphone called out, "Single file. We will escort you in."

The squad herded the group into a line, grabbing them above the elbows.

"Don't touch me!" Leah said.

"Standard protocol," the man restraining her responded. He bowed his head toward a radio attached to his chest and said, "Six incoming. Three and three."

They marched through the gate and past the wall of heavily armed soldiers. Massive guns on swivels lined the road on either side of the overpass. Beneath them, Paul saw floodlights, tall fences, and more soldiers stationed along the highway that led to Deltaport.

"Wow. How far does it go?" Paul asked.

"The peninsula is secure," the woman on his left answered.

At the bottom of the overpass stood a large white marquee. Troops clad in hazmat suits waited outside.

"What is this place?" Jocelyn asked.

The soldier to her left answered, "You are going into quarantine."

"What?! For how long? We told you, we weren't bitten." Her voice wavered.

"Jocelyn, it's alright," Paul said over his shoulder.

"I just want to go home!" Leah called. "Please, my mom is going to be worried."

"Our personnel will notify your emergency contacts."

Two people in hazmat suits approached them. "We'll take them from here," one of them said, his face obscured behind a medical mask and plastic face shield. "Ladies first, follow Private Anderson, please. Gents, you're with me."

"What? No, please, you can't split us up!" Jocelyn pleaded.

Paul turned to Jocelyn and found her hand. He gave it a squeeze and kissed her softly, and said, "Follow their instructions. We'll be home in no time. I'll see you soon, okay?"

Jocelyn's eyes shone. She nodded and wiped a tear from her lashes. Leah and Amy stepped forward and joined her, following Private Anderson. Paul, Blane, and Shawn followed the unnamed man. The entrance forked into two paths. Anderson led the women down the hall to the left. With pleading eyes,

Jocelyn looked back at Paul one last time. He nodded at her and held eye contact until they were out of sight.

They were led into a room lined with plastic sheets and hoses coiled along one wall. More officers in hazmat suits filed in after them. Each one grabbed a hose.

"Alright, men, we need you to strip down. Place everything in these bins. You'll get your belongings back. Doubt you'll want those bloody clothes though, eh?" He nodded at the blood splatter coating Paul's shirt.

"Strip? Nah, man, I'm not into that," Shawn said as he crossed his arms over his chest defiantly.

"We must inspect you for wounds and sanitize any traces of tainted blood. You *will* comply."

Paul led by example and pulled his clothing off. The two teens reluctantly followed suit.

"Line up against the wall. Over there. Hands behind your heads, spread your legs."

Paul sucked in a deep breath when the cold water hit him. Goosebumps crept across his body.

"Turn. That's it. Not so bad, now, is it?"

Blane scowled at the man spraying him. "It's freezing! Come on, man."

A man with a large cartridge strapped to his back stepped forward. It had a coil of hose that connected to a wand in his hand. He sprayed them down with a substance that smelled like a concoction of alcohol and other chemicals. Paul held his breath.

"Turn."

They did. The spray made Paul's skin tingle. Water washed over him again and rinsed the sanitizing mixture off.

"Turn." The man approached Blane and examined him more closely. Satisfied, he nodded to his colleague, who handed Blane a towel. He continued his inspection, clearing Shawn, and then stopped to study Paul's left deltoid. "Interesting scar, how'd you get that, son?"

"Don't remember. I was very young."

"Either someone was very cruel to you as a child, or I'd say that looks like a vaccine scar. It's very intricate though, how curious. Robert, after the report, pull up his medical records."

Shawn and Blane looked at Paul curiously.

Good luck finding this on any records. Thanks a lot, Mom.

ANA
1 JULY 2018
06:13 PDT
BARKLEY SOUND, BC

Turquoise and teal swirled around her. She plummeted down, down, down toward the bottom of the ocean where kelp swayed in the current. It coiled around her ankles and pulled Ana deeper. Her heart beat so heavily she could feel it thumping in her ears.

Hands joined the kelp: bloody, broken, water-bloated hands. She kicked at them, but they were too strong. They pulled her closer until she could see their faces: Eddie, with pieces of Flo's flesh still stuck between his teeth. Flo, with shattered glasses and a gaping hole for an eye. A crab scuttled out of the hollow socket and across her cheek. Bubbles drifted from Ana's mouth when she tried to scream.

A third face came into view. It was Harvey with a bullet hole in the very centre of his forehead. Blood seeped from the hole and diffused through the water, until it surrounded her in a swirling gradient of crimson, purples, and blues. The blood overtook the ocean and became a pool of red. He grabbed her shoulders and said, "I loved you too."

Ana woke with a start, drenched in cold sweat and encased in a layer of blankets. Her eyes were uncomfortably dry from a night of sleeping in contact lenses. She listened to the sound of her breath, rising and falling in unison with someone else's. *Another dream?*

She felt an electric tension that only the feeling of skin-to-skin connection created, and realized she was practically naked. She looked at the arm wrapped around her. Long, sinewy, and covered with dark hair. *Why the hell am I in bed with Skylar?* She turned toward him and bashfully pulled the blanket tighter across her chest.

Her stirring woke him, and his dark eyes fluttered open. He drew in a long breath.

"Thought we would lose you, An. How did you fall in?"

She tried to recall what happened. *I was speaking with Paul, and then...icy water*. "I don't know exactly. I was hoping you could tell me." Then she remembered the distinct feeling of two hands on her back. "I didn't fall in. I was pushed."

"You were... What? By who?"

Ana raised an eyebrow. "Mikey and Patrick."

"No... Why would they? How could they... The boys were in bed!"

"Of course it wasn't them, Sky! It was Kat! She must have overheard me telling Paul what happened to Harvey. I was trying to be discreet. I thought she was asleep in the cabin."

Skylar pushed himself up. He scanned the area for his clothing and said, "That bitch. She's gotta go."

Ana put a hand on his chest to placate him. "If it were the other way around and she'd been the one to do it... I can't even tell you how I would react. I would do the same, or worse."

"Doesn't matter. You don't throw a person overboard into frigid waters and just get off the hook."

"Skylar, please, don't do anything brash."

He manoeuvred across her, found his shirt and shorts, and pulled them on. Skylar stormed out of the cabin and Ana heard him yell, "Get up!"

She sighed and looked around for her clothing. The muscle shirt and basketball shorts were nowhere in sight.

"I said get up! Greg, please take us to shore. Kat won't be accompanying us any farther."

Ana hastily wrapped herself in a blanket and followed him. "Skylar, please."

He turned to Ana. "Throwing someone overboard is unacceptable. We're all here trying to survive. She tried to kill you!"

"Just like how Ana killed Harvey, right?" Kat hissed at Skylar. She sat on the bench next to the startled boys.

"What's this all about?" Greg asked as he blinked sleepily.

"Ana didn't fall overboard last night. She was pushed." Skylar glared at Kat.

"Kat, is this true? Why would you do such a thing?"

"She overheard me speaking with my brother. I told him what happened between Harvey and I."

"What did happen, exactly? You just couldn't stand that he was with someone else, with me, so you executed him?"

Ana's eyes welled up as she said, "Those monsters had us surrounded. I didn't mean to hurt him. I...I love him. Even if we weren't together, I always would've. Always will." She pulled the blanket tighter around herself, her eyes dropped to her feet.

"You're a killer! You murdered him!" Kat yelled as she stood up from the bench.

The boys watched with wide eyes as they cradled each other beneath their blanket.

Skylar took a step forward, placing himself between the two women. "Enough!" he called. "It was an accident. Greg, I am not comfortable staying on this boat with her any longer. Ana and I are the ones who got this rig to the water, who brought you to safety out of those monsters' reach. You are the captain. This is your call."

The old man pondered. He wrinkled his nose as he pushed his glasses up. "Skylar is right. I cannot have someone on board who will endanger the other passengers. I'm not comfortable with Ana's actions either, but that was clearly a sorely regretted mistake. Kat, your actions were intentional and malicious. We will bring you to shore."

"You can't be serious." She glared at him.

Greg nodded silently.

"Fine! I don't want to be anywhere near that murderer anyway." She sat at the back of the boat and folded her arms over her chest.

Greg started up the engine. Skylar sat next to him and

rolled a cigarette with shaking hands. Tobacco flakes fell to his lap.

The crisp morning air gave Ana goosebumps. “Do you have any spare clothes, Greg?”

He looked at the woman, wrapped in nothing but a blanket, and said, “Oh, yes, yes, of course. Port-side cupboard above the bed.”

Ana stepped down into the cabin and found sweatpants and a t-shirt. She dressed, swapped her uncomfortably dry contact lenses for glasses, returned above deck, and sat next to Skylar. Everyone was silent as the boat cruised toward Salmon Beach.

The ocean glimmered with tones of turquoise, grey, teal, and green as they approached the shore. Rugged rocks bordered the beach. Western sandpipers ran from the gentle lapping of waves on the grey sand. The area was otherwise uninhabited.

Skylar approached Kat at the stern and cupped his hands as he lit his smoke. He inhaled twice to get it going. “If you want, you can take the boys,” he whispered, so they wouldn’t hear.

“I don’t know those kids. I don’t want them. They were only with us because heroic Harvey towed them along. I’ll go alone. I hope you all get eaten alive.”

When the water was shallow enough, Kat, still clad in her lilac wetsuit, lowered herself in and waded to shore. She didn’t look back, and there were no goodbyes.

MIKEY
1 JULY 2018
06:30 PDT
BARKLEY SOUND, BC

His shoulders sagged as he watched the dark-haired lady wade to shore. She had been with him and Patrick since their mom died. It'd only been a day, but he trusted her. These people were strangers.

"What are you doing? She won't be safe!" Mikey yelled, his little fists in balls at his sides as he jumped down from the bench. "Those monsters, they'll get her!"

Skylar knelt down next to Mikey. "We're far away from the monsters now. There's a community nearby. She'll be safe there."

Mikey didn't believe him. He saw how quickly people became monsters. How the monsters had hurt his mom, and how she became one of them and hurt his brother. *I wonder if the baby in her belly turned into a little monster too.*

He looked at Patrick, wrapped in a blanket on the bench. His little brother suckled his thumb while the oversized life jacket cradled his chin.

"Hey, kid. Some pretty scary stuff has been going on, but you know what? You're pretty brave! Your brother, too."

The man exhaled a stinky cloud of smoke that drifted past Mikey, who wrinkled his nose.

"Oh, sorry." Skylar repositioned himself downwind of the children. "Hey, you boys wanna see a map? Check out where we're headed?"

"Sure," Mikey said with a strained smile. Patrick continued sucking his thumb.

Skylar threw the butt of his cigarette overboard.

"You shouldn't litter," the young boy called out.

"Uh. That one doesn't have a filter. But, yeah, you're right. Sorry, kid." He walked over to Greg and grabbed a map from a cubby next to the captain's seat. Skylar returned and sat on the bench next to Patrick. Mikey hopped up next to Skylar and nestled back into his blanket. His finger traced lines on the map as the boat coasted away.

"This is where we are, see? Salmon Beach." He pointed to the map, and Mikey's little finger followed Skylar's. "See all those little islands out there?" Skylar pointed southwest.

"Uh huh."

"Those are the Broken Group Islands. Lots of people go kayaking there."

"Cool!"

Patrick leaned over for a better view. His head rested on Skylar's arm. "We'll pass by those islands, and then go down the coast and past Victoria."

Mikey looked up from the map. The blonde lady's eyes didn't leave the shoreline.

"An, she'll be fine," Skylar said.

Ana shook her head wordlessly.

"Here we go, boys, hold on!" Greg called over his shoulder.

Skylar responded, "Aye, Captain!" The boys giggled.

The boat accelerated until streams of water sprayed out behind it. Mikey watched the beach shrink into the distance.

"Goodbye, Kat," he whispered.

PAUL
1 JULY 2018
07:00 PDT
QUARANTINE TEST FACILITIES
LADNER, BC

The fluorescent lights that illuminated the sterile white walls were blinding. Paul was unsure how long he'd been cooped up, isolated, in his tented holding cell. The guards had clothed him in a grey sweatsuit. He sat on a narrow cot and waited for what felt like hours. *I'm so freaking tired. What the hell is taking so long?*

He habitually ran his hands through his hair. Paul hadn't slept. He stood up and paced the small room. His body protested, his back sore from the fall in the heritage house. Finally, two people in hazmat suits joined him in the tented room.

"Greetings, Mr. Zuessen. I am Dr. Hayde, and this is my assistant, Nurse Perri." He gestured toward the woman on his right. "Thank you for your cooperation. Some of our other *patients* have been somewhat less, well, patient." His voice was slightly muffled beneath the layers of protective rubber and plastic.

"Whatever gets me home sooner," Paul responded. "How long will I be in here? Where is Jocelyn?"

"Our emergency response plan is to quarantine each patient individually for forty-eight hours, after which we will release folks to return to their homes. Please, take a seat."

Paul sat. "Forty-eight hours? You've got to be kidding me. Have you seen those things? People turn in a matter of minutes once they're bitten."

Nurse Perri answered, "Whether a subject is bitten, scratched, or absorbs the contagion through an orifice seems to affect the incubation stage. There are other biological markers at play as well. We can't risk this disease getting into Vancouver and beyond. We are taking every precaution. This is standard protocol."

Dr. Hayde's eyes bore into Paul's. "We would like to know your participation in yesterday's events."

"My *participation*?"

"Yes, Paul. Where were you when the helicopter crashed? We would like to hear about your experience. Please, be thorough. As I'm sure you can imagine, these events will be rather historic, and any information we can gather will help us to understand the nature of the spread."

"How do you have time for this? Forty thousand people live in Ladner and Tsawwassen. Do you have enough space to hold us all?"

Nurse Perri and Doctor Hayde exchanged a look.

"We haven't had many survivors come through the perimeter yet," Nurse Perri said.

Paul inhaled deeply. "I was at the mall when the helicopter crashed. I saw what I can only guess was the first chain of attacks on the mainland. It was Rocket, you know, that adrenaline junky social media influencer? He was in the helicopter. A fireman pulled something out of his pocket. It looked like a vial."

Nurse Perri took notes as he told the story.

"What's the situation in Tofino?" Paul asked.

"Vancouver Island is in a more precarious situation," Dr. Hayde said. "With a tsunami and an outbreak occurring simultaneously, it has been challenging to set up a perimeter as we have done here. There are outlying communities, and people travelling on boats. Rest assured, our teams are working diligently to keep the situation contained."

"My sister is in Tofino. You took my phone, and I want it back. I need to be sure she's safe."

"We will have to discuss that later. Tell me more about this vial."

"It was cracked and leaked purple goo. That's all I know."

"Sephonia, send someone in to find this relic. I wish to inspect its contents." Nurse Perri nodded and handed the doctor her clipboard before exiting the room.

"Now, Paul, my colleague Mr. O'Hara tells me you have a rather *unique*-looking scar." He pulled a file from the back of the clipboard and flipped through it. "Your medical records show measles, hepatitis, tetanus, diphtheria, all the standard vaccines administered on schedule. What can you tell me about your scar?"

"I don't know what it is."

"This will be a lot easier on us both if you don't lie."

"I'm not lying." Paul clenched his jaw.

"Please remove your shirt. I would like to inspect it myself."

Paul pulled the grey sweater over his head. He rotated so that his left shoulder faced the doctor, who moved closer and inspected the pink scar tissue: a star with seven dots encircling it.

"There are no standard vaccinations that would cause this. Perhaps it was experimental?"

"I told you, I don't remember."

"And your parents never told you anything about it? Children are curious creatures. I'd be *surprised* if you told me you never inquired with them."

"Our parents were hardly ever around. They were always away for work. We had a nanny."

"I see. Excuse me for one moment." The doctor exited through the white door. Paul could hear wheels rolling along the makeshift matted floor. Dr. Hayde returned with a trolly containing empty vials and a string of tubing attached to a butterfly needle.

Paul eyed the contents of the tray and looked up at the doctor. "What the hell is this?" he asked.

"We're going to take a few blood samples. We're doing so with all of our patients."

"Is that so?" *Then why didn't you come in with it?*

"Yes, Mr. Zuessen. You, especially, should be concerned. Blood droplets speckled your face when you arrived here, and judging by your lack of injuries, I suspect it was not your own. If so much as a drop entered your eyes or another orifice... Well, you know what could happen. Now, please, give me your arm. This is standard protocol."

The more you say that, the less I believe you. Paul offered his arm to the doctor and watched as the vials filled with his blood.

SKYLAR
1 JULY 2018
11:00 PDT
STRAIT OF JUAN DE FUCA, BC

The ocean was calm as the boat sped along its smooth surface. The sun neared its peak as midday approached.

Skylar joined Ana on the bench at the back of the boat. They were silent until her stomach let out an audible growl.

"Hungry?" Skylar asked.

She shrugged. He followed her line of sight to a duffle bag tucked under the bench across from them. Skylar stood up and grabbed the bag. He unzipped it to find snacks packed amongst various articles of clothing. Skylar pulled out some jerky, handed it to Ana, and then rummaged through the bag to find a couple small shirts and pairs of shorts.

"Here, boys. Change back into your clothes." He tossed the clothing to the boys, who caught them and headed below deck.

Skylar dug further into the bag and pulled out a hunter-green shirt and a periwinkle dress. He saw a sadness fill Ana's eyes when she glimpsed the clothing in his hand.

"I don't feel right about leaving Kat like that."

Skylar sighed. "Would you prefer having someone on board who would like to see you drown?"

"We left her with nothing. No protection, no food or water." She gestured to the contents of the backpack. "Not to mention how uncomfortable that wetsuit must be after wearing it for so long."

"Ana, she's far away from the outbreak. She'll be fine."

The boys returned from the cabin wearing their street clothes.

"Better?" Skylar asked as he handed them each a handful of jerky.

"Way better. That thing was getting itchy."

Skylar noticed that rashes had formed on the boys' arms.

"That looks painful. Why didn't you say anything?"

Mikey shrugged as he nibbled on the dry meat in his hand.

"Well, if you're ever hurting or something is bothering you, you speak up, okay?"

"Mhm!" the boy mumbled through a mouthful.

Skylar brought some jerky up to Greg.

"Ahh, thank you, Skylar. We're going to need...some gas..." Greg said in between chews, his moustache curling with each bite. "But we should make it to Sidney by this afternoon."

"Where do we go for gas?"

Greg pointed to a GPS on the dash. "We're nearing Port Renfrew. We can fuel up there."

Skylar nodded. "Would you like a break? I can take over."

"Thanks, Skylar." He slowed the boat and moved to the passenger seat, leaning back with a heavy sigh.

As they continued southeast, Skylar watched their destination inch closer on the GPS screen.

They passed a great rock jutting of the water. Sea lions basked in the sun, occasionally barking at one another. Skylar slowed the boat and cruised by the colony.

"Wow! Look at that, Patrick!" Mikey exclaimed. "They're huuuuge!"

"Here, have a better look." Greg reached into the cubby beside him and handed a set of binoculars to the boys.

"So cool!" Patrick said. "He has whiskers, just like Spot!"

I think that's the first time I've heard the poor kid speak.

Footsteps approached faintly from behind him. Skylar turned when he felt a hand rest on his shoulder.

"Sky, could you please..." Ana gestured to her phone charging in a USB port on the boat's console.

"Here you go, An." He handed it back to her. "Lucky it didn't go over with you!"

The screen was cracked from its fall during the incident between the two women. Ana nodded as she poked at the broken glass. She held the phone up to her ear, and after a few moments of silence, spoke into it. "Paul, it's Ana. We're on a boat heading to Sidney. I think we need gas." She raised an eyebrow at Skylar, who nodded and mouthed *Port Renfrew* to her. "We'll be stopping for gas in Port Renfrew. Paul, I hope you're okay. I'll check in again later. Call me back."

She returned her cell to its charger on the dash. Her shoulders sagged. Skylar put his arm around her and gave her a little shake. "He's fine," he said.

"None of this is fine." She pulled away and returned to her seat at the back of the boat.

Skylar sighed and called, "Everyone get settled. We're going for it." He sped the boat away from the barking sea lions.

As they neared Port Renfrew, Greg took over at the wheel. "You're doing a fine job, Skylar, but making berth is a delicate procedure. Perhaps I'll teach you someday."

Skylar walked to the starboard side of the boat as the marina came into view. He grabbed a rope and readied himself.

Two men stood on the dock, watching their approach intently. They brandished the firearms in their hands.

Greg directed his boat toward them and manoeuvred it until they were parallel with the dock. "What's all this? Not the welcome I usually receive here," Greg called.

"We aren't accepting visitors. Where are you coming from, and what do you want?" one of the men called. He spat in the water and tightened his grip on the shotgun in his hand.

"We just need some gas, and then we'll be on our way."

"Is anyone infected?"

Greg gestured to his peaceful passengers. "All clear."

"You didn't answer my first question. Where are you coming from?"

"Tofino."

Couldn't have lied, Greg?

The two men exchanged a look. "We'll provide gas, then you leave. Understood?"

"Clearly."

Skylar made a move toward the dock.

"Nobody docks. Hand me the rope." The man slung the shotgun's strap over his shoulder and held his hand out.

Skylar did as he ordered.

The man pulled the rope, dragging the boat several metres, then stopped walking, allowing it to drift toward the gas pump at the end of the dock.

Greg chatted with the man at the pump while he filled their reserves.

"So, what was it like?" the man with the rope said flatly to Skylar.

Skylar exhaled heavily. *Hell.*

"Can't have been too bad if you have *women and children* who survived."

"Listen, you ignorant piece of—"

Skylar turned and grabbed Ana by the shoulder before she could finish her sentence. He gave her a pleading look as if to say *Shut up!* before he turned back to the man.

"It was chaos. I can't even fathom how many people died, men included. And yes, it was *that bad.* This woman has brilliant aim, probably better than yours. The children were with a group of strong survivors as well."

"Not strong enough if they ain't here now."

Skylar felt the anger that radiated from Ana.

"Have you ever had to run for your life? Kill or be killed?" Skylar asked.

"I was stalked by a cougar once."

"Well, imagine that, but instead of one predator, there's one hundred."

"Huh. How many did you kill?"

"There wasn't time to count how many we killed. Not to mention those were people, you insensitive bastard," Ana lashed out.

"I'd keep track. Bragging rights with the boys."

"Bragging rights? For exterminating someone who could've been family, a neighbour, or a friend?"

She was red in the face. Skylar saw her hands curl into fists.

Ana, don't do anything stupid...

"It's all about protecting me and mine, lady," he said, giving his gun an acknowledging nudge.

Ana looked like she was ready to pounce. Skylar put his hand on her arm and guided her away from the altercation.

The man at the pump handed Greg a jerry can.

"Well, we owe you a thanks," Greg said. "We've enough gas to get us to Sidney and back!"

The man holding the rope spat in the water again and said, "Just to Sidney. Don't come back."

KAT
1 JULY 2018
08:27 PDT
SALMON BEACH, BC

The dry neoprene chafed the back of her calves where it rubbed against her skin. Kat ignored the discomfort and ventured northeast along the coast. The warm morning sun shone down on her as she scanned the perimeter of the beach. Her thirst increased with each step.

She heard it before she saw it: a stream seeping from the forest to her left, trickling in harmony with the rhythmic sound of the lapping waves. Kat waded upstream, following it into the woods. She dipped a finger in the water and brought it to her mouth. Satisfied that she was far enough from the ocean, she looked around to ensure she was alone. *Trees, ferns, and more trees.* Kat submerged herself in the stream. Water seeped under the neoprene at her wrists, ankles, and neckline. She knelt on the smooth stones and drank cool water from her cupped hands.

A twig snapped to her right. She flinched and grabbed a large stone, then exhaled deeply when she saw the raven.

"You scared me," she said.

It cocked its head, then ran its beak along a stick it stood next to. The raven let out a low clicking sound.

"Okay, okay, I get it. I'll be moving along soon."

When it spread its great black wings, Kat noticed it had one prominent pure white feather. It took flight and swooped down over her left shoulder. She watched it flutter toward a shadowed figure, and she gasped when she saw the man.

His eyes were crimson and his pupils dilated. Bloody dribble ran down his chin when he opened his mouth and hissed. Lurching forward, he stumbled into the water.

Kat scrambled to her feet and threw the rock in her hand at the infected. It crawled through the water, and reached a gnarly hand toward her. She retreated and ran back to the beach.

How? How can the creepers be here, too?

Once she was out of the woods, Kat turned to see the monster staggering in her direction. *Shit. I have to get rid of you.* She looked around and found a long stick nestled amongst the driftwood at the high-tide line. She took it in her hands and tested its strength. Satisfied that it wasn't too brittle for the task, she waited as the infected approached.

The raven soared ahead of the man and landed on a log near Kat. It hopped down the length of the wood toward her.

"Waiting for your next meal, huh? Who's it going to be, him or me?" It cocked its head at her question and let out a low caw.

The infected man drew closer.

She held the stick like a javelin and readied herself.

"It will *not* be me!" Kat cried as she drove the end of the stick at the infected man's head. The muscles in her arms clenched as she forced the tip through the monsters eye. Its hissing ceased as it fell to the ground. Kat put a foot on its chest to brace it while she withdrew her weapon.

She took a step back and waited. The raven didn't approach the corpse.

"Smart bird. This is worse than carrion. I wouldn't eat it either, if I were you."

It stretched out its wings and displayed that prominent white feather once more.

Kat looked around and noticed indentations in the sand close to shore. She approached them, while periodically checking over her shoulder. *Footprints. Maybe they'll lead me into town.* She stopped where the footprints turned into a scrambled mess. It looked like someone had rolled and writhed on the ground. Drops of a purple substance speckled the area. *What the hell happened here?* The footprints leading away looked laboured, as if their creator had dragged their feet.

Kat walked up the beach with her weapon doubling as a walking stick until she found a path. It led to a road that curved through tall coniferous trees. The area was quiet, and Kat realized she was alone again. The raven had stopped following her. *Maybe you were hungry enough after all.*

The short trail led her to a village. She stopped in her tracks and scanned the area. It seemed quiet. Kat searched for signs of life. Or signs of death. There wasn't another human in sight. She walked past the first house on her left. Its door bore a rusty crimson smear of dried blood.

She felt a tingle at the back of her scalp. *No, please, not here too. What the hell am I supposed to do?* Panic set in. She looked over either shoulder, trying to find someone, anyone, who could guide her to safety.

Footsteps approached from behind her. Slowly at first, and then their pace quickened. Kat tightened her grip on the driftwood stick and held it in a defensive stance as she turned toward the sound.

It was a young woman, around her age. They were of a similar height and had the same hair colour: a black so deep it nearly shone blue. The woman could have been a mirror image of herself, except her reflection's skin was clammy and dark circles hung beneath her almond eyes.

Something metal protruded from her chest near her heart; her clothes were stained, yet her wounds no longer wept. She opened her lips and coughed a mouthful of blood in Kat's direction, which fell to the ground between them and spattered the pavement. A nauseating scent filled the air.

Kat pulled the stick back and drove it with all her strength at the infected woman. *Through the eye, destroy the brain.* Kat's hands vibrated as the stick pierced its target and struck the back of her skull. She watched the lifeless corpse fall to the ground.

Another sound caught her attention. Kat looked up to see a parade of infected marching down the street toward her. Her feet reacted before her thoughts did. She couldn't think clearly, didn't consider which direction to run in. She just ran.

Kat reached the end of the paved road. She didn't let the gravel slow her, though it tore at her bare feet. The road narrowed until it was just two tire tracks along a dirt path. The grass, clover, and pineapple weed were a welcome change in texture. She looked over her shoulder and, convinced that she was alone, slowed her pace.

Kat let out a long exhale just as something light bounced off her head. *What the hell?* A LEGO man landed on the ground at her feet. Kat looked up and was surprised to see several round faces peering down at her from a treehouse nestled in the branches of a great maple. She heard a rustling, and a rope ladder lowered beside her.

PAUL
1 JULY 2018
12:00 PDT
QUARANTINE TEST FACILITIES
LADNER, BC

"Where's Jocelyn? I want to see her!" Paul demanded as Dr. Hayde entered the room.

He didn't look up from the clipboard in his hand.

"How long have I been in here? Come on, man, you can see I'm not sick! I'm not one of them!"

"I already told you, Jocelyn is in quarantine, as are the others." Dr. Hayde walked forward and sat on a stool across from Paul. He finally lowered the clipboard, and said, "Paul, I feel as though you're withholding some valuable information from me."

"I already told you what happened. We witnessed the attack and ran for it. I killed a couple zombies in the hunting store. Saved some kids from a house that is probably burnt to rubble by now. What more can I say?"

"Tell me about the *Regina Vitae*."

Paul feigned ignorance. He tried his best not to react, to not even blink. "*Regina* what now?"

"This will all go much easier for you if you comply, Paul. Tell me what you know, and I'll give you a few minutes to make a call."

Ana. How much time has passed since we spoke last? What happened to you at the end of our last conversation? Paul sighed. "My parents worked aboard the *Regina Vitae*. It was a floating lab. They were based offshore, conducting their research on international waters."

"Why is that?" Dr. Hayde asked. "What was their primary focus?"

"To hell if I know. I was a kid. My parents didn't tell us much about their work."

Dr. Hayde unclipped a page from his notes and turned it around to show Paul. It was a photo of a broken vial oozing purple goo. A crack in the glass ran along the etched emblem of a phoenix wearing a crown. "Does this look like the vial taken from Rocket's person?"

"Yes, I think so. I only saw it very briefly, and from a distance. That looks like the same purple stuff though, from what I can tell."

"Did you know this vial has a button? Just here." Dr. Hayde pointed to its top rim. "It's a trigger that releases a needle. Well, seven needles actually."

Paul noticed Dr. Hayde's eyes were on his scar. "I did *not* know that. *Why* would I know that? As I told you, I didn't get that close."

"I think you know from experience."

"What are you saying?"

"I believe your resentment toward your parents stems not only from abandonment issues but also from anger toward them for experimenting on you as a child. Is that correct?"

Paul clenched his jaw.

"And your sister too, perhaps? Where is she? Tofino, you said?"

"She was. Could be anywhere now. Could be dead."

"I want you to get ahold of her. We want to bring her here, where she will be safe."

"The island has nearly a million people on it. Why do you want to save *her*?"

"To find out if her blood is as *special* as yours. I suspect it is."

"*Special*? What do you mean?"

"Well, that is interesting. There are bacteria in the infected blood samples that have parasitic tendencies. We can see under a microscope that, when mixed with the blood of the infected, *your* blood carries antibodies that withstand their attack. We have tried with several other samples, my own included. All others have been overtaken. Except for yours. Your blood tells us a very interesting story, as does your scar. This vial," Dr. Hayde gestured to the photo again, "only has seven needles. Do you remember where the central scar came from?"

Paul didn't answer his question.

"If there truly is a connection between your scar and this vial, you could potentially save lives. Don't you want that?"

"Yes, but I won't let you experiment on us like some lab rats!"

"We would only require a small amount of blood now and again. There would be no further tests done to either of your persons. You truly have nothing to fear."

"Why do you need both of us? Why can't you just use mine?"

"Genetic variability: the more viable samples we have, the higher our chances of developing a cure."

Paul said nothing. He weighed the doctor's words as he stared at his feet.

"Her safety is in your hands. People do unspeakable things to survive. If she finds herself on the wrong doorstep...well, any number of things could happen."

Paul sighed and ran his fingers through his hair. "Let me see Jocelyn. And speak with my sister. *Privately*. Then you'll have your answer."

"I'm afraid I can't do that."

"Can't do which?"

"Let you see Jocelyn. We have released her into the second-level quarantine: no infection. She will remain there until our transportation team has time to deliver her safely home."

"I thought you said you'd be holding her for forty-eight hours? I want to see her."

"Jocelyn has passed all our lab tests and has been cleared for release. Paul, listen to me. Technically speaking, you are infected. You will not be leaving my custody any time soon. I can make this very comfortable if you cooperate."

"And if I don't?"

"Either way, we will find your sister and bring her here. The choice is yours. Would you rather she be welcomed like a hero or treated, as you say, like a *lab rat*?"

ANA
1 JULY 2018
13:00 PDT
STRAIT OF JUAN DE FUCA, BC

Wind tugged at wisps of hair that had fallen from Ana's braid. Midday sun glimmered off the water in every direction like an oceanic kaleidoscope. A freighter passed in the distance, but their journey was otherwise without company. The placid horizon looked unsuspecting, as if it couldn't possibly produce the kind of chaos and destruction it brought to shore less than twenty-four hours earlier.

The boys had taken to Skylar and listened intently to his stories about surfing and life on the west coast. Ana tuned in and out of their chatter, but her ears perked up when her cell phone started ringing.

"Hey, Ana, I think this one's for you, dear," Greg called over his shoulder.

Ana walked across the deck as Greg cut the engine. She lost her footing and grabbed the back of his chair to steady herself. Greg put a hand on her arm to stabilize her, then handed her the phone as she sat down in the passenger seat.

Her brother's picture illuminated across the cracked screen. *Thank god!*

"Paul?"

"Ana! Where are you?"

"We're on the boat still, making our way to Sidney. I think we'll be there soon."

"Where *exactly* are you, An?"

"What, you want coordinates?"

"I can get you out of there."

Relief flooded through Ana's troubled mind, until her twin continued.

"I'm with... I don't even know what to call them. The officials. They have Jocelyn and I in quarantine. She's been cleared, but they're holding me for further testing. It's our blood, Ana. They think we can help."

"What do you mean, *'it's our blood'*?"

"Remember that time Mom and Dad took us on board the *Regina Vitae*?"

Though she had spent many nights trying to forget, Ana remembered. Only once did their parents bring them on a tour of the ship.

Ana could recall the excitement she felt at visiting a *real* science lab, and she was so proud of her parents and their seemingly important jobs. Her excitement faded when a ring of seven needles pierced her arm and caused searing pain to run through her veins.

Dr. Zuessen never told her children the truth about what she had injected them with. *"Just a flu shot, my sweet. All the kids get them at this time of year."* Their mother's words echoed through her mind even still.

She told Ana the swelling from the first injection was a hallucination, but Ana knew that was bullshit. Even twins wouldn't have the same hallucination in two separate rooms.

A man in scrubs burst into the room Ana was being "treated" in and whispered something in her mother's ear. *"Run the second course now, you fool! Before it's too late. I don't care if he's struggling. He's eight. Figure it out!"* their mother had hissed through gritted teeth.

Ana ran a finger over the tattoo that concealed a star-shaped scar with the seven small punctures that encircled it. Paul had the same scar. Matching keepsakes of their brief time aboard the *Regina Vitae*. But he hadn't covered his up.

Ana looked up and realized everyone on board was staring at her.

"Ana? Are you there?"

"I'm here. Of course I remember. Are you...sure it's safe there?"

"I hope you know I wouldn't drag you into this if I thought it wasn't."

She turned her back to everyone and discreetly said into the phone, "What will they do to us?"

"They'll just need blood samples occasionally."

"Paul, I don't know if I'm comfortable with this..."

"It's safe here. We'll be protected. The peninsula is under quarantine. They set perimeters up. They think they can use our blood to help develop a cure, An. Think about how many people we could help save. We can help stop all of this."

"Paul...I need a little time to think this through."

"Okay. I have to turn my phone back over to *them*. I'll let them know you need some time. Call you back in an hour?"

"Sure, Paul. I'll talk to you then." She set the phone down and rubbed her face with both hands.

"What was that all about?" Skylar asked.

"My brother is with some officials who want to bring me in. They think they can develop some kind of vaccine or antidote from our blood."

"Why the hell would they think that?"

"Because of some experimental shots my mom administered to us as children."

"So the purple goo didn't affect you because...you were already infected," Skylar said.

"No, I don't think so. Maybe I'm just...immune."

"How do you know for sure?"

"I *don't* know. The purple goo didn't affect me, but a bite may be an entirely different story."

"How long have you known...that this was all related to your scar, to your mom?"

"When Rocket pulled the vial out of his pocket, I saw the logo for the company my parents worked for, Regal Phoenix Pharmaceuti—"

"And you didn't think it was important enough to mention?"

"What was I supposed to say? *'Oh, hey, Skylar, I have a sneaking suspicion that I have family ties to the impending apocalyptic outbreak. Shall we take a moment to find out if I'm immune?'* I wasn't about to offer my arm as a snack to one of those monsters to test it out! They were still coming after me!"

"So, they think they can make some kinda vaccine from your blood?"

She shrugged. "I guess they wanna try. Who knows how long it'll take though. I sure as hell don't want to become their guinea pig." Her brain flooded with images of being restrained, strung up with IVs and prodded by needles and worse.

Greg looked at Ana sternly. "Your choice could change the course of life on Earth."

"So, what, I give myself up and let them bleed me dry? I don't want to be experimented on!"

"Don't be so selfish, child!" The old man's face was red. "This is your opportunity to help your country... Hell, humanity! I won't have you hiding aboard my ship with so much at stake!"

Ana looked out at the horizon.

"Greg, this is Ana's decision to make. You don't need to raise your voice." Skylar stood between them. "Ana, sounds like you have a little time to consider it." He guided her past Greg and toward the stern of the boat.

The boys watched apprehensively as she walked past them.

"Will Cap'n make her walk the plank?" Mikey asked.

Skylar shook his head. "No, Mikey. No one else is walking the plank today."

KAT
1 JULY 2018
10:38 PDT
TREE HOUSE
SALMON BEACH, BC

Kat reached the top rung of the ladder and peered around the room at the faces looking back at her. Four kids sat in a circle around the opening in the floor. She pulled herself onto the wooden platform of the treehouse and lay still for a moment, catching her breath.

"Gross, you got blood on our ladder," one of the children commented as he hauled the rope back up. He closed the trap door.

"I'm...sorry?" Kat offered.

"Don't get mad at someone for being hurt, Roger. Are you okay?" The young girl looked sympathetically at Kat.

Kat rolled over and inspected her feet, which were covered in lacerations. *Shouldn't've looked.* The pain kicked in when she saw the damage caused by the gravel.

"Here, use this," the girl said.

"That's my towel!" one of the boys cried.

"Would you rather she bleed out in your fort, Stu?"

Stu shook his head silently, frowning as he watched the terry cloth Teenage Mutant Ninja Turtles sponge up the sticky crimson from Kat's feet.

"I'm Milah, and this is Stu, Roger, and Adam. Where did you come from?"

"Tofino. Name's Kat. How long have you kids been up here?"

"Overnight. Since they all...became monsters. How'd you get here from Tofino?"

"By boat."

"You have a boat? Can you take us away?" Roger asked.

"No, they ditched me here."

"Oh."

"Where are your parents?" Kat looked around the room. None of their eyes met hers.

"They're monsters now," Adam said through braced teeth.

Great. I get to be the babysitter again. "I'm sorry. Do you all live around here?"

"We were staying at Stu's family's cabin for the weekend," Milah answered.

"Do you have food? Water?"

"I have a granola bar," Adam said.

The other kids patted their empty pockets and shrugged.

Kat sighed deeply. *Here we go again.*

"Why are you wearing a wetsuit? Mom said there was a tsunami headed for Tofino. Were you surfing?"

"No." Kat grimaced as she continued patting her feet with the towel. "You kids aren't going to last long up here without any food."

"We were gonna wait it out until that herd of deadies leaves town."

"Well, kid, they're still there."

"It's Adam."

"Right, Adam."

"We can pick salmon berries, and the red huckleberries too!" Milah said matter-of-factly.

"I know how to fish. Papa taught me. My rod is back at the cabin," Stu said.

"That's great, but you guys are thinking way too long-term. We need to pack up some food and get the hell outta here."

"*We*? So you're coming with us?" Milah beamed at Kat.

Roger's stomach growled audibly. "She's right. We won't last up here much longer. We need to make a plan to get into Stu's cabin. We'll pack as many snacks as we can carry, and find her some shoes." He gestured to Kat with his thumb.

"Wouldn't mind some clothes as well," Kat muttered.

"How many monsters were down there, Kat?"

"Oh god, I don't know. Dozens? I didn't really take the time to count, kid."

"I told you, it's *Adam.*"

"Okay, okay. Adam, Stu, Robert, and Mulan."

"Milah!"

"Roger!" they said in unison.

Man, this group is feistier than the toddlers. "Sorry, guys, I have a lot on my mind at the moment," Kat said as she rolled her eyes.

"Okay, here's the plan. We run up Front Street and split into two groups. One group will distract the monsters, and the other group makes for the cabin," Roger suggested.

Kat scoffed. "Who's going to volunteer to be the bait?"

The kids simultaneously lifted their fingers to their noses. Their eyes met as they tried to determine who had lost the draw.

"Adam is the fastest," Stu said as he poked himself in the belly. "Look at me, I'm a meal on two legs. Besides, I know where everything is in the cabin."

"Milah should go to the cabin with you." Adam flushed when he said it.

"Oo-ooh!" Roger and Stu chimed.

"I'm a fast runner too, Adam!" Milah protested.

"It's too dangerous! You and Kat should go with Stu. Her feet are in no condition to run anyway."

"I ran here, didn't I?"

His only response was a raised eyebrow and a nod toward the bloody towel.

"Yeah, okay, I'll go with Stu and Milah."

"Roger, you're with me," Adam said.

His face went ghostly white, but Roger nodded in agreement. Stu lifted the hatch door and lowered the rope ladder.

"Wait! What happens after?" Milah asked.

"I was thinking we meet up back here?" Stu said.

"For what? Live out the rest of our days? I don't think so.

Can you drive?" she asked Kat.

"Yeah."

"Great. We'll take Stu's mom's minivan."

"Where are we going to go?" Roger asked.

"A night in the treehouse was fun, but I want to go home," Milah said.

"Where are you guys from anyway?" Kat asked.

"Port Alberni."

Great, not too far. I can dump them there and get out of babysitting duty. "Yeah, I can get you there."

ANA
1 JULY 2018
14:05 PDT
STRAIT OF JUAN DE FUCA, BC

The tree line swirled in a feathered flurry as they raced down the coast. Skylar checked on her from time to time, but mostly, Ana had spent the last hour in silent contemplation at the stern of the boat, watching the spray of its wake.

Paul, what have you gotten us into?

Skylar held the railing as he made his way toward her. He nearly lost his footing when Greg hit a wave, but held fast and steadied himself.

Ana looked up at Skylar as he took a seat next to her.

"Have you...come to a decision?" Skylar called over the roar of the engine.

"About whether to save the planet or my own ass? Yeah, I think so."

He held his hand out. She scooted closer to him on the bench and took it in her own.

"I'm scared," she told him.

"I know. But I'd bet they'll treat you like royalty, An. They'll probably make a statue of you afterward."

"Arms outstretched, surrounded by little bronze zombies?"

"Yeah, something like that."

"Will you come with me, Skylar?"

His eyes didn't meet hers when he answered, "Sure, An."

They slowed to a stop. When the engine cut, Ana could hear her ringtone. The boat rocked as gentle waves lapped its starboard side.

Greg gave her a stern look as they walked past one another.

"Paul?" Ana said into the phone as she rested on the captain's seat. A wave of nausea washed over her. She couldn't decipher if it was caused by seasickness or the prospect of becoming a test subject.

"Hello, Diana," a steely voice answered. "I am Doctor Hayde."

"What? Where is my brother?" she nearly yelled into the phone.

"He's nearby, Ana. I will let you speak to him, but I wanted to connect with you first."

His voice made the skin on the back of her neck crawl. Ana turned around and looked wide-eyed at Skylar. He nodded at her reassuringly.

"Alright, Doctor. I'm listening."

"Ana, I'm sure I don't need to reiterate the importance of your decision, but I do hope you'll join us. The outbreak has gotten significantly worse on Vancouver Island. We have it contained, for now, on the mainland. We can only pray that more of these biohazardous vials your mother created don't start popping up on our shoreline. It's only been a day since the outbreak began, and the damage we've already witnessed is astronomical. I don't wish to scare you by telling you how the authorities want to deal with the situation, but it's along the lines of total eradication, unless I can provide hope that this can be corrected. Ana, you are that hope."

"Total eradication? Of what, the island? Everything? There's no way all the isolated communities and outlying islands are infected! And what about the old-growth forests? How can they even consider that?"

"Large trees do not supersede the importance of the survival of mankind, Diana. The final decision hasn't been made as of yet, but your compliance can help dissuade those in favour of *eradication.*"

Blood crept into Ana's cheeks as she fumed at his tactics. "How dare you! I was already planning on agreeing to come. Did you really think guilt and manipulation were the right tact to get me down there?"

"I am pleased to hear that you will join us. Someday, what's left of your country will thank you. After you've spoken with

Paul, please have your captain give my assistant your coordinates." The phone was silent for a moment.

"Ana?"

"Paul, what the hell was that?"

"What was what? I just got in the room."

"Your friend, *Dr. Hayde,* guilting me into coming."

"Are you?"

"Yes!"

"That's a relief. Ana, I was so worried. You can't imagine."

"Oh, yes I can!"

"Why are you yelling?"

Ana sighed and leaned back in her chair. "I'm sorry, that guy has terrible bedside manner."

"Yeah, he is rather assertive. Well, I'll see you soon, alright?"

"Sure. See you soon."

There was a moment of silence, and then, "This is Nurse Sephonia Perri speaking. May we have your coordinates please?"

"Just a sec," Ana said. She stood, held the phone up, and nodded to Greg. "They want coordinates."

Greg took the phone and relayed, "Hullo there. 48.37 degrees north by 123.94 degrees west." He nodded and ended the call.

A heavy silence loomed over the boat. Ana retreated into the cabin. She flicked on the hanging flashlight. *What the fuck just happened? Oh god, what am I getting myself into?* She rubbed her eyes beneath her glasses. Her heart thumped rapidly against her ribs as a tightness formed in her chest and a thirst for air consumed her. The dim cabin felt suddenly like a cage, with its curved walls closing in on her. *I gotta get outta here.* She turned and collided with Skylar, who she hadn't heard come in.

"Hey, An, it's going to be okay. You're doing the right thing." His eyes narrowed as he reached out to give her arm a squeeze. She stepped toward him and his long, sinewy arms wrapped around her. "Shh, shh, breathe, An."

They stood together, silently embracing, letting time pass until they heard a roaring engine in the distance. When it grew closer, Ana and Skylar parted.

"Sounds like your ride is here."

"So quickly?"

"They must have expected your answer and already been in the area."

A fresh wave of anger washed over her.

"Come on." He held her hand and led her above deck.

"Wow, look at that, Patrick!" Mikey said as he pointed to the silver seaplane that soared above them. It flew in a smooth arc and descended toward the ocean's surface.

"So cool!" Patrick squeaked out when he saw it. He hoisted himself up and stood on the bench.

"Come on, Pat, sit down or stand on deck. You'll go overboard that way," Greg warned him.

Mikey gave Patrick's hand a tug and pulled him back to his seat.

The plane glided above the surface of the water until its floats made purchase. Mist flew into the air above the wake of the plane. The boys cheered as it taxied toward them.

"Yer doing a noble thing, Ana," Greg said. He patted her shoulder as he walked past her, and set to putting fenders out on the port side of his boat to create a barrier for the approaching plane.

"Yeah, we'll see."

Ana realized she was squeezing Skylar's hand. Her palm felt clammy in his, but neither of them let go until the plane nudged the fenders Greg had set out.

Skylar pulled the duffle bag out from under the bench opposite them. Harvey's hunter-green shirt lay at the top of the bag's contents. Skylar handed it to Ana, who took it while blinking away tears.

She looked up at Skylar and said, "You're coming with me, right?"

"An, come on. I'm not wanted there. They have no use for me."

"You said you would come with me!"

"Paul will look out for you. I'll see you again soon, okay."

"Diana Zuessen?" a commanding voice called from the plane.

Ana looked up at the man, who wore an armoured uniform with a tinted face shield that made his features nearly indisernable. He held out a gloved hand.

She stole one last look at Skylar. He stepped toward her and took her in his arms.

"At least we get to say goodbye this time," he whispered into her hair. His embrace felt rigid, and Skylar was the first to pull back.

Ana's knees trembled as she made her way toward the plane.

The old man nodded solemnly and the older boy waved at her.

Ana took the hand of her military escort. He guided her to step onto the float of the plane, and she climbed into the aircraft's cabin. The scent of aged leather filled her nostrils. A pilot wearing a helmet and visor turned and nodded at her in acknowledgement. The man in uniform closed the door behind them and settled in next to Ana.

The copilot spoke into his headset. "We've retrieved patient zero. No issues. Over."

Patient zero? What the hell. I didn't start this outbreak.

The propellor spun when the engine roared to life. Ana's chest tightened as the plane taxied away. She kept her eyes on Skylar, who lit a cigarette at the back of the boat. He lifted one hand to bid her farewell and was out of sight when the plane turned. They sped up and Ana felt that fleeting moment of weightlessness as they lifted into the air.

"You ever been on a float plane before?" the man beside her asked.

Ana shook her head.

"You get used to it. Taking off isn't so bad. It's the landing that's a little unsettling the first couple times."

"Great, I'm so glad we have that to look forward to."

"Don't get me wrong, it's safe and all. Probably the safest thing you've done in the past twenty-four hours. I think it's fun now."

Ana didn't respond. She watched the view beneath them change from grey ocean to rocky coast to dense rainforest.

"What was it like...back in Tofino?"

She looked over at him. From what she could see beneath the tinted polycarbonate, the officer appeared to be around her age. She sighed and shook her head. "Have you ever had to run for your life?"

"Well, we go through rigorous training—"

"That can't compare. The stakes aren't high enough in training. Have you ever had something coming after you, bloodthirsty, and you had no choice but to fight, run, or die? Have you watched your friends tear each other apart and eat each other's entrails? Have you heard the screams of women, children, and grown men as they were eaten alive?"

"No, ma'am. I can't say I have."

"Well, *that's* what it was like."

"I'm sorry you went through that."

Yeah, me too. I'm sorry I came out here this weekend. I'm sorry I killed Harvey. I'm sorry my mother tried to play God and got us all into this whole mess.

KAT
1 JULY 2018
11:30 PDT
SALMON BEACH, BC

Kat and the kids stood behind the tree line at the edge of town, overlooking Front Street, where they noted the positions of the infected roaming about.

"Our biggest threat is that cluster over there, by the corner of First Avenue." Stu pointed. "Adam, you and Roger lead them to the end of Front Street and turn on Second Ave. There's a path through that patch of woods about halfway up the street. It cuts to Victoria Street. Follow Vic up to Fourth. We should be in and out by then, and we'll meet you on Elizabeth."

Adam nodded along in acknowledgement. "I think I got it. You really know this place, huh?"

Stu shrugged. "Small town. I spend a lot of time here. And I like maps." He stepped out from behind the trees and signaled for the others to follow.

Kat winced. Her feet throbbed with each step. She tried to keep up with the kids, who moved as a tightly knit unit. They cut across yards and stayed close to the houses to avoid being exposed on the street.

When they drew near the group of infected, Adam and Roger turned and nodded at the raiding crew—deemed Team Cabin—and ran up the road.

"Hey! Heya, dummy! Over here! Yeah, I'm talking to you. This way, this way!" Adam called.

"He's so brave," Milah whispered.

Kat rolled her eyes and limped after Stu, who was heading toward a rustic-looking cabin. He ascended the steps to the porch and knelt to reach under the doormat for a key. After unlocking the door, he disappeared inside.

"Kid, hold up. How do you know if this place is secure?" Kat asked in a harsh whisper.

"I know it *isn't*, but the quicker I move, the more quickly we have a gun in our hands."

Kat and Milah followed the boy inside.

"I'll wait here until it's clear," Milah squeaked as she closed and locked the door behind them.

The entryway opened to a living room. An overstuffed black leather couch sat in the middle of the room. The floor was covered in broken glass and blood spatter.

Stu reached into a closet and pulled out a lever-action rifle. He held it with a confidence that told Kat it wasn't his first time holding the firearm. After loading a round into the chamber, he walked down a hallway lined with several doors, each of them ajar. He toed the first one open. Kat watched Stu scan the room and move on to the next door. It creaked on its hinges. The second room was empty as well.

A thud sounded farther down the hall. Stu opened the last door on the left. A shrill hiss cut through the silence. He lifted the rifle and fired, reloaded and fired again, repeating this action several more times, then signaled to Kat to follow when he entered the room.

Stu knelt over the corpse of a middle-aged woman. He rummaged through her pocket and pulled out a set of keys, which he handed to Kat. His lower lip trembled, and he didn't look up at her.

"Check that closet for whatever you need. Milah and I will pack some food."

As he walked past, Kat noticed the curve of Stu's upturned nose matched the dead woman's. *Oh fuck. Is this his mom? Poor kid.* "Stu, you didn't have to—"

"Yes I did."

"I could have—"

"No, it had to be me." He sniffled and walked out the door.

Kat limped past the woman of the house's corpse and opened her closet. She grabbed black sweatpants, a tank top, and a cardigan, and then noticed a bag on the floor. Kat emptied its contents and packed another sweater, jean jacket, and shorts. *Better stock up. Who knows where I'll end up after I dump these kids in Port Alberni.*

She grimaced as she peeled the wetsuit off. Sores formed where the neoprene had rubbed her soft skin for too long.

Wish I had time to shower. Kat sighed. The pants were too long for her petite stature and bunched at her ankles.

She rifled through a rack of shoes and selected the smallest pair in the pile: black and white sneakers. She pulled them on and took a couple steps to test their fit, accidentally treading in a pool of their previous owner's blood. Kat grimaced as she left crimson footprints on the cream carpet.

Who gets such light carpets in a cabin? They're so easily soiled.

Kat looked around the room for anything else that might be useful. She spotted a stack of CDs and grabbed a couple that looked tolerable. *Going to be a long drive, I'll need something to drown out those kids.*

She stepped over Stu's mom and walked back down the hall toward the kitchen.

"Not that. Come on, Stu. Do you know how long it takes to cook? We need food that's quick and easy."

"Whatever, Milah, just take everything! But hurry, Adam and Roger are probably getting close to the checkpoint and we don't want to leave them waiting."

Kat entered the kitchen to find the two kids stuffing bags with food.

"Hey, lady, there's a cooler in the pantry. Start packing up the perishables."

"So you give me shit for calling you *kid*, but it's okay to call me *lady*? Seems like a double standard." She rolled her eyes but followed his instructions. Kat packed a carton of eggs, a brick of cheese, several packs of smokies, and a pre-cut fruit and veggie tray.

"Score!" Stu called when he pulled a box of cookies out

from the back of the highest cupboard. "Found Dad's stash! Alright, let's get the hell outta here!"

Kat closed the fridge and lifted the cooler, then followed the kids to the front door.

Milah stood on her tiptoes to peer out the peephole while Stu reloaded his rifle. "No deadies in sight."

"That doesn't mean they're not there. You two get the groceries loaded. I'll cover you," Stu instructed as he handed over his bags. He stepped past Kat and opened the door.

Kat hurried down the driveway and clicked the fob's unlock button. The van emitted a soft beep that caught the attention of several infected who stood on the lawn of a neighboring cabin. Their moans filled the air as they began shuffling toward the van. Stu readied the rifle as Milah and Kat loaded the supplies.

"Save your ammo, get in!" Kat called as she shut the liftgate.

Milah slid the side door open and let Stu climb in before her, then pulled it closed as he scrambled into the front passenger seat. Three infected had reached the driveway, snapping their jaws in hungry anticipation.

"Kat, hurry!" Milah called as Kat approached the driver's door.

She jumped in, slammed the door, and flicked the power lock switch. Bloody palms pawed at the window. The keys rattled as her shaking hand searched for the ignition. Nothing happened when she turned the key. Kat looked down at the positioning of the three pedals. *Three? Oh...shit.* Her face fell.

"Let's go!" Stu called as more infected hobbled up the street. "What's the hold up?"

"You didn't mention the van is *manual*!"

"Are you serious? So you can't drive it?"

"I didn't say that... Just give me a second!" Kat closed her eyes. *Think. Think! Left is the clutch. Press the clutch while you're shifting gears.* She put her left foot on the far-left pedal and turned the key again. This time, the vehicle revved to life, aggravating the monsters outside. They clawed the glass with more fervour.

"Are the windows going to hold?" Milah wailed.

Kat ignored the children and pulled down on the gearshift. She set it to first gear and pushed on the gas as she released the clutch. The engine failed and fell silent.

"Oh my god. You're going to kill us because you can't drive a manual! Did you really just stall out?" Stu looked with wide eyes at another group of infected shuffling down the road.

"Shut your mouth! Unless you think you can do better, keep quiet. I'll get it!"

"Ease off the clutch more slowly," Milah whispered.

Kat tried. This time she made it into first gear without losing power to the engine. The van inched up the driveway, forcing several infected near its hood out of the way. Kat pressed down on the clutch again and pulled the gearshift to second. They moved a little faster, then stopped with a lurch.

"Watch it!" Stu called.

Milah shushed him and gave him a warning look.

The horde of infected caught up to them and bloody hands once again rapped upon the windows.

Kat swore as she put her foot on the clutch again. She put it in neutral and started over. *First gear, second, third. Yes!* As a half-dozen more infected staggered toward them, Kat brought the van up to speed. She hit the accelerator and knocked a few of them down. They heard a sickening crunch beneath the front wheels.

"Let's get the hell out of here!" she exclaimed. Kat followed the curved road onto Second Avenue.

"Left on Elizabeth Street!" Stu pointed.

At the end of the road, Kat took a wide turn. There were two silhouettes in the distance, sprinting in their direction.

"It's them!" Milah called.

Kat sped toward the kids. She slowed down and stalled,

shaking her passengers in their seats yet again.

Milah pulled the sliding door open and climbed to the rear bench to make room for her friends. Roger and Adam dove into the van.

"Go...please...go..." Adam got out in between breaths.

Stu looked his friend up and down. "Where did the blood come from, Adam?"

"It...isn't...mine... Go!"

Kat looked in the rearview mirror and saw dark figures emerging from the forest. She shifted without fail and continued down Elizabeth Street.

"Right on Fourth, then right on Barkley!" Stu called to Kat. "Adam, where did the blood come from?"

"Look at yourself, man. You're splattered too." Adam pulled his shirt off and rotated his arms. "See? No bites."

Kat glanced over as Stu's eyes dropped to the blood on his shirt. He pulled it off to show his unscathed limbs to his friend and then silently pulled his shirt back on.

Kat called over her shoulder, "Hey, kid. See that blue bag back there? Pass me one of those CDs."

PAUL
1 JULY 2018
15:40 PDT
QUARANTINE TEST FACILITIES
LADNER, BC

The warm afternoon air held the pungent scent of a nearby farm. Paul scrunched his nose when it greeted him. He followed Nurse Perri out of the tented pavilion and walked toward a set of chairs in a fenced yard.

"Please, Mr. Zuessen, have a seat. Dr. Hayde will join us shortly, and your sister should arrive any time now."

He felt restless, but Paul sat to resist the urge to pace. "How kind of you to let me have some fresh air, Nurse Perri. Do you treat all your patients to such freedoms?"

"My patients are either cleared and released, or they are infected and exterminated. You are an exception, Mr. Zuessen. We will treat you humanely."

"Humanely? Great, thanks." He looked at her closely, trying to distinguish her features beneath the thick hazmat suit. *She's young... Patient, but rigid. How is she so...robotic?* Paul realized he was staring and began plucking at one of his nails instead.

"Paul!"

He turned to the sound of his sister's voice and a wave of relief washed over him. Paul stood from his chair as Ana ran across the yard toward her brother, her long braid trailing behind her. The twins embraced, and he felt his sister's shoulders fall as she sighed.

"An, I can't tell you how worried I was." He pulled her to arm's length. She looked tired, with dark bags under her eyes, but otherwise unharmed.

"Me too, Paul. What...is this place?"

"Some sort of testing facility. I haven't had the luxury of a full tour yet. Nurse Perri here leaves me in my cell, mostly."

"Your *cell?*"

"A precaution, Miss Zuessen, though cell is not the word we'd use for it," the nurse interjected. "It's true that his accommodations have been somewhat cramped, but our patients' quarters weren't designed for long-term stays. We're discussing relocation, but I'll let Doctor Hayde fill you in on that." She nodded at the doctor as he approached. "Miss Zuessen, I'd like to introduce you to Doctor Hayde."

Ana turned to see the man who approached their group. The plastic of his protective suit made slight swishing sounds with each step he took.

"Hello, Diana. Thank you for coming. I am Doctor Hayde. I see you've met my assistant, Nurse Perri."

"Uhh, hi."

"If there is anything I can get you, please don't hesitate to ask Nurse Perri. It won't be long now until we transfer you to our other facilities."

A man in a military uniform approached and whispered something to Doctor Hayde.

"Ahh, yes. Thank you, Sergeant. Diana, Paul, I will be with you again shortly. I have another patient to prepare for our journey, and then we can further discuss the logistics of our move."

Ana watched as Doctor Hayde walked away. "Another patient? That's weird. Do you think someone else could be immune?"

"I have no idea." Paul raised his eyebrows. "Unlikely though, unless some other unfortunate kids toured the *Regina*."

"It's more of a specimen than a patient, really," Nurse Perri said. She pursed her lips and looked at the twins. "That's really all I can say about that though. I'll leave you two to catch up. Miss Zuessen, meet me at the nurses' station when you're ready, and I'll have you outfitted." She turned and walked across the yard.

Paul and Ana looked at each other.

"I don't like the sounds of that," Ana whispered.

"Come on, An, sweats aren't very flattering on anyone, but... What is it you're wearing?"

Ana looked down at Greg's oversized t-shirt. "I wasn't talking about the sweatpants! I meant the *specimen*."

"Well, I suppose they need zombie blood to test with, as well as immune blood."

"I guess so. Doesn't feel safe though. Having one of *them* in here."

"There are armed guards everywhere. We're safer here than anywhere else."

"Sure. Where's Jocelyn?"

"They released her, but they haven't given me an opportunity to contact her. I feel a bit like a prisoner in here, An. I think you made the right decision though, agreeing to come. We're doing the right thing. They would have found you anyway, if you had disagreed. They would have brought you either way."

Her cheeks flushed. "Paul, you're kinda scaring me."

"I'm sorry. I'm just...overwhelmed." He ran his fingers through his hair as he lowered himself to the chair. Ana sat a few feet away and absent-mindedly picked at the blades of grass beside her.

"Do you...want to talk? About Tofino?" Paul looked at his sister with concern in his eyes.

"Not particularly. I'm exhausted, Paul. I'm not ready to relive it right now."

"You look tired."

"I *am*. I avoided the tsunami and survived the zombie apocalypse, only to be pushed off a boat and nearly drown."

"You were *WHAT*?"

"Look, I'm fine, alright?"

"Who did that to you?"

"Kat... Harvey's new girlfriend or whatever. She overheard

me telling you about...what happened..."

"An, that wasn't your fault. It was an accident."

"Isn't it ridiculous? I was there...for him. To be with *him*. For fuck's sake, he taught me how to shoot. What sick fate is this?" Ana let out a few sobbing laughs and wiped her lower lashes.

"CODE WHITE... CODE WHITE... ALL PERSONNEL REPORT TO YOUR STATIONS!"

"What the fuck..." Ana looked up in alarm. "Paul..."

He stood from his chair and scanned the yard. Ana jumped up and stood next to him.

"What now?" he asked. Paul looked around for an escape route. The fence around the yard was ten feet high. They were trapped.

Screams erupted from within the tent. A beastly, disfigured man with a barrel chest sauntered through the tent door.

No... It can't be...

A monstrous roar echoed across the yard. His forehead glimmered silver in the bright summer sunlight. He dragged a disembodied arm, which he lifted to his mouth, tore off a strip of flesh, and then let out a low, rumbling growl, threw the arm aside, and sprinted toward his new prey.

"Ana, run to the fence, now!" Paul shouted.

She turned and ran. "Paul, it's too high! We won't make it!"

He ran after her. "I'll boost you!"

"What? No! Paul, I'm not leaving you."

"Move it!" he shouted.

When they reached the fence Paul cupped his hands for Ana to step onto. "GO! NOW!" he yelled.

Ana placed a foot in her brother's hands, and Paul hoisted her up. She pulled herself to the top of the fence, and tried to balance there, but failed and fell over to the other side.

"Save the twins!" Doctor Hayde called across the yard.

A unit of heavily armed officers filed onto the grass.

“Paul!” Ana screamed from the other side of the fence, blind to what was happening.

He didn’t have time to run. Paul turned around and punched Rocket, but his assault had little effect on the rabid man.

The charred monster bore his blood-stained teeth at Paul, causing blisters around his mouth to crack and ooze. Rocket grabbed Paul by the wrist and bit down on his forearm.

MOLLY
1 JULY 2018
14:40 PDT
GAS STATION, HWY 4
NW OF PORT ALBERNI, BC

"Come on, Molly. You don't get free food or drinks during your shift, right? Why would you now? Don't be so presumptuous." The gangly young man in a bright yellow and red uniform snatched the soda bottle from her hands.

"I think, considering the situation, you could be a little more lenient, Jeremy...in order for us to, you know...survive? We're kind of trapped here," Molly responded with disdain in her voice. She wore the same dated uniform.

"That's right. Until a gale sets us free, we're becalmed here, and I am your captain."

"That's a stupid analogy. A captain would allow his crew rations."

"If you have a problem with the way I do things around here, I suggest you see management." He smiled at his younger colleague. "There is a way you could *earn* this beverage, however."

He walked across the blemished white tile floor. Jeremy turned the deadbolt and a bell clanged as he pushed the door. He was careful to only open it wide enough to let his arm through and released his grasp on the pop bottle. It flew across the pavement and landed next to the third pump, which was vacant. They were all vacant.

Low moans answered the sound of the rolling bottle as three infected lurched toward it. The closest one was missing an eye and a stream of bloody saliva ran down its chin.

"That, Molly, is your target! These are your weapons. Use them as you see fit." Jeremy held up a basket of oranges.

"When does your shift end?" a girl asked from behind Molly.

"Same time as the apocalypse, I suppose," Molly said to her friend.

"You're endangering us all. There's plenty of soda to go around. Why are you making her do this?" an elderly woman called from the back of the group.

"Oh, come on, Rosa, play along. Aren't you guys getting bored just sitting here? I'm helping you build survival skills for the new world we live in." He gestured out the window toward the infected.

"Whatever," the teenager said, and helped herself to an unnaturally blue slushy.

"Hey! Haven't you been listening? That isn't free! Did we just find our first volunteer?" He pushed his glasses up, his narrow eyes blinking quickly behind them.

"No way, loser. I'm not playing your game." She took a long, slurping sip of the frozen fluid.

"I'll go," Molly said.

"You'll...what?!" her friend gaped at her.

"I *am* bored. And thirsty."

"My star employee! I knew you'd set a good example. Now, here are your oranges. Only take three, yes, that's right."

"I'm not *your* employee, Jeremy," Molly said.

"Yes, yes, a matter of diplomacy."

"Are you all seriously going to let this happen?" The teenage girl looked around at the others in the room: three young boys, the elderly woman who had lost her previous bout of courage, and a middle-aged man who no one had heard speak. No heroes in their midst.

"It'll be fine, Kayla. I'll be back real quick, and that'll be the best tasting pop we've ever had."

"Don't need it, I've got a slushy." She stuck her bright blue tongue out at Molly, who was pocketing her oranges.

Molly peered outside, scanning the station for anything she could use for a weapon or diversion. The monsters had dispersed from the landing site of the pop bottle. Only one of them remained in sight.

"Tell you what, Mol. I'll even throw in a corn dog if you get me a salmonberry from the bushes by the highway." Jeremy unlocked the door once more. "But it has to be ripe!"

Molly squeezed through the barely open door. A metallic screeching echoed across the pavement as the door closed against its grimy frame.

The infected near the fourth pump began lurching toward her. One step forward on its right foot, followed by a slow drag of its broken left foot. It inhaled a hissing gasp.

Poor thing, it's so slow.

Molly jogged across the pavement past the pumps and looked up the deserted highway. *I'd probably be better off making a break for it.* Dense forest lined either side of the gas station that was located miles from town. *Who knows what the hell those trees are hiding though.*

She watched as the other two infected revealed themselves from around the side of the building. They shuffled much faster than the monster with the broken, dragging foot.

Molly picked a few berries and placed them in the breast pocket of her uniform. As she reached for one more, a thorn pricked her finger. She gasped when a small dot of blood welled where the thorn had pierced her skin.

The monsters moved faster, invigorated by the scent. She stuck her finger in her mouth and, with her other hand, threw the first orange at a bucket above the ice machine. The bucket fell over and made a racket as it bounced across the pavement.

The three infected turned in unison and as they hobbled toward the fallen bucket, Molly ran to pump three.

She picked up the pop bottle, opened it, and as the pressure released, she heard a satisfying *tsssst*. After taking a long sip, she turned to the window and bowed at her audience. She still had two oranges left. *This is too easy.*

Once the infected realized the bucket wasn't edible, they turned back to Molly, who feigned yawning before she grabbed a squeegee from the window washing bucket. She swung it by her side, whistling as she walked toward the nearest infected: a one-eyed man in a plaid jacket and torn jeans. *Time to say goodbye to the one-eyed lumberjack.* Molly swung the squeegee like a baseball bat, impaling his remaining eye, and he fell backward. She stepped on his shoulder to brace the body as she removed her weapon from the depths of his skull. Molly brought the squeegee down on him several more times, letting out a primal scream with each strike.

She looked back at her spectators. The elderly lady had stopped watching. The three young boys had their hands and faces pressed up against the glass. Kayla was pointing at something behind Molly. She turned to see the second monster drawing near.

Molly removed the second orange from the side pocket of her black cargo pants. Recognition flooded her mind as she looked more closely at the advancing infected. It was the local kindergarten teacher, Mrs. Knight. *Wow, last time I saw you we were singing pat-a-cake.* She allowed the infected woman to lurch closer, and Mrs. Knight snapped at her former student. Molly shoved the orange in Mrs. Knight's gaping jaw.

"I'm so sorry. You deserve better," Molly said and raised her squeegee in the air. It took several blows to knock her down. Once she did, Molly stomped on the orange, and Mrs. Knight lay still. A mix of juice, pulp, and coagulated blood coated Molly's runner.

The infected with the broken ankle lurched forward. Molly took a few quick strides out of its path and crossed the cement until she was at the front door. "Open it! Now!" she said as she slapped her palm on the window.

Jeremy unlocked the door and opened it wide enough for Molly to squeeze through. The bell chimed, and she was in.

"Well done, Molly! You put on quite a show! Who's next?"

When Jeremy tried to close the door, Molly wedged her foot in it. "Oh, no, you don't." She reached a hand into her breast pocket and pulled out the salmonberries. "I got the juiciest, ripest berries I could find. I taste-tested a couple, and they were amazing. Here, would you like to try some? All you have to do is use this orange as a distraction, or weapon, or whatever, retrieve these berries, and then you may indulge. Questions?"

"Hey, come on now. I was just having a bit of fun. No need to be like that, Molly."

She threw the berries out the door, turned, and grabbed Jeremy. He was much taller, but she was stronger.

"Kayla, help!" she called to her friend.

Kayla, looking momentarily horrified, stared at Molly and Jeremy before she stepped forward and grabbed Jeremy by the other arm. They pushed him farther through the doorway.

"Ahhh! Help! This is mutiny! This is uncalled for! Someone, please help!"

The elderly lady rose from a seat she had taken near the coffee station. She walked over with a scowl on her face.

"Oh, Rosa, thank you!"

Rosa furrowed her brow and helped Kayla and Molly push Jeremy. He held onto the doorway so tightly that his nails tore.

The three young boys ran over and began pummeling Jeremy's hands. He lost his grip and was out the door.

"Molly! Molly, how could you? I'll have you fired for this!"

"That's fine, Jeremy. See management," Molly said. She smiled as she locked the door behind him.

The infected latched onto him, and sunk its grimy teeth into his flesh as it pulled Jeremy to the ground.

He was screaming as the van pulled up. It entered the station slowly at first, and then the driver accelerated toward Jeremy and the monster. Both were pinned under the vehicle.

The group inside watched as four children filed out of the van and ran to the building.

The girl yelled, "Shotty first!" The locked door didn't budge as she tugged on its handle. "Hey, can you let us in?" she called through the glass.

Molly unlocked the door, and the kids scurried past her to the washrooms.

A petite woman with raven hair stepped out of the vehicle and limped after them. Molly held the door open for her.

"You have something orange on your cheek," she commented as she passed through the doorway.

KAT
1 JULY 2018
15:00 PDT
GAS STATION, HWY 4
NW OF PORT ALBERNI, BC

Now's my chance. Kat looked around the storefront. *They'll be safe enough. Lots of provisions, all with extra preservatives. They'll last forever here, as long as those windows hold up.*

"Hey, lady, what's going on out there? We've been cooped up in here all night. We called for help yesterday, but nobody has shown up."

"Everybody needs help. It isn't coming. Got any coffee?" Kat muttered without looking at the uniformed teen.

"Back corner. Where did you come from?"

"Salmon Beach. Do you have oat milk?"

"This is a gas station, lady."

Kat patted the empty pockets of her borrowed sweatpants. "I, umm, don't have my purse."

"It's fine. Take whatever you need."

She read the teen's name tag. "Thanks...Molly. I'm sorry about your colleague out there."

Molly pursed her lips. "Don't be. We threw him out. He was starving us in here. Power tripping."

"Wow. Bold move." *Time to make my own bold move.* "Thanks for the coffee," Kat said as she walked to the door. She winced with each footfall as she made for the van and stepped gingerly over a limp arm that protruded from beneath its wheel.

Kat pulled out of the gas station and turned left onto Highway 4 toward Port Alberni. The road was abandoned; she drove a few kilometres without crossing paths with anyone, infected or alive.

They'll be fine there. Grandma in the corner looked like the wholesome type. She'll take care of them. Kat looked at the bags of food shoved between the back seats. *Oh, who am I kidding? That one chick already fed someone to the zombies. It's going to be* Lord of the Flies *in there before the sun sets.*

A gunmetal-grey truck approached from the opposite direction. The truck slowed down, and the driver signaled to Kat to roll down her window.

"Wouldn't go that way if I were you, little lady," the man behind the wheel said.

"How bad is it?"

"Bad? Well, there ain't nothing good to be found in that town. Not anymore. Those monsters have taken over. Where is it you're coming from?"

"The coast. It's overrun there too."

"I suggest you find yourself some supplies and get up a logging road if that vehicle permits it. Safest thing would be to wait this out."

"How long does one *wait out* something like this?"

He shrugged. "Don't think it'll be in the short term that there'll be a solution."

"Where are you going?"

He hesitated, then said, "Got a houseboat on the lake. I'm meeting my brothers there, my ma, some other folks too. You're welcome to follow, if you can pull yer weight."

"Thank you... I've got some friends I need to go find though."

"Hope they're still alive when you get there."

"Me too," Kat said as she began shifting the gears.

"If you change your mind, we're just up by Taylor Arm."

"Thanks." Kat mustered a weak smile. She crept forward as the truck drove off, then pulled a U-turn once he was out of sight. She cursed herself as she drove back to the gas station.

Kat heard the bell chime as she stood at the pump.

"Kat, what are you doing?" Milah asked.

"Just filling the van up."

"I...I thought you left us here."

Oh, I tried to, kid.

"Why did you come back?"

"Couldn't leave you kids alone, not with that *psycho* Molly inside. You know she pushed this guy out here?" Kat nodded at Jeremy's corpse.

"It's just as bad in town, isn't it?" Milah asked.

"I didn't get very far, but I ran into someone who confirmed that. I don't think it's worth investigating any further."

"Now what?"

"The man I just ran into... He said they had a houseboat on Sproat Lake. We could go check it out..."

"Well, well, look who came back," Stu called as he walked through the door.

Kat rolled her eyes. "Hey, kid. Grab whatever you guys need from inside and let's get going."

Stu retreated into the station and returned with Adam, Roger, and a jerry can. "Here, lady. Fill this up too." He handed her the orange vessel.

She smiled as the kids filed into the van. When she finished filling up, Kat walked around to the driver's side and climbed in.

Kat followed the highway toward the Taylor Arm Provincial Park turnoff. She pulled down the side road, nearly missing it amongst the overgrowth of alders and salal. A hundred metres from the highway the pavement ended, and the terrain became gravel, which soon became dirt, until finally Kat found herself manoeuvring between protruding roots and large rocks.

"Where the heck are we going?" Adam asked from the back seat.

Where are we going, indeed. Kat second-guessed herself until she saw the dark grey truck parked up ahead. "This is it," she called over her shoulder.

"And why are we trusting these people?" Stu asked. "We don't know them."

"You don't really know me either. We're trusting them because they're alive, unlike the rest of the town."

"Right, that's reassuring," Stu said.

"They have shelter. We have each other, and your gun, Stu," Milah chimed in.

Once Kat parked the van, she turned to face the kids and said, "I think we should leave a bag of provisions in here, you know, in case we need to split. The rest we take. They'll expect us to contribute."

The boys nodded. Milah chewed her lower lip.

Kat exited the van and walked to the water's edge. A small skiff floated in the distance, its reflection elongated on the rippled surface of the lake. With her fingers in her mouth, Kat let out a low, loud whistle, which caught the attention of two figures in the boat. She could see the silhouette of one looking back at shore through a set of binoculars. Kat waved both arms high in the air, and the kids mirrored her.

The boat slowly turned and chugged back toward them. It stopped within thirty feet of shore and bobbed gently.

"You changed yer mind?" the man called through cupped hands.

"Yes. Can we join you?" Kat yelled across the water.

"I didn't realize there'd be so many of you," he said. "And so...young."

"Ace, what's all this about?" the woman steering the boat asked in a hushed tone, but the water carried her deep, raspy voice.

"Ran into her on the road. Offered her shelter. Didn't realize she had a full litter with her."

"They're children, for god's sake. Of course they can come!"

The engine churned the glassy surface of the water as they glided toward shore.

Relief washed over Kat as the children removed their shoes and waded to the boat.

"Steady, steady," the woman said as Stu climbed in. Adam

was next, who gave a hand to Milah, and then Roger followed.

Kat picked up the cooler and took a step into the water. She shuddered as her mangled feet dipped into the brisk shallows. When she reached the skiff, the water was up to her knees. Ace took the cooler before offering her a hand into the boat.

"You're limpin' pretty bad, miss. You hurt?"

"Yeah. I had to run for my life barefoot on gravel."

He inhaled sharply. "Sounds awful painful. Mama Jean here is pretty good at patching folks up. She can take a look at ye when we get back to the houseboat."

"That would be appreciated, thank you. Are you a nurse?"

"Nah, but raisin' three boys will teach you a thing or two about actin' like one," Mama Jean responded as she guided the boat away from shore.

The mid-afternoon sun illuminated the lake. The children took turns pointing out the beautiful scenery: a loon that dove beneath the surface, a log that protruded from shore that could act as a diving board, a swing in a nearby tree. Kat listened to their childish banter and, for a moment, forgot the pain in her feet and the worry in her heart.

They followed the lake west along the shoreline. After a few minutes, the houseboat came into view on the horizon.

"Wow, look at that!" Stu exclaimed as they approached the dwelling.

The compact houseboat had two stories. Its walls were covered in cedar shake and dotted with small, round windows. A large deck hosted planters full of nasturtiums, strawberries, herbs, and other plants.

"How many people can it sleep?" Kat asked, concerned that the five of them would be a burden.

"Comfortably, I'd say about ten. Not to worry, there were only four of us before you lot joined in: Mama Jean here, and my brothers. There'll be more on the way, but we'll sort that out later."

Mama Jean cut the engine. The skiff pulled up beside the

houseboat and gently nudged the fenders along its port side.

Ace climbed on board and reached down to give the kids a hand.

"What's going on? Found some tagalongs?" a voice called from within the house.

"Hey there, brother. Yeah, they're in need of shelter. Figure we can give 'em a hand for a day or two."

"Mhm, mind you remember that: a day or two. And don't have them overstay. We don't have too many provisions ourselves."

"Oh, come on, Billy. I taught you better than that," Mama Jean scolded her adult son as she climbed up over the railing of the boat.

Ace offered Kat his hand again. She took it, and stepped up to the houseboat's deck.

"Come along, miss. I'll show you to a room. You look awful tired," Ace said.

"I'd be lying if I said I wasn't." She stumbled over her wet, dragging pants, steadied herself, and followed Ace into the houseboat.

He led her through the common room, along a narrow hallway, and opened a door revealing a guest room. "Here you go, get yourself some rest, and I'll send Mama Jean in to patch up your feet. We're all safe now. And don't mind Billy, you all are welcome to stay as long as you need."

"Thank you, Ace." He closed the door behind her and Kat looked around the tiny room. There were bunk beds in the corner next to one of the round windows. She lowered herself to the bottom bunk. Kat lay her head on the soft pillow and, for what felt like the first time in days, felt safe.

ANA
1 JULY 2018
15:58 PDT
QUARANTINE TEST FACILITIES
LADNER, BC

Hearing her brother's scream felt more painful than if the monster had bitten into her own flesh.

She pounded the fence with her fists. "Paul! Please, somebody help!"

A growl rumbled in her ears. She heard shots on the other side of the fence, followed by the crackling static of electricity, another inhuman growl, and finally, a thud.

You're too late. So much for protecting us. She fell to her knees. Her twin moaned in pain just feet away from her, yet so far out of reach.

"An?"

"Paul?" she called through the fence.

"Fuck, that hurt!"

"Oh my god, Paul! Are you okay?"

"I'll tell you one thing: they'll definitely be quarantining me after that... Shit. There's a lot of blood."

"Mr. Zuessen, I see you met our other patient. My apologies that things got a little...*out of hand.* I can assure you, that won't happen again." Ana could hear the smooth voice of Doctor Hayde through the fence.

"You can't assure anything!" Paul snapped. "Don't make promises you can't keep. This is the fucking apocalypse."

"Not yet. Not if we can prevent it. Paul, where is your sister?"

"I'm here!" Ana called through the fence. *But I wish I wasn't. I wish I could run far, far away from here.*

"I'm pleased to hear that you both made it through unscathed."

"Unscathed? That asshole took a chunk out of my arm! Can

you get Sephonia to give me a hand here before I bleed out?"

"Charles, get Nurse Perri. You'll be fine; it's only a flesh wound. It's rather curious though. Seemed almost like a shark attack. Often when a shark bites a human, it is a case of misidentification, with the predator believing its prey is a seal or the like, but once it has a taste of the flesh and realizes its mistake, it loses interest. That must be how your immunity works."

"Great, so a horde will still tear me apart, but after they each have a taste, they'll leave me alone? Fuck, this hurts!"

Four heavily armed men approached Ana. Two grabbed her under the elbows and pulled her to her feet.

"Come along, Miss Zuessen."

She took a step and inhaled sharply when pain jolted up her leg. Amid the excitement, she hadn't noticed that her ankle had twisted upon the impact of her fall. Ana limped slowly next to the officers.

"Ma'am, with your permission," the man beside her said as he held his arms out. She recognized the voice of the young man that had escorted her during the flight.

Ana nodded and sighed heavily. The officer bent down and lifted her over his shoulder. *Well, this isn't quite what I thought he had in mind.*

They marched Ana back into the tented compound and into a space that resembled a doctor's examination room.

Paul sat next to Nurse Perri, who, despite the thick layers of protective rubber she wore, was stitching his arm with precision.

"Paul!" Ana cried as the man lowered her to the floor. She limped to his side. A fresh surge of adrenaline coursed through her when she saw the wound, his flesh torn nearly to the bone.

Paul winced as Nurse Perri coaxed his muscle tissue back together.

A wave of nausea ran through Ana. The private who carried her in brought a chair over, and Ana sat next to her brother.

"Ma'am, it's probably best if you don't watch," he said to her with a look of concern on his face.

"Sir, it's probably best if you don't call me *ma'am* again." She raised a hand to her forehead and closed her eyes.

Paul scoffed. "Give the guy a break, eh, An?"

Doctor Hayde entered the room. "Well, that's dealt with. The patient has been sedated and restrained. He won't cause you two any more trouble."

"Doctor, why is it you keep calling that *monster* a *patient*?" Ana asked.

"He will become an important part of our research. He shows a stamina that is unique from that of others with the affliction and could provide valuable insight into the condition's reactability."

"That, or you can't take him down. I faced zombie Rocket in the mall... Shot the bastard in the head and my bullet ricocheted off his stupid metal plate."

"Wait, that charred beast is *Rocket*?!" Ana asked in disbelief. Paul nodded.

"I assure you, we have the ability to *take him down*. Nurse Perri, once you have finished patching up Paul, please escort the Zuessens to the launch pad. We depart at seventeen hundred." Doctor Hayde stood and made to leave.

"Doctor, hold up a sec. I'd like to speak to Jocelyn before we go anywhere, and I want to know exactly where it is we're going."

"You may call Jocelyn when we arrive at my ship, the *Rex Vitae*." He turned and marched out of the room.

Paul and Ana's eyes locked. The skin on Ana's neck crawled, and her stomach dropped. *He worked with Mom... this whole time.*

PARTING WORDS

Thank you for reading my debut novel, Waves of Undead! I hope you enjoyed being immersed in the chaotic world I've created.

The greatest gift you can give an author is a rating and review. I'd love to hear your thoughts on Goodreads, Amazon, or wherever you picked up your copy of Waves of Undead. If you enjoyed the book, a quick review helps others find it too.

Thanks again for your support. It truly means the world to me.

ACKNOWLEDGEMENT

I'd like to thank everyone who's ever uttered the words "how is your writing going?" My heart swelled whenever those words reached my ears, even if I bashfully answered, "I haven't written in six months". I am grateful to have such supportive friends and family.

To my beta readers, thank you for reading this work in its roughest form, and for your valuable opinions and insight.

My dear cousin Cait, thank you for your continuous support throughout this project. From sensitivity and beta reading, to poring over maps, to blurb suggestions and beyond — thank you. Every time I asked, "Can I ask you a quick question about X?" you went above and beyond to help me find an answer.

To my Mom, thank you for all the support and encouragement you've provided through this journey. From verbal encouragement, to formatting, to setting up meetings with the printers, I appreciate you more than I can say.

Thank you to my Dad for always encouraging me to follow my dreams.

To my husband, Iain, thank you for loving me despite the chaos and horror that I choose to create through the keyboard.

Before I close, I would like to acknowledge that none of this would have come to fruition if it weren't for my brother, Steven, who submerged me into the world of zombies at a young age. He recruited me as his emotional support viewer while he played video games like *Resident Evil*. Not long after that, the dreams began... One of them even made it into the pages of this book (See Management). Thank you for the childhood we shared, emotional damage aside.

ABOUT THE AUTHOR

Rebecca Cuthbertson, author of *Waves of Undead,* is a nature enthusiast intrigued by stories of survival. As a child, Rebecca spent endless hours watching her older brother play apocalyptic video games such as *Resident Evil* and *Silent Hill.* For decades she was afflicted with nightmares of zombie outbreaks (and still is).

At the age of twenty, she moved from her hometown of Ladner, BC, to Tofino, BC, where she enjoyed life on the rugged west coast while often contemplating "what if?" scenarios. Her love of hiking, surfing, and the great outdoors inspired the setting for the *Undead Waters* series. Rebecca now lives in the Lower Mainland with her husband and toddler, where she feels unsettled living amongst more people than trees, lest an apocalyptic "what if" scenario should occur.

STAY UP TO DATE on the *Undead Waters* series and other projects by Rebecca Cuthbertson by signing up for her newsletter or following her on social media.

Instagram, Threads, TikTok
@rcuthbertson.writes

Facebook:
RCuthbertson Writes

Newsletter sign up:

CONTENT WARNINGS

Please be advised that the story in your hands contains potentially distressing content, including but not limited to:

Abandonment
Animal death
Automobile crash
Boating accident/near drowning
Body horror, blood & gore
Bushfire
Cancer
Contagions
Depression
Drugs, alcohol & tobacco use
Eyeball trauma
Firearm use
Grief, death & loss
Harassment/assault
Helicopter crash
Medical treatment & procedures
Murder
Needles
Physical injuries
Pregnancy/loss
Reference to animal testing (not depicted)
Scars
Tsunami/flooding
Zombies/cannibalism